Closet Full of Bones

By AJ Aalto

PIXIEGRIND
INK
PUBLISHING

CLOSET FULL OF BONES
BY AJ AALTO
COPYRIGHT 2017 A.J. AALTO. ALL RIGHTS RESERVED.

PRINT ISBN: 978-0-9952004-5-6

Cover Design by Dean Samed
Edited by Rafe Brox
Formatted by Kody Boye

This is a work of fiction. Names, characters, places, brands, media, and incidents are either the product of the author's imagination or are used fictitiously. Any resemblance to similarly named places or to persons living or deceased is unintentional.

Author's Note

This is a work of fiction partially inspired by true events. All places, dates, times, and names have been altered to protect the victims, although it could be argued that there are no innocent parties in this tale. Thanks are due to the many individuals who confided in me during the course of this difficult situation; these individuals will be protected by the author and therefore cannot be thanked by name.

For R., for her inspiration, patience, strength, and undying sense of humor.

Chapter One

Saturday, October 11. 3:00 A.M.

She had the dump site picked out before she'd made up her mind to kill him. Not that she'd ever admit it aloud, but if she was honest with herself, the idea of his death began squirming like a night crawler in the back of her mind the moment he'd crossed her invisible but inflexible lines of impropriety.

An imperious pre-dawn text. Such a small thing to become a death sentence.

Such a small thing to most people. A pebble in a shoe. A minor nuisance, best forgotten. But it wasn't the only pebble, and it wasn't forgotten, and she wasn't most people. Involving her had been Travis Freeman's biggest mistake.

The text came early enough to wake her from a paralyzing sleep, the type that always followed one of her savage, day-long migraines. Though the master bedroom was darkened by heavy blinds and drapes, she knew by the weight of her limbs that it must still be nighttime. She'd been dreaming of red wine, dark chocolate, and a man without a face, but this slipped away, the pleasant blur marred by electric rattling; hard plastic against oak and brass, the phone vibrated against the lamp's metal base. Her hand shot out from under the pillow and fumbled for it, yanking it off its charger.

Assuming it had to be an emergency of one sort or another, she felt for her glasses, knocking them off the nightstand, and they went skittering under the bed. She squinted at the phone's bright backlight and tried to read the text through blurry eyes, cursing her poor vision as she moved the phone closer.

For a moment, she was baffled by the sender's name. It made no sense. At that intimate hour, in the privacy of her bedroom, a text from that name felt like a breach, an invasion, a perforation of a boundary that ought not to be pierced. This was a man she barely knew and certainly did not like. Her right eyebrow throbbed warningly. The text made her lips tighten into a pale line.

You're gonna tell Frankie to return my calls, Featherweight.

It was the "you're gonna," that stirred anger behind the teeth, made her molars grind together until they squeaked. A slow roll of nausea woke her further and she slid upright in the sheets, pulling her knees up to her chest, leaning her sore head against the padded, velvet headboard. Her left hand drifted toward the lamp but stalled midway; experience had taught her that the low, dull ache in the back of her skull could easily roar back to life if she aggravated it with more light.

More than the baffling new nickname for her, his "you're gonna," with its implied "or else," tipped her mood from inconvenienced to indignant. Later, she would recall the thought, *careful, boy,* pressing into her mind, as though she could transmit it from her perennially pitch-black bedroom to wherever he was, this man who believed he knew her well enough to call her by a disparaging, patronizing epithet or intrude on her precious, hard-won sleep. She was sure she'd mentioned her migraines to him; politeness had forced her to find fodder for small talk on the rare occasions they'd crossed paths, and it was one of the few things she'd discovered they had in common.

On the heels of her mental warning was a seconds-long consideration, *might have to do something about this.* She almost texted him back. Suspecting he was trying to stir trouble, though, she didn't; she would be no man's puppet. Games like his should be beneath notice. What would Dad say in his lucid moments? She whispered it in her black bedroom with a bittersweet smile. "Don't feed anyone who doesn't feed you."

Her heavy eyelids reminded her of the hour, and of the pointlessness of getting agitated by someone else's break-up. A general weariness with Frankie's ever-changing dramas won out. She trusted that Frankie was old enough to deal with her own issues; if not, she'd ask for help. Frankie always came to her for help. *Until that happened, what could she do?*

She abandoned the phone on the empty pillow beside hers, the one that would forever belong to her beloved, though her lover was no longer there to warm that side of the bed. She nestled down under her heavy blankets, to return, hopefully, to the land of food she'd never again taste, of a lover she'd never again touch, of whimsical dreams where reality couldn't worry her. The last thing she needed, she thought as she drifted, was the trouble of trying to get rid of a problem that would probably resolve itself in time if left alone.

But then she did wonder, just a little, if a second murder would be easier than the first.

Chapter Two

Saturday, October 11. 10:00 A.M.

Alibi Alley was the only coffee shop in Derby Harbor, its tiny patio half-wedged into an alleyway between the bank and the old library, which now served as the shop's winter abode. All summer long and into late fall, the wrought iron tables and chairs were pushed out onto the cobblestones and set with ashtrays and little vases of Gerbera daisies, because the owners of Alibi Alley — Misty and Gerald Volk — liked to imagine they were in Paris and not a small village near Lake Ontario. Mrs. Volk was a mystery buff, and also owned a tiny independent bookstore called Cozy Reads that held biannual murder mystery dinner theater productions in a long room above the shop. The Volks owned half the city's real estate, but enjoyed dividing their time between the bookstore and café rather than dealing with boardrooms and stakeholders' meetings. These were their retirement years, but they showed no signs of slowing down.

Their grandniece, Evelyn, had been raised to respect hard work and the almighty dollar, and even at eighteen, she knew precisely what she wanted from life. Today, sitting at a café table as a cool autumn morning became a crisp afternoon, what she wanted from life was to pack up and actually *go* to Paris, to escape small town life, to study art and love in equal amounts. The only thing stopping her was the sale of one final piece of property, which her grandmother had left her, and which her lawyer, Mr. James, was helping her unload. The senior Volks did not want anything to do with the rundown old place. The pair of ladies sitting across from her at the small table crowded with legal documents, did.

Frankie Farmer was the younger of the two sisters, and had been the last to arrive. She'd pulled up on a bicycle with a big floppy turquoise purse in a straw basket on the handlebars, looking out of breath and windswept in a lavender layered dress of chiffon with satin cuffs. Her bleached blonde hair was feathered *a la* early-80's Farrah Fawcett around a pale, heart-shaped face with enormous brown eyes. She ditched the bike without a care against the café's railing and bounded to the table to give her sister, Gillian Hearth, a noisy smooch on the top of her head. Evelyn, adjusting her paisley ascot and making sure her jacket buttons were in place, watched this arrival with as much stiff disapproval as one of her age and eccentricity could muster. Frankie's purse remained in the basket, open to the world, unzipped, contents flashing: a hairbrush that didn't look to be used often, a red patent leather wallet, a big sketchbook.

Across the road behind the older sister was Higgins River, the wide swath of water that spilled into Lake Ontario at Higgins Point, named for a valiant British soldier who fought in the War of 1812 and spent much of it rescuing his fellow military men from certain death. Valor Station, where the trains once stopped, was also named for Captain Higgins.

Today, Higgins River provided a crisp blue but silent backdrop, not a ripple in sight. The wind did not stir, as though it dared not disturb a hair from Evelyn Volk's tight braid. As the blonde newcomer leaned across the table, flashing straight white teeth in an open-mouthed smile and sticking out her hand to enthusiastically pump the lawyer's, Evelyn found her hands clenched in her lap and had to unfold one finger at a time to reluctantly accept the handshake thrust upon her.

The waiter appeared behind Frankie like a polite shadow. One of her fine hands fluttered to the nape of her neck as she caught her breath from the bike ride, and she dazzled him, too, with one of her attention-getting grins.

"Surprise me," she told him. "No dairy, but anything with caffeine. Have fun with it."

The older sister, Gillian, smiled behind her tea cup and sipped her green tea without comment, eyeing their company to calculate their impression of Frankie.

"You sure?" the waiter asked, aiming his pen at her and putting his little notepad away in his apron.

Gillian mouthed some words fondly before her little sister could say them, and it irritated Evelyn somewhat, though she couldn't have said why.

"Life's short. Live a little," Frankie told him with a wink, swinging into one of the wrought iron chairs.

Her sitting was accompanied by various clinks and jingles; multiple brass bracelets shook on both wrists, her dangling earrings tinkled prettily with every shake of her head, and the belt around her waist hung with tiny crystals that clicked. Frankie Farmer was not someone you missed, either when she arrived or when she departed. This also irritated Evelyn Volk.

The lawyer opened his mouth to speak but Evelyn's voice silenced him.

"Is this how you always arrive to a business meeting, Ms. Farmer?" Evelyn asked primly, breaking off a tiny piece of biscotti and tapping off the crumbs on her plate. "Sweaty and disheveled and dressed like a fairy princess?"

"Awww, thanks, sweetie!" the blonde answered, beaming. Her brown eyes said she'd heard the disapproval but was choosing to be flattered. "So, what are you, twelve?"

"Frankie," Gillian whispered, swinging one denim-clad knee to bump that of her sister.

"Eighteen this Thursday," Evelyn answered coolly, showing a restraint beyond her years. She turned her focus to the older sister, who seemed far more reasonable, if less interesting to look at. "My Gran was really special to me."

"I'm so sorry for your loss," Gillian said sincerely, putting down her tea cup a careful distance from the documents. "I understand her passing was sudden. This must be a difficult time for you."

Evelyn softened inside but caught it immediately and brought her formidable defenses back up. "Yeah, well. She left her estate to me, but suggested that you might like to buy the house. I thought that was generous of her, considering how often you two bullied her about it."

Gillian made a moment's business of scratching at something on the side of her teacup. The lawyer looked to be ignoring them, counting sugar packets for his coffee, letting his client's tongue run wild.

Frankie swiped at the ends of her hair, where a stray leaf had become tangled in the curly mess. "Bullies, eh? Wowsers. That sure sounds like us."

Gillian came to the rescue. "We asked too often. We're eager. I do hope she didn't feel we were... haranguing her out of malice."

"Let's cut the shit," Evelyn said, to the surprise of both sisters. "Gran was annoyed. She said you were a plague. Nonstop phone calls, notes… I have your notes with me in the car. A whole bundle. Would you like to see them?"

Frankie snapped. "What's done is done. No sense rehashing old arguments. What is your idea of a fair price?"

Evelyn turned her focus back to Gillian, whose right hand had disappeared below the table. Eve thought she might be squeezing her sister's kneecap warningly, and it pleased her a bit. Her chin rose and she nibbled her biscotti chunk thoughtfully, as though she hadn't already decided. She needed at least four hundred grand to secure her *pied-à-terre* in Paris, and she couldn't afford to give them a break.

"I'll sell it below market value," she said, "but I have an 'if.' Or rather, Gran had an 'if.'"

Frankie turned in her chair, tossing all that hair over her shoulder to beam up at the waiter as he delivered her surprise drink: an earl grey soy latte with a sprinkling of vanilla sugar, accompanied by a baby blue meringue cookie on the house. She rewarded him with a little delighted squeal that set Evelyn's shoulders up stiffly with displeasure.

Gillian ignored all this to calmly inquire, "If your grandmother mentioned us to you and had a final wish regarding us, especially in regards to the house, we would of course—"

Frankie squawked with an open mouth at her, and Gillian leveled a stern glare at her, effectively squelching further comment. Frankie's lip turned up; she was not good at keeping things off her face, no better than the eighteen-year-old real estate magnate who currently held their future dreams in the palm of her hands.

"We would, of course, hear you out," Gillian finished smoothly. "I can't imagine we would be rude enough to not honor her final wishes."

Evelyn wriggled a bit in her chair without realizing it, a pleased little *aha-gotcha-now* move that someday she would tame. She flicked her gaze at her wisely silent lawyer, who was only there to help her dot the Is and cross the Ts and witness paperwork.

"She wanted you to do the clean-up," Evelyn said. "You. Not a hired company. And you have to sign this contract saying you will do all the cleaning yourself. No maids. No friends. No family. Just the two of you."

"What did she do to the place," Frankie drawled, "booby-trap it?"

"Yes," Evelyn said, and snickered despite herself. "Rolling boulders and pits of vipers."

Frankie started, "Well why else would she—"

"She thought if you wanted something," Gillian supposed aloud, "you should have to work hard for it. Right?"

"And she thought you'd never worked a hard day in your life, by the look of you," Evelyn said, aiming this indictment at the younger rather than the older sister. Gillian Hearth had soil under her nails, and Evelyn didn't think it was from being dirty; she thought this one looked physically toughened by the outdoors, and maybe had a job that required getting her hands in the soil. "So I guess the question is, ladies, how badly do you want this property?"

The lawyer finally spoke. "Ms. Volk is asking four hundred seventy-five thousand for the house," he said. "It's a lakefront property and worth a good deal more, as you know. There are other offers on the table, *higher* offers, but she's giving you this chance because it's what Mrs. Blymhill wanted."

Frankie's unusually large eyes were bulging now as she craned slowly to stare in disbelief at the side of Gillian's face. Gillian was doing quiet mental calculations, but Evelyn could see her answer already written there. The elder wanted it; she was not going to let go. She had her deal, and she was going to Paris, and the future was bright, and everything was perfect. She allowed herself to eat the rest of the biscotti, calories and crumbs be damned. Higgins River glowed behind the sisters Hearth and Farmer, and Evelyn imagined that the autumn sun warmed a touch to celebrate her victory.

Gillian said, "Frankie, will you go inside and get me another green tea, please?"

"Get it yourself," Frankie said on a laugh.

Gillian aimed her sister another sidelong glance, which prompted Frankie to swish from her chair, tossing her hair, and jingle on into the café on her quest for tea. The lawyer watched Frankie's hips sway and then tore his gaze from them and back to his papers.

Evelyn, on the other hand, was watching the older sister struggle with her words, sure she wasn't going to like what came out next.

"Your price is fair," Gillian replied. "More than fair. I know it. And your grandmother's final wish is... unusual, but I accept it. I have one small request of my own."

"Which is?" the lawyer asked, wary. His hands went almost unconsciously to his fountain pen and spiral notepad.

"A few years back, I fell down the stairs and injured my shoulder and right arm. This makes your clean-up request a bit difficult for me, physically. My sister is..." Gillian gave them a knowing look that summed up an unspoken judgment that Evelyn nodded in immediate agreement with, and felt herself warming to the elder sister a touch. "I have a coworker who is very sturdy and would pitch in where needed. His name is Bruce. I'll do most of the work myself, I swear to that. But the heavy lifting…" She showed them her hands in a gesture of helplessness.

Evelyn had her *pied–à–terre* money and Gran's final wishes mostly fulfilled, and she spoke before the lawyer could. "I believe we have a deal, Ms. Hearth. One helper. Only for the heavy stuff." *What the hell do I care? I'll be in Paris.*

Gillian smiled gratefully, and Evelyn thought she should try it more often; it made her face far more interesting and her eyes, fern green with a sharp outline, brighten and come alive.

Frankie returned with a steaming cup of green tea and her step slowed; she stared off into the distance, her color draining.

"Ms. Farmer?" the lawyer said, looking over his shoulder. "Is there anything…?"

Frankie shook her head, looking troubled but setting the tea in front of her sister. Evelyn looked around, too, but didn't see anything but a few customers coming out of the deli across the street and an older gentleman with a leashed Yorkshire terrier on the walking path by the river. Wind tossed red and yellow leaves from the trees. A dry leaf skittered across the cobblestones near the younger sister's bicycle.

Gillian handed Frankie a pen and took her tea without noticing the worry.

"You sign here beside me," Gillian told her, and pointed at the second flagged line.

Frankie said, "Gillian, are you sure this is…"

"Life's short," Gillian said with a forced smile that seemed to convey a private message between them. "Live a little."

Chapter Three

Saturday, October 25. 10:00 A.M.

Seagulls spun in lazy circles above the glittering water of the Welland Canal at Lock Six, screeching overhead in the wake of a passing ship as Constable Dean Jagger strolled through the small parking lot toward the food truck. Stones crunched under his boots and he kept his step light and casual, admiring the covered picnic area and the whitewashed lattice wrapped tidily around the trash bins to hide them. The smells of deep fryer grease and rotisserie hot dogs belched from a nearby food truck's exhaust vents. One of the back doors was propped open, and there was a fat bald man in a stained white apron smoking a cigarette on the cinder block that served as a step from the truck to the ground.

In the order window, a woman with a heavy bosom and long, kinked blonde hair leaned on the high counter; being fairly tall, the counter came up to Jagger's chin, but he could imagine his kids craning their heads back to look at the lady. She greeted him warmly, and her smile made a plain face somewhat pretty; good skin and excellent teeth made up for a teased, crimped eighties hairdo. He ordered a large basket of fries and a diet Coke, and while she set the fries to cook, he took his can of pop to the closest picnic table and sat facing the truck, swinging his attention between her and the blue, rippling canal. A boat had recently gone through, and the gulls swooped excitedly at the churned up water behind the propellers.

"Busy?" he asked.

The lady squinted up at the sunny sky. "Nah, not this late in the season. Only people besides you today were a regular who likes hot Italian sausages with sauerkraut, and my grandson. He drives in for a hot dog and onion rings on Saturdays on his lunch break." She looked at him expectantly.

He scoffed with a gracious frown, "You're not old enough for grandkids that can drive."

She waved her hand at him in a *go-on-you-scamp* motion and smiled again, pleased.

"Get a lot of regulars from the parks department?" He nodded his head toward the park and the public cemetery property behind it, which blended into a protected green space a little further in – a swath of trees and local wildflowers planted and maintained by the city, with support from a private conservation fund.

"Once in a while," she answered, "but mostly I get folks from the canal, workers on break or at the end of their shift. Or people stopping on their way to the big outlet mall."

"Sailors ever get off the boats?" he asked.

She shrugged. "If their ship is tied up long enough."

"If I showed you a picture or two," he said, "think you could say if you'd seen someone?"

Her gaze sharpened beneath the light blue eye shadow on her lids. "Maybe. If you showed me a badge."

He did. Then he brought out the pictures, starting with his missing person, Mike Deacon: thirty-four years old, Caucasian, five-nine, one-eighty, brown eyes, dark brown hair. The blank look on her face told him "no" before she said it. Then he showed her a picture of sisters, one blonde and one brunette, smiling side-by-each with the sun in their hair. She stared at it for a long time without speaking, but he could see she wasn't trying to place the faces; she'd already fixated on the brunette and was carefully choosing her next words.

He used his protective voice accordingly. "Everything okay?"

"See your badge again?" she asked.

He showed her, and gave her one of his cards, which she promptly squirreled away. He had no doubt she'd be calling to verify his badge number.

"Another guy asked about her." She pointed at the brunette. "Different picture, though. One on his phone. Small. He had to do like this." She moved her fingers apart to indicate zooming in on a picture in a smartphone. "I didn't feel right about him."

"He wasn't a cop," he guessed. "Did he say he was?"

"Implied it. He wasn't up to no good, whoever he was." She tapped the picture. "She's real quiet. Works close to here. Drives a Jeep, an older one. Not especially friendly, but that don't mean she's trouble. Always has dirt under her nails, not filth but good clean soil, if you catch my meaning. Works hard for her money. Likes to get her hands dirty."

"No fancy gloves for her," he said, picking up on her train of thought. "A farmer from across the canal, maybe?"

"Or something. Nice Tilley hat most days, but sometimes a faded old baseball hat. Big for her. A boyfriend's hat, I got the impression."

He asked, "No name for her?"

She shook her head. "Doubt she'd give it to me if I asked. Quiet," she repeated. "Skittish, like." She turned to bellow, "Dave, fries!" then thumped the picture, this time with a thick forefinger, her fingernail painted with gold glitter. "I didn't think she'd like that guy knowing anything about her." She shook her head and her kinked hair barely moved. "No. Fuck that guy."

"Mind describing him for me?"

"Skinny. Five-ten. White hick. Dark hair. Couple day's stubble. Coors Light t-shirt, jeans. Dark eyes, I think. Drove a big black crew cab, loud as hell. Shiny. Big ol' wheels like he's out to prove he's Mr. Bigshot. Chrome out the ass. Back in my day, a big truck like that meant a tiny pecker."

"What did he ask about her?" Dean asked.

"If I'd seen her a lot. I told him she didn't look familiar," she said, and sucked her teeth before repeating, "because fuck that guy."

"Have you mentioned to this woman that the man was asking about her?"

"Haven't seen her yet since it happened, but my gut tells me it's the kind of information a girl should have, even if she won't like to hear it." She studied him a minute. "Think I should?"

The bald smoker handed forward a heaping cardboard box of steaming fries, glistening with grease, and Dean's mouth watered. "Always listen to your gut," he advised.

She gave him extra salt and ketchup packets and another diet Coke on the house. "And what about you? Should I tell her about you?"

Dean smiled. "Always listen to your gut," he said again. He took his fries to his car to eat in silence and collect his thoughts.

***

Paul Langerbeins sat in his silver Audi, eating the last of his hot Italian sausage with sauerkraut, and watched the plain clothes police officer walk back to his personally owned vehicle, a black SUV; he recognized the walk, the routine with the pictures, the feigned indifference when an investigator hit solid on a lead.

"What are you working on, you busy bee?" he wondered aloud, his interest piqued. He was about to snap a picture when his phone rang in his hand; blocked number. He answered with a curt, "Yes."

"Where is she?" A low growl, altered using voice manipulation. "Where. The fuck. Is she?"

Paul wet his mouth with a sip of ginger ale and paused long enough to hear the breathing on the end of the phone become ragged and stressed. Only then did he reply. "Who is this?"

"Where are you hiding that slut, that *fucking whore?*" The man on the other end of the line was so angry that he sounded like he was choking on his words.

Paul, who was hiding no one, wondered if his most recent client had decided to take his advice and go stay at a friend's house or a motel for a few nights until things with an ex cooled off.

"Nice voice. You're the one hiding things. How did you get this number?" Paul asked.

"I can get anything, you crippled fuck."

He's seen me walk, Paul noted, and then, wryly, *Or try to walk. Okay. So he's been outside Frankie's place when I've come or gone. Where is he now?* With half his focus, Paul continued to watch the unfamiliar officer in his SUV, munching fries, and making notes.

"Keep harassing me, son," Paul said, "see what happens."

"Keep fucking my girl, see what happens," the caller spat.

Fishing for info. Paul could have confirmed or denied, but said, "You don't scare me at all."

"Gonna try to have me arrested like a little bitch?" The mechanical-sounding voice was a grating rasp. "Pussy."

Paul put on his sweetest, most condescending tone. "Have a marvelous day, kid," before coolly hanging up, and then switched his phone to vibrate for a while, putting it on the car charger and turning the car on. Immediately, the texts started shaking the phone, one after another, a furious barrage. He drove slowly through the parking area, slowed by a trash bin, threw out his lunch garbage and a couple of empty coffee cups, and set off down the canal road heading south, toward home.

***

Constable Dean Jagger jotted down the license plate of the man in the silver Audi, the date and time, and a brief description.

Chapter Four

Saturday, October 25. 10:00 A.M.

"Heads up, Gills."

Gillian's right hand was up before she saw the water bottle, snatching it out of the air. The impact gave her bad shoulder a twinge that she knew would cause her trouble later, but for now, she would ignore it. The air was warm and damp in the greenhouse and smelled thickly of loam and peat. She used the cool condensation on the plastic bottle to wet her brow, willing away any remnants of last night's disrupted sleep, nodding a thank-you at Bruce Wertheimer. Rearranging the landscaping tools onto the back of the ATV trailer, she kept him in her peripheral vision. A big man, broad through the shoulders, thick in the middle, long-legged and impressively strong, Bruce kept a handsome face hidden beneath a heavy but well-kept beard.

They'd have three hours before the noisy riding mowers and leaf blowers started up in the cemetery. End of the season clean-up was always noisier than early spring plantings. Someone had brought out the CAT Multi-Terrain Loader and hadn't parked it properly, leaving it beside the greenhouse overnight, the keys still inside. *Stupid*, Gillian thought, *or lazy.*

Other than the loader being left out, the morning was typical for mid-October; chilly, damp, but so far free of frost at daybreak. But for Gillian, something felt different, a subtle shift that she couldn't quite peg down. Chalking it up to lingering effects of restless sleep, she tugged her Tilley hat so that the brim would shade her eyes when she got in the sun outside.

"Gillian," Bruce called, jerking his head to the side at the back office. "Phone's ringing."

She smiled and waved that it was fine. She never answered her cell phone while she was working, and everyone knew to leave a message. Most likely, it was Frankie, up early with an idea for an art project for their new home, wanting to ask a question about colors and mood, or to vent about her most recent break-up, or solidifying plans for their "sisters only" dinner date later.

They had started calling it "sisters only" after a disastrous fish and chips meal the previous month. Frankie's sons were with their father, her ex-husband Henry Farmer, for the weekend, and she had invited Gillian over for a Friday night movie and dinner; Gillian had picked up two dinners from a local fish shop, but when she showed up at her sister's house, she was disappointed to see Frankie's boyfriend Travis's black truck parked in the driveway behind the red Fiat. Frankie tried to give him polite hints that they were having a girl's night. He'd grilled them about what they were planning, as if they were going to snort a bunch of cocaine and rob a bank or something; his attitude had been so surprising that Gillian had laughed out loud and rolled her eyes, made a crack about male strippers, and went into the kitchen to dish out the *two* dinners onto *two* plates, pouring *two* cups of Pepsi.

Irritated that Travis was trying to dictate their activities for the night, and frustrated that it wasn't her place to kick him out, Gillian had bitten her tongue after that. The sisters had put on a movie as they'd planned to. Travis sat brooding and mute while they ate; the discomfort in the room had grown as the silence stretched interminably. It struck her as completely out of character for Frankie to not speak her mind. There had been an ugly undercurrent that Gillian hadn't seen before.

That evening, she and her sister had eaten not just dinner but also ice cream in front of him, the silence increasingly uncomfortable, feeling monitored, intimidated, punished for daring to want girl time alone together. And while Gillian's sense of propriety had nagged her to offer him some of her dinner, she'd dug her heels in and refused to give in and do so; she couldn't reward bad behavior or encourage him to stay longer. This was her night, not his, and she wasn't in the mood to share. After going outside for a cigarette, Travis had eventually driven away, and Gillian remembered feeling like she could breathe again. Gillian wanted to ask her sister then why the hell she wouldn't put her foot down and tell him to get lost, but Frankie had been in a funny mood after he left, and Gillian had let it go. They'd put on a movie, choosing Sleeping With The Enemy; the mood had become increasingly awkward until the only solution had been turning the movie off halfway through and switching to Breakfast Club, an old favorite of Frankie's.

Their next girl's night was called "sisters only," and if Travis had given Frankie grief about it or had gotten the hint, Gillian didn't know. By then, though, Travis Freeman was on the way out of Frankie's life. He just didn't know it yet.

"Phone hasn't stopped," Bruce advised her from the other end of the greenhouse.

The new guy, Aaron, piped up, "Someone's phone!"

In case it was something regarding the real estate deal, Gillian removed her gardening gloves and whistled to the driver of the ATV to wait for a second while she jogged to the back office, opened her locker, and looked at her phone.

Three missed calls. Two from a blocked phone number, and one from an old friend she hadn't heard from in a long time. *Three years, four months, and four days to be exact,* her conscience piped up, always terribly aware of the date. *What does she want?* The thought of reconnecting with Bobby McIntyre lit a fire of anxiety in Gillian's veins that stalled her hand. Bobby had never been a stable member of their social group; a whirlwind of drama and paranoia and flat-out fabrications, Bobby drained the energy out of the bubbliest friends and set the unhappier ones on a downward spiral. It

Closet Full of Bones

happened every time.

But that's not the only reason you're avoiding her, the dark part of her mind nagged. *What does she want? Can you afford to ignore her?*

There were two voice mail messages. She resolved to listen to them on her lunch hour, put the cell phone on vibrate, stuck it in her back pocket, and hurried back to the ATV. Bruce had loaded the last of the tools, and the driver had the ATV rolling forward before Gillian was fully in her seat. She slapped one hand atop her hat and held on tightly. They rattled out along the little cemetery roads until they got to the next row that needed work.

A few hours of removing dead annuals and trimming perennials on the graves, and her back was sore with good, hard work and her right shoulder only ached a little. Gillian called a lunch break, and the crew started back to the greenhouse as the sun gilded the heavy woods to the north.

Chapter Five

Saturday, October 25. 8:00 P.M.

On the south side of Lake Ontario, dotted between Derby Harbor and the Niagara River, buildings that had once been summer cottages had been winterized into homes, and larger luxury houses had sprung up in the jagged land between, perched on rocky shorelines or tucked into forested glens. The homes in most of this area could only be reached by one-lane paths, numbered fire-lanes that were little more than winding dirt trails, barely wide enough in some spots to allow the passage of a car. Gillian and Frankie's maternal great-uncle had owned many of these cottages back when they were run-down shacks, and fortune had left a few to be divided between the girls. After Frankie's divorce, she and her two young sons had settled into one that required the least fixing-up, where she'd made a cozy home off the beaten path. They were close enough to town to run in for groceries in under half an hour, depending on whether or not the bridge at the canal was up or down, but far enough from the city of St. Catharines to feel like they were living in their own lakeside retreat.

On a soft autumn night, with an unseasonably warm breeze pushing the maples and cedars around and casting shadows on the driveway, Gillian expected her sister's windows to be open. It did not escape her notice that they were shut up tight, a detail that might have been missed by some; Gillian had spent eight years married to a cop, and her attention to details had been finely honed by the time of Greg's death. As she approached, the smell of old wood and decades of embedded polish and wax hung heavy in the air. Most of the old cottages smelled like churches, she'd always thought, especially Frankie's, with her love of incense.

Frankie did not greet her at the door, but yelled, "Come in?"

More a question than permission. It forced Gillian to dig out her house key and let herself in. Her sister was bundled in a ball on the couch, and turned brooding eyes up at her. Wary. Exhausted.

"He's been texting non-stop." Frankie said.

"I see you're finally locking the door like a normal person. Why didn't you let me in? Where's the dog?" Gillian asked, tossing her purse and key ring on the hall table. There was an odd smell in the air under the old church-wood scent, one that didn't register at first because it was so unusual in this house: sweat. Frankie was surrounded by empty cans — ginger ale — several half-eaten sleeves of soda crackers, and a bottle of antacids. "Stomach bothering you?"

Frankie's hand drifted to her face and Gillian noticed it tremble. "Seriously, like every ten seconds, another text."

"Who?" Gillian said, her nose wrinkling. *Oh, the break-up. Travis.* "Just ignore him. He'll get tired of it."

"Did I do the right thing?" Frankie asked tiredly. "Maybe I made a mistake."

"You should have stayed with him because he's harassing you?" Gillian asked, narrowing her eyes. "That's your logic here? Stay with Mr. Control Freak because then he'd... leave you alone?"

"No, of course not," Frankie sighed. Her phone dinged. Her short, blunt fingernails dug into a spot on her cheek, picking; it was a nervous habit Gillian hadn't seen her employ since she was a kid. "I know. It's stupid. I just can't take this."

Gillian rolled up her sleeves and kicked off her shoes, and began picking up soggy wads of Kleenex and tossing them in the trash. "Don't pick," she said almost absently. "What have you taken for your stomach?"

"Nothing, just Tums."

Gillian pointed at the phone, which dinged as if on cue. "Turn that to vibrate. Where are the munchkins?"

"At Henry's," Frankie said, and the relief in her voice was contagious. "He wanted them for an extra week and promised to take them to the zoo."

Gillian nodded once that this was good. The air in here was toxic with tension, and her sister was a jittering bag of bad nerves; this was no atmosphere for two little boys. As much as she didn't see eye-to-eye with her ex-brother-in-law, she was certain that Matthew and Kirk would be better off out of town with Henry Farmer for the time being. He'd take them to the track, of course, and give them an unfortunate lesson in losing a cartload of money on the ponies, but the boys loved the dust and action and animals. There were worse things to see.

"I'm opening at least one window," Gillian said, "unless you're prepared to put the air conditioning back on. It's like a sweatbox in here." She cracked the front window. They could watch that one, make sure no one was slipping through it. She lowered the blinds on it so no one from the yard could look in, locked the front door and put the chain on, then turned on the porch light. *Oh, for heaven's sake*, she mentally chided. *Do I think really think he's lurking out there? Or have Frankie's histrionics made me paranoid?* She wasn't sure.

Frankie was wringing her hands as Gillian took away the empty pop cans and crackers. "I'll make you some dry toast, maybe get you some applesauce if you have it. You've got to eat something."

"I'm too stressed. I could barely swallow a few crackers. My throat keeps tightening up." Frankie sat up straight on the couch as a fair breeze pushed through the blinds, rattling the slats. "How do I know for sure I've done the right thing?"

Gillian paused on the way to the kitchen, showing her sister an encouraging smile. "Underneath the fear, how do you feel?"

Frankie thought about this, cocking her head and pushing damp strands of blonde hair off her forehead. The lamp beside her turned the strands into spun gold. "Free," she said with a sheepish little laugh. "I can do whatever I want, now."

You should always *be able to do whatever you want*, Gillian thought angrily, but she was careful not to say it. It was too soon to lecture Frankie; there would be plenty of time for that later. The red flags had been there. Maybe not right away, but Gillian had spent the last few months alarmed at the fast-tracking of the relationship and the increasing isolation of her baby sister from the family and her friends.

If Greg had been alive, he'd have sat Frankie down and pointed the signs out, and she would have listened to him. She'd always equated his badge with some secret precognitive abilities, like he could spot a bad apple immediately. Gillian knew this wasn't true, or Greg would still be snoring away in bed beside her every night, drooling into his pillow. She used to hate that. Now she'd give anything to be washing his sleep-drool out of their pillowcases. For a moment, her grief returned full force, surprising in its ferocity. It had been like that since the funeral, even after three years, popping up out of nowhere, triggered by the silliest things. She almost gave over to it, her eyes stinging hotly.

Instead, she cleared her throat and glared at her baby sister's phone, vibrating against the glass coffee table relentlessly. Another text. Another. Desperate for attention. Pushy. Gillian gave Frankie a questioning lift of her eyebrows to ask permission before touching the phone, then swiped it up off the table and silently read the texts, deleting them one at a time as she went through them.

Where are you? Delete.

Who's with you? Are you alone? Delete.

I know you hear these. Delete.

What's his name? Delete.

Why won't you just answer me? You don't have to talk, just tell me you're okay. Are you okay? Delete.

I'm worried about you. Delete.

Should I call an ambulance?

This one made Gillian mutter, "ugh," and roll her eyes before she caught herself, and she shook her head to tell Frankie to never mind. She deleted this text, too. The phone continued to shake in her hand, the texts marching before her eyes like soldiers positioning for war.

You need to get control over your mental problems. Delete.

You need to call me. Now. Delete. Gillian's eyebrows crept up, feeling her anxiety rise. "Frankie, was he always so demanding?" she asked, but thinking back to their awkward, monitored fish-and-chips meal on that "sisters only" girl's night, she supposed it was a silly question. Frankie didn't answer, but her lips crumpled inward in silent acknowledgement.

This isn't like you. I'm worried. Delete.

Are your pills screwing with you? Delete.

You're not seeing things straight. Delete.

You can't just turn off your feelings, baby. I know you better than that. Delete.

Gillian felt a chill wash through her. He seemed frantic. The texts kept coming with a vengeance, each question worded carefully to make her doubt her decision, doubt her options, doubt her own sanity.

"Holy shit, Frankie." *Where do you meet these guys?*

"Right?" Frankie laughed breathlessly. "You probably thought I was exaggerating."

Gillian had, in fact, assumed that her sister was being overdramatic, and admitted it with a guilty little smile. She glanced in the kitchen, where Frankie's mostly-deaf, eighteen-year-old Golden Labrador lay sleeping under the little round oak table. "What would you be expected to do tonight, if you were still with him?"

"Expected," Frankie said with a mid-air jab of her finger. "Exactly. He'd have it all planned. Watch something on TV, like NASCAR."

Gillian said, "I never knew you liked racing."

"I don't," Frankie said, "but Trav thought we should have things in common."

"His things. What about your hobbies?"

"He said his were more interesting," Frankie said, her eyes straying to her latest stained glass creation, a six foot orchid window, special-ordered by a customer from the fall craft festival.

"To him," Gillian said with a disgusted laugh. "Because they're his interests. And yours are interesting to you, so shouldn't he make an effort if you made an effort?" Gillian stopped herself, hearing a lecturing brewing. "Sorry, I just heard mom's voice coming out of my mouth. Did you?"

Frankie forgave that with a one-shouldered shrug. "After the race, we'd eat something super-healthy, because God forbid I gain weight, and take a bath at precisely ten, with the lavender salts of course, and then slip into something pretty..." She let that hang, but the sour lift of one corner of her lip told Gillian more than she wanted to know. "You know, he used to fill the bath for me, and get the nightie out, and light candles. At first, I thought it was really sweet. But after a while, it was like, hey what if I don't *want* to take a bath? What if I don't even want you to spend the night at my house?"

"Did you ever say that?" Gillian asked.

"No way. If I didn't take a bath, he'd sulk." She did a fair imitation of his voice. "Other girls would *loooove* it if their boyfriend paid them this much attention, and pampered them. There's something wrong with you, you're getting frigid in your old age. You're letting yourself go. No pizza for you."

The texts stopped coming in, and Gillian looked down at the phone in her palm. The last one was long-winded and rambling, littered with spelling mistakes, a single run-on sentence with no punctuation, peppered with demands, and a troubled Gillian didn't waste time reading the whole damn thing. She put the phone back on the coffee table after briefly considering turning the vibrate function off.

"What do you want to do about this?" Gillian asked.

"Well, don't think I'm crazy or anything," Frankie said, "but I've spoken to a private investigator. Someone Bobby recommended."

"Oh, not Bobby," Gillian sighed, her shoulders falling. "Don't bring her back into our lives. She called me this morning. I didn't even listen to the voice mail. I can't bear it."

"She'd hired a detective before, after her mom died, remember?"

"Yes, she thought her mother was murdered. Olivia McIntyre died of a heart attack, not anything mysterious," Gillian said with a sigh. "This is the kind of thing I'm talking about. Bobby's made of drama."

"But I knew she'd have a recommendation," Frankie said, gathering up her wild blonde hair and wrapping it with a black, velvet elastic strewn with silk flowers. "Anyway, this investigator is going to check Travis out and see if there's anything that I really need to worry about or if he's all piss and wind."

Smart, and better than hiding under the bed, waiting for this to be over. Frankie had a couple of his business cards on the coffee table, and Gillian scanned one quickly before slipping it in her pocket. She nodded that she'd drop it, though her guard dog instincts still wanted her pacing by the front door, protecting her sister.

"So. What do you want to do tonight?" Gillian asked, and forced her lips up in a bright smile, ignoring the burst of fury at Travis and hoping it did not show on her face.

"We need to talk paint colors for the bed and breakfast," Frankie said happily, brightening. "I can't believe you talked me into buying that ugly old pile of bricks."

"It's a steal at that price, and you know it," Gillian said, echoing her sister's excitement with a smile. "But we need to get in there and explore before we can pick a palette and start choosing drapes and bedding. If you could do anything *else* tonight, what would it be?"

Frankie's cell phone started vibrating again, loud against the glass, over and over; she did a fairly good job of ignoring it, though her forehead grew lines with each buzz. Her hand drifted back to her face, to a new spot, this time on her chin. She scratched there, *pick pick pick.*

"Let's not let that idiot ruin our night," Gillian said.

Frankie nodded once, decisively. "I want to watch a movie with my sister, and eat pizza." Frankie grinned, and though it wobbled a bit, she managed to keep it. "And garlic bread. And hey, I think the kids left some oatmeal cookies in the cupboard."

"Pick out a movie, I'll order," Gillian said. "Ham and pineapple or pepperoni mushroom?"

Frankie took a deep breath, checked to make sure none of the texts were from her boys or her ex-husband, scratched at the spot on her chin, and said, "Surprise me. Life's short."

Gillian nodded again. "Don't pick," she said, and went to get the flyer for the pizza place.

Chapter Six

Sunday, October 26. 4:15 P.M.

Paul Langerbeins studied the woman before him with interest. She sat on the very edge of his client chair like she wasn't committed to being there, ready to take flight at any moment. A contradictory determinedness in her gaze told him she wouldn't; she had made her decision, had booked the appointment, had marched up those stairs, had opened his door, and she wasn't leaving until she'd at least vented to him. There was self-assurance, there, a battered, wary resilience that had bolstered her through loss and tragedy that might have conquered some people. Gillian Hearth did not look conquered. Maybe a stubborn streak kept her upright.

He'd thought her cold at Detective Greg Ellis's funeral, but he saw now he'd been wrong; pride had stayed her tears then, and pride stayed them now, though three years later the loss of Greg still showed flinching-fresh around her eyes. They were pale green, the kind that were likely to change with her mood or outfit, reflecting the things around and within her, light irises that were circled by a dark outline and strikingly framed by thick lashes and dark brows. She wore no make-up or jewelry. She was not looking to attract attention. Paul wondered if she'd ever been a make-up, hairdo, high-heels kind of woman. Greg's partner Kenneth had once remarked that Gillian Ellis, as she was known then, was the kind of woman who seemed plain at first glance (*no, "plain in public," that's what he'd said, and I'd been forced to wonder if Ken had ever seen her in private*), but who could play up her natural beauty to stunning effect if she chose to do so. Paul thought it would take a lot for this hard woman before him to melt into a soft, playful vixen, but once his mind discovered that intriguing track, he found it difficult to remember why she was here. Her thick, espresso-dark hair was tamed by a simple tie-back. He wondered what it would look like spread across his desk, what it would feel like wound around his fist.

"You're staring at my face," Gillian noted, cutting through the bullshit and making him smile guiltily. "Is there a problem, Mr. Langerbeins?"

"I apologize. You don't remember me, I take it?"

Gillian placed her thumb between her eyebrows and rubbed firmly a few times. Her right eye fluttered closed for a second. "I'm sorry, should I?"

"It's been a long time, and you've been unwell, so I don't expect you to," he said. "We never met, not officially. I only saw you briefly, at Greg's funeral. When the shooting happened, I was their new partner."

"Right," she said. "The Rookie."

"Greg and Kenneth never called me anything but, and I've only got my initials on the business, so I don't blame you for not knowing."

Gillian swallowed and he heard a dry click in her throat. "Paul."

His lips turned up in a pleased half-smile. "That's right."

"You were also injured…"

He bobbed a nod. "Took two in the hip. I walk like an old man now, but it could have been a lot worse."

Greg took two in the head, and Kenneth had his chest blown out. They'll never be old men. You're damn right, it could have been worse. Paul felt like an asshole for having said it. As the rookie, he'd been out front, in the car, where he belonged, where he'd been ordered to stay.

He'd worked through a nasty case of survivor's guilt with the chaplain. If Gillian blamed him for not being there, for not being able to save her husband's life, she didn't show it.

"Are you feeling better?" she asked, and he felt her interest was sincere.

"Never mind me," he said, "we're here to talk about you and your sister."

"How did you know I've been unwell?" she asked.

"Greg mentioned it once or twice. Had to take a few days off training at least a couple times for hospital trips? Confessed he was worried about a brain tumor." Paul studied the pallid face of the woman before him, sizing up possible strengths, calculating weaknesses. "How'd that turn out? Everything okay?"

"Headaches. Just the result of a neck and shoulder injury," she said. "Do you mind terribly if we focus on why I'm here?"

"Of course. Tell me what I can do for you, Ms. Hearth? What have you come to me about?"

"My sister hired you to look into her ex-boyfriend, to make sure there's nothing worrying in his past." She could no longer seem to open her right eye for the pain, and Paul wondered if it was possible for her to drive home like this. He didn't think Greg would like that. "She recently broke up with a man that I believe may be stalking her. I want to know for sure that he's not."

"You want me to keep tabs on him for a bit," Paul said, noting the deep furrow of her brow. He turned off the banker's lamp over his desk, letting the room's overhead lighting stay. "Do you want a glass of water?"

"No, thank you."

"Does the pain get worse if you focus on it?"

Gillian let out a shaky breath and answered, "Yes. Maybe we should pick this up tomorrow. I'm sorry. I have a remedy at home. I didn't expect…"

"I've got a better idea." Paul stood. "I'll give you a lift home, see that you get in all right. We'll get you your remedy. I'll sit with you for half an hour or so and look over your notes, jot down any questions I have. If your headache doesn't go away, we'll call it a day, pick up tomorrow."

Gillian looked like she could have wept with relief, but Paul had gathered there was no way she'd show that sort of weakness in public, especially in front of a stranger. She collected herself, waited until she was sure she could speak without her voice betraying her emotions. "That sounds fine, thank you."

She had not hidden her emotions well at all, not from Paul Langerbeins.

***

Red Maple Drive was so named long before the row of maples was planted, the only one of the fire lanes to have a name. A few land owners on Red Maple Drive had replaced their maple trees with frilly Russian Olives and the effect was magical, creating a burgundy and silver canopy where the road dipped behind a row of greenhouses. Gillian remembered, through her fog of pain, how Greg had loved their little sanctuary at the very end of the dead-end lane; surrounded by mature trees and their own small pebble beach, tucked away from the world. The front door was painted bright green and was hugged by matching honeysuckle vines, now overgrown, perfuming the night.

She kept the window rolled down for the fresh air, a crisp distraction from what was building to be a whopper of a headache. Mr. Langerbeins drove in silence, for which she was grateful. They pulled up to the house and Gillian didn't think twice about handing him her keys.

Where Greg had been a great bear of a man, Paul was slight and wiry, with long arms prone to darting out. Despite his quick and agile movements, Gillian felt instinctively safe around him; she didn't feel the need to watch where his hands were going.

She followed him in, kicked off her flats, and stumbled in the direction of the couch.

He shut the door behind them with a long, unhappy sigh. "Gillian... what would Greg say about this?"

Nearly blinded by pain, she whimpered, "What?"

"Gillian, you just invited a strange man into your home when you're clearly vulnerable. How well would you be able to defend—"

He had to move quickly when he saw her in motion, lunging forward to grab her as she fell. Her foot hit the coffee table and she toppled. He eased her safely forward onto the couch.

"We hired you," she said, wrapping both arms around herself and bending at the waist.

"You're dealing with a scorned ex who seems unhinged. How do you know *he* didn't hire me first?" Paul said ominously. "Greg would want you to ask these questions. If this man has gotten a reaction from you, you can't underestimate him."

"Maybe I'm only being silly." She didn't believe it, but it felt good to say it. "Maybe I've over-stated the problem."

"You were a cop's wife. Give yourself some credit. What does your gut tell you?" He gave her space to respond, but talking was hurting her head even more. "I'll tell you what your gut is telling *me*. Neither you nor your sister would have called me if you didn't think this man was a serious problem. I ain't cheap, and you're not rolling in dough. You told me on the phone that your sister has had bad relationships before, bad break-ups... but you've never called me about any other ex-boyfriend. This one worries you. Why?"

Gillian whispered, "Acetaminophen, aspirin, strong coffee. Please."

He went to the kitchen and started her coffee maker. It was a small pocket kitchen, and he leaned a hip on the doorway while he waited for the coffee to percolate. "Why does this guy worry you?" he repeated.

"His mood seems to shift from needy to angry in the space of a split second. In the texts I've seen, anyway," she said softly. "And he's constantly insinuating that my sister is crazy and just not thinking straight. That's not entirely true."

"Entirely?"

He saw her lips curve in spite of her headache. "Let's just say, Frankie's a tad flighty. She has challenges. Who doesn't? But she's thinking straight. We both are."

"Good to hear," Paul said, turning to fetch the bottle of aspirin and acetaminophen kept right beside the coffee maker and bring them to her.

"She knows what she wants, Mr. Langerbeins. She wants Travis Freeman gone." *And* I *want Travis Freeman gone.*

"And he doesn't want to get gone," Paul said.

"He doesn't want to hear it."

"Would it surprise you to know that the same morning that your sister hired me," he said, "I got a very angry phone call from a blocked number? I think your instincts are good, Gillian. He's seen me, which means he's watching her."

Gillian paled and her hand kneaded her eyebrow. She dry swallowed two acetaminophen and two aspirin and took the mug of black coffee he handed her, blowing the steam.

"Should I put milk in that to cool it off?" he offered.

She shook her head, barely able to make decisions through the throbbing pain. She might have, any other time, said yes. As it was, she just needed the mug in her hand, the caffeine in her system. She sipped the hot coffee tentatively.

"I have another concern," she admitted. "You've dealt with a client named Bobby McIntyre?"

"I don't normally discuss former clients," Paul warned gently.

"I understand that. But I'm very concerned with having this person back in Frankie's circle of influence. She's a former drinking buddy, a vortex of drama, and not trustworthy at all." Gillian drank more coffee, her nervous guts giving a hard twist. "It's not my place to choose my sister's friends or lovers, and I know I sound overprotective. Frankie's in such a good place right now. Her creative output is high, she's clean and sober, and we've just bought a grand old house together to run as an artist's retreat, bed and breakfast style."

"A local house, or out of town?"

"The old Blymhill place at Higgins Point."

He nodded for her to go on.

"Frankie has a lot to look forward to," she said. "I don't want to see her derailed by negative people. Getting rid of Travis Freeman from her life was smart, very smart. Keeping Bobby McIntyre at a distance would be just as wise. I need to know if you see Miss McIntyre around my sister."

Paul appeared to consider this for a long stretch while Gillian finished her coffee and contemplated turning on a lamp. A late afternoon storm was rolling in across the lake, from west to east, and the room had grown dim.

"I can't stress this enough," Gillian said, putting her mug down. "I really can't have Bobby swooping in while my sister is struggling to rid herself of this toxic ex-boyfriend, while her judgment is off, while she may be vulnerable to 'help' from bad places. Do you see what I mean?"

"I can certainly appreciate your concerns, and if you want me to report on this person's whereabouts, I can do that." Paul gave a sorry smile. "But since your sister hired me, I can't very well watch her and report her whereabouts without informing her that this is what you've asked me to do."

Gillian shook her head. "No, I see. Yes, that is fair, of course. Please report on this Travis Freeman person, and let me know where Bobby McIntyre might be."

Paul nodded, and they made some notes together. When they were through, Paul accepted an envelope of cash from Gillian, and made sure her house keys were in her hand.

"I should get home for dinner. Your remedy seems to be kicking in?" Paul said.

Gillian exhaled slowly. "It always works."

"Caffeine, acetaminophen, aspirin," he said. "I'll have to remember that for next time I have one of my headaches." He tipped an invisible hat and went to the door, limping heavily. It made her wonder why he didn't use a cane, and then recognized the signs of pain being angrily ignored as it crossed his face.

Gillian moved to the door, watching him get into his car. She had no reason to believe that Travis Freeman might be watching her in addition to her sister, and felt no fear of the deep shadows that played in the heavy brush across the road and in the ditches on the unkempt neighboring property. Evenings were coming earlier and earlier as October tilted to run downhill toward November, and the dusk swallowed Red Maple Drive once Paul's headlights retreated. When she turned off the porch light and paused to listen to the evening breeze in the trees, letting the sound soothe her, there was no feeling of unfriendly eyes. Instead, she felt completely alone. Tonight, that was a blessing.

She returned to the coffee table to shake one of the pill bottles. The "acetaminophen" was almost gone; that bottle contained only a few more OxyContin tablets. But she still had plenty of Vicodin in the aspirin bottle, enough to get her through the next wave of pain that would come before bed. She prepared for the worst by digging out her heating pad and pulling the blinds, ordering Thai delivery, and filling the coffee pot.

It would be a long night for Gillian Hearth.

It would be an equally long night for her sister.

Chapter Seven

Sunday, October 26. 9:15 P.M.

Travis Freeman's gut was a tight knot of rage as he watched the house through cold, blue eyes that his ex-wife had once described as empty. A frigid old cow, Susan Freeman was, constantly overreacting and outright disrespecting him. And now she thought she could live without him, and she was finding out the hard way how awful that was. He almost felt sorry for her.

The front door of the house opened. One man left, the one with the limp. Twenty minutes later, another man arrived but did not go inside. Instead, he went around to the back of the house. Travis assumed he entered through the rear entrance.

The temperature outside dropped rapidly but Travis didn't notice his breath fogging the truck's driver side window, nor did he notice the wind rustling the silvery Russian olive trees or the moon appearing briefly between heavy cloud banks. He had only his hot ball of hatred and that woman's face in his mind.

Her lights went out. *That woman.* His stomach churned. *That uppity bitch.* She was going to learn some things the hard way, too. Soon.

Travis stewed and smoked a cigarette in the dark.

***

Bobby McIntyre let herself into the side door at Frankie's little cottage, calling out for the kids, or Doogie, the nearly deaf dog, or her best friend, singing, "Woo hoo, where is everyone?" and pocketing her key ring.

She did not consider that it was after nine on a school night, nor did she think about waking up the dog, which would no doubt bark and wake the neighbors. What Bobby *did* think about was how excited she was to see her best friend after so many years apart.

She jogged up a short flight of stairs, her flats slapping the old vinyl tiles, to the landing where the half-bathroom was. For a moment, she paused and listened. The dog hadn't barked the way he should have. Her eyes were dragged, almost against her will, down the long basement flight of stairs, one hard step after another, disappearing into darkness to that cement floor surrounded by sentinel doors into tiny, empty rooms. There had once been a big chest freezer down there, at the far end of the basement, but Bobby doubted Frankie had kept it. Not after everything. And if that freezer was still down there, Bobby didn't want to know it. Some things were best forgotten.

She heard a sound she didn't immediately recognize, and went down the hall to the living room and the kitchen, passing the sleeping dog, who didn't so much as twitch, seeking the source of the noise. *Running water. The shower.* Frankie was in the shower. Now Bobby could smell soap on the misty, humid air in the hall. She leaned against the wall there, hands in the pockets of her jeans, lingering for a moment, not sure where she wanted to wait. She sidled over to poke her head in the kids' rooms, establishing that they were empty. She moved on cat-quiet feet into Frankie's bedroom.

The bedroom walls had been freshly painted, and Bobby didn't like that she hadn't known about the change; when had it gone from a soft, spring yellow to eggplant, rich and sultry? There was a time, back in their early art class days, that Frankie and Bobby were a team, and decorating and art decisions were made together. There was a new oil painting over the bed, a sunset over an unfamiliar body of water, palm trees and wetlands. Frankie didn't like to work from photographs, she preferred to go to a location, to soak it all in. Had she gone on a vacation? The possibility that she'd been kept out of the loop hit Bobby's gut like a cold fist. *When did this happen? Where had she gone?* She peered at the signature on the painting and was relieved to see it wasn't Frankie's work.

But she purchased it, then. Where? When? From whom? If Frankie still kept a diary, the answer would be in there. But Frankie was also seeing that Travis fellow, last Bobby had heard, and she didn't want to stumble across anything written in the diary about him. The thought made her sick to her stomach.

Bobby went back to the kitchen, unsettled and tempted to sulk, to make herself a drink. Going through all the cupboards, she found no booze. *Since when does Frankie not have a bottle of Captain Morgan on the goddamn counter?* She settled on a Pepsi and added ice, and went to plop on the couch, put her feet up, and turn on the TV to wait. She flipped through the channels, settled on the news, grabbed a People magazine off Frankie's coffee table, and noticed the unusual mess. Odd for Frankie, the poor thing. She wasn't quite herself. Bobby would fix that.

The shower turned off and the old pipes in the bathroom gave a deep, clanging rattle. Bobby flipped through the magazine, half-interestedly digesting the news about stars and various crimes and issues. She didn't see Frankie in her robe in the dark hallway right away, and when she did, she yelped.

Frankie had a crowbar, and her eyes were crazy-wide. She bellowed, "Bobby! Jesus! You scared the fuck out of me."

"Me?" Bobby slapped the magazine down on the couch, swinging her feet down. "You're the one coming at me with a weapon. What the hell is wrong with you?"

"Why are you here?" Frankie demanded, putting the crowbar down, leaning it against the white leather loveseat. "How did you get in?"

"I have my key, honey," Bobby said with an astonished laugh. "Hey, you're really scared. What's wrong?" She got up. "I knew it. I knew something was off when I talked to you. Christ, what's happening?"

Frankie's shoulders slumped. "It's only a dumb break-up. It's just..." She burst into tears, and Bobby was quick to close the distance between them with hugs and soft, sympathetic cooing.

"Sit, sit," Bobby said. "Look, I'm sorry. I know you told me not to come. But you need support, my *gawd*, just look at you! Sit on the couch. Let Bobby take care of you. Lord have mercy, you're a sight. Seriously, your color is off, you look like you've lost a thousand pounds."

"Me? You should talk," Frankie laughed weakly, shaking off the contact. "We always did say you're light as a feather. You never gain an ounce."

"You're picking your face," Bobby scolded. She felt Frankie move to put more distance between them and didn't like it one bit. "Look at all those marks."

"I'm fine," Frankie said weakly.

"My ass, you're fine. You wouldn't be calling me for that Langerbeins prick's number if you were fine," Bobby stated, hands on her hips.

"Thank you for that," Frankie said, sinking onto the couch, chewing her bottom lip. A worried frown rippled her forehead.

"Tell Bobby what's wrong," Bobby said, taking the blanket off the back of the couch and draping it over her friend.

"Bobby is talking about herself in the third person again," Frankie said with forced humor, and then added, "It's just that I really need to be alone right now."

"Alone is the *last* thing you should be," Bobby said sternly, feeling that urge to sulk again. She softened her tone. "Are you kidding me? Honey, seriously."

"I'm not in any danger. I'm exhausted and I'm just going to bed."

Bobby studied her critically. "How about a night cap? Help you sleep?"

"No!" Frankie said, a little sharply. "No, thanks. I'm dry."

Bobby's eyebrows shot up. "Oh, is that so? Huh. Well, I suppose that's not a bad idea," she replied uncertainly. "I could crash on the couch tonight, in case you need company."

Frankie set her lips in a firm line. "No, I'm afraid I'd like you to go, Bobby. I want some alone time. It's nothing personal. I just need to process. And rest. You know? Clear my head."

"Oh," Bobby said, rocking back on her heels and cramming her hands in her jeans pockets. "Oh, right. Clear your head. I get it. Yeah, that's fine. I'll check on you tomorrow, okay?"

As Bobby retreated to the side door, Frankie called, "Hey, Bobby, could you leave me that extra key you've got?"

Her back to Frankie, Bobby grit her teeth. "Oh yeah, sure. No problem."

"I just need an extra to give to someone," Frankie said lamely, "for tomorrow. Won't have time to get a spare made. I'll get it back to you!"

My ass, Bobby thought, but she said with forced cheer, "Of course, honey. It's your key. Whatever you need." She took one of Frankie's keys off her key ring and set it on the kitchen table, then continued on to the side door. "Call you soon, babe."

Chapter Eight

Sunday, October 26. 10:30 P.M.

Frankie wrapped a blonde lock of hair around one finger and twisted until the ends made a satisfying snap. She let her hand wander until it had parceled out another lock to just the right thickness and snapped that, too. The broken ends of hair drifted to her lap and she swept them onto the carpet. When she felt well enough to unfold from the couch, she'd vacuum them up, along with the fingernails she'd chewed off and spat, and the corner of the Kleenex she'd shredded. A clean-freak, the unfortunate results of her nervous habits drove her every bit as crazy as the constant vibration of Travis's text messages arriving. Sometimes, the texts slowed. After Bobby left, the texts had increased, as though Travis knew she was alone again.

Want me to come over?

You shouldn't be alone right now. You're too fragile to handle this.

Have you called a doctor?

I'm worried, baby, that's all.

I'll just check on you and then leave. Okay?

Should I come now?

Answer your goddamn phone.

Paul had advised her to stop deleting the texts, to keep them as proof of harassment should she need to go to the police. Frankie just wanted to sleep, but how could she with his constant pestering? The house was quiet but for the sound of waves crashing on the pebble beach behind her property. She'd meant to get up and close that window now that the breeze was picking up and the temperature was dropping. She just hadn't managed to convince herself to get up yet, to unfold from the tight, comforting self-hug she was in under her blanket.

Gillian had been at her house every night this week. For that, Frankie was eternally grateful. She often thought of Gillian as her own personal pit bull, small and savage, fiercely protective. When they were growing up, Gillian would walk her to school, holding her hand when crossing the street, giving bullies the stink eye until they afforded both girls a wide berth. After their mother died, Gillian took over. Even now, if Gillian was unwell, she would take her to doctor's appointments, or intervene on her behalf with lawyers and Henry when they got too greedy. Gillian had rallied in her defense so many times that sometimes Frankie couldn't imagine dealing with life in her sister's absence.

She'd mentioned this to Travis once, when they'd first started dating. Gillian the champion. Gillian the pit bull. Travis had laughed hard and long, not bothering to hide his disbelief. (*"What does she weigh, a buck and a quarter?"*)

Later, when Travis had taken to mocking Gillian behind her back, Frankie had warned him, "You don't want to get on Gillian's bad side." Again, he'd laughed, delighted by how ridiculous he found this.

"What's she ever done?" he'd asked.

And Frankie had blurted it out, or half of it, The Big It, if only to wipe that smug, superior smile off his face. *Blurted it right out*, she thought, recalling the dread she'd felt after the words escaped.

But he hadn't believed her. Not for a second.

Now, Frankie regretted ever telling him. She wondered if he remembered. He seemed to remember every goddamn thing, like each slight was written in a mental log book, counting against her on some relationship scorecard, hash marks tallying her failures or his grievances, real and imagined. She was always letting him down, falling behind, making him wonder aloud, "Why am I with you?" and "Why do I put up with this?"

She'd never had an answer. She hadn't been aware that she didn't need to answer, that she didn't owe him an explanation, that she didn't owe him a damn thing. That her answer could be "Go, then." That hadn't occurred to her until Gillian pointed it out.

Once again, Gillian to the rescue. The pit bull chomping at the bit to defend her. Frankie had always been quick to laugh, quick to love, quick to cry. If someone stubbed their toe, *Frankie's* eyes would well up before theirs would. *Too soft,* Frankie thought about herself; maybe she had a bold and fearless heart but she also had raw nerves. Maybe she didn't give enough thought about tomorrow in her rush to love today.

Gillian, on the other hand, had a strong outer shell which Frankie admired and longed for. Nothing fazed Gillian. Gillian was careful to withdraw and analyze, to take things slowly; if you weren't willing to wait for Gillian, you'd miss the depth of a heart that had decided to commit, to give its all, for better or worse. Gillian took time to decide whether or not to be devoted to you, but once she was, you could depend on her for anything, forever.

How could I ever repay her? Frankie thought. And then she heard her sister's voice, very clearly: *You don't have to. We're sisters.*

Frankie took a look around the messy room with its litter and low light and locks done up tightly, and shook her head, dangling earrings tinkling pleasantly. She lifted one fluttering, nervous hand to push her wild hair back from her face.

Her sister shouldn't have to come here and play nursemaid. She had a job and a new business and her own life to live. *This is silly. Turn your phone off and get back to it, Miss Frankie.* After three hours curled up sweating and nervously picking her face and snapping her hair on the couch, Frankie finally got up, and set about putting things right again. Her first order of business was to text her sister good night and then turn off her phone.

Chapter Nine

Monday, October 27. 10:15 A.M.

Dozens of questions go through the mind when digging up bones. The first time, people assume it's just an animal; a family pet, perhaps, buried in a shallow grave near the honeysuckle. The second time, suspicions arise about the size. Around the ninth or tenth time, though, start putting them right back where they were found, and quickly; superstitious or not, it's unwise to muck about with bones or otherwise disrespect the dead.

Gillian knew all about digging up skeletons, or planting flowers to mark their place. To honor the dead, whether they deserved to be remembered or not. Her work at the cemetery was peaceful and she took great pride in beautifying and remembering. She patted the earth back over the last bone — *probably just a beef bone Mrs. Blymhill never got around to turning into broth,* she told herself — and picked up the garden shears to trim an invasive peppermint plant.

"The old Italian lady next door watches me," Frankie said abruptly, using the back of her gloved hand to wipe sweat off her forehead and sweep some stray bangs off her temple.

Gillian snort-laughed, sounding a lot like their father. "She does not."

"*Does.* Her husband brought us grapes the first day, remember?

But she yelled at him to come away. Now he ignores me, and she stares at me funny."

"Well, you're funny-looking, can you blame her?" Gillian asked.

"Maybe she wants me," Frankie said, winking.

"Doesn't everybody?" Gillian drawled, only half kidding.

"Only the ones with good taste," Frankie said, and waved at the fence line. The neighbor's curtain twitched closed. "Oops. No waving allowed, apparently."

Gillian heard a crash inside of what she still thought of as Mrs. Blymhill's house, and rested on her haunches in the herb garden to survey the back door, propped open and spilling some classic rock from a battery-powered radio into the yard. She'd asked Bruce from the cemetery planting crew to help haul out some old pieces of furniture to the curb for garbage pick-up and to tear down a few old cabinets and toss them into the construction dumpster she'd rented. He swore at something gruffly and there were two more thuds, then the crackling of wood giving way. Gillian peeled off her gardening gloves and gave her sore fingers a rub, noticing without surprise that her sister hadn't so much as tugged a weed or clipped a dead bloom.

The wind stirred the foliage and the dull glint of something metal caught her eye. She squinted, parting the mint with her gloved hand, cocking her head. "Hey, Frankie?"

Frankie made a half-interested *hmmm?* She stepped closer and leaned over, peering at the rusty metal object barely peeking through a thick patch of herbs. "Huh."

"What is that?" Gillian asked.

"Looks like an old bear trap," Frankie said, standing straight and demonstrating with her clawed hands snapping shut. "You know?"

Frankie's ex-husband was an avid hunter; she enjoyed shooting, whether it was at game or in the shooting range with one of his many handguns.

"Take a picture and send it to Henry, ask him how to disarm it so I don't accidentally tear my arm off," Gillian said. "And hand me that solar light. I'll use it to mark the spot."

Frankie handed her the little solar powered lantern. Gillian stuck the pointy end in the ground near the trap, if that's what it was, to mark the danger zone. She looked around more carefully and spotted another one lurking between two hybrid tea roses, their limbs heavy with rose hips.

"It's not the only one. Looks like a couple more by the back fence," she told her baby sister. "I'll mark them with more lights. But better not wander into the garden off the path in case there are others, okay?"

Frankie rolled her eyes, and the gesture said *as-if-I-would*. She got a picture on her phone and texted it to her ex-husband with their question. "Mrs. Blymhill was a weird old coot, eh?"

This place had been their dream since they lost their mother to the bottle and their father to depression. They envisioned a retreat where writers and artists could get away and pursue their creative pursuits without interruption. Frankie, an artist working in both oil paint and stained glass, wanted a studio. Gillian, who dabbled in poetry and pottery, was charmed by the idea of helping other people in the creative community. Hearth House wouldn't be the only bed and breakfast in the quaint lakeside village of Derby Harbor, but it would be the only one jutting into the lake on Higgins Point, and it would be theirs.

Frankie answered a call on her cell, giving an exhausted-sounded puff into the phone. "Absolutely, no, I could use a break. I'm *wiped out!*"

Gillian rolled her eyes as she put her gardening gloves back on and examined the stubborn, overgrown mint plant before her.

Frankie said, "See ya Saturday? Yeah, you gotta see this place. The dining room walls are legit old growth dark walnut, floor to ceiling. And what a ceiling. Pressed copper. Fucking gorgeous. Yeah, it's dark, but it's just stunning. Same thing up the big staircase, and in the hallways. The granddaughter left all sorts of antique furniture to go with the house. Hopefully, the throw rugs can be salvaged, because they look like genuine Turkish beauties. I've got a guy coming to look at them."

She's got a guy coming to look at them, Gillian thought wryly, noting it had been an hour since they discussed the possibility and it had been Gillian's idea.

Frankie went on excitedly, "Oh, and it's *full* of weird shit. I'm talking taxidermy-level weird, monkeys in little clown outfits, a beaver on the mantelpiece. The bedroom I liked most came with a bonus: creepy dolls! About three dozen of them. Those are *going*, ASAP, I don't care what my sister says. I'm tossing them right in the damn dumpster before we have a full-blown Chuckie incident on our hands. I'm not sleeping in this house with century-old dolls staring at me from the shadows with their glass eyes, no thank you."

Gillian rolled her eyes again and this time directed a sigh at her sister.

"Yeah, no," Frankie rambled on, "even the back yard is loopy. Crazy old bat must have really liked cooking. Half the yard is a maze of overgrown herb plants. Dried herbs hanging in bundles in the kitchen. You can barely walk in there."

Gillian thought this an overstatement, but not by much. Mrs. Blymhill had been a bit of a hoarder. Gill was equally dismayed to find the once-manicured yard overgrown with ivy and honeysuckle and trumpet vine and spider webs, but she saw as much potential here as she had three years ago when she stumbled upon the big Victorian house on a boat cruise along the shore of Lake Ontario. As the boat had slipped through silent, midnight-dark waters and the other partiers sipped champagne, nibbled finger foods, said a goodbye to the man they'd come to mourn and celebrate, Gillian had leaned on the boat's railing and watched the passing lights in the homes and the few lighthouses along the coast and wondered where her husband's ashes would wash ashore. The big house had loomed in the darkness at Higgins Point, only a single light on in a main floor window, and Gillian thought it seemed a lonely place, as lonely as she'd felt since her husband Greg had been killed in the line of duty. It was there, she decided, that the current would probably take his ashes, having been spilled into the lake not fifteen minutes before. And it was there, in that old, rambling house with its peeling paint and wrap-around porch and its broken-down dock and its boulder-strewn shoreline, that she wanted to live.

Frankie was still chatting on the phone, strolling toward the house, wrapping one long curly blonde lock of hair around a finger. A clean finger, Gillian noted, certainly untouched by dirty work.

You haven't been down to that shoreline, something teased in the back of her mind. She fought it off by taking her garden shears to the mint and trimming it unforgivably short.

Frankie gasped and insisted, "Stop it! You're horrible!" But her tone was teasing and delighted.

Gillian cleared her throat. "Bruce could use a hand, I'm sure."

Frankie didn't entirely ignore her. She shot her a *do-you-mind* look and continued to gab. After a few minutes of watching her sister battle mint while taunting her latest boyfriend about various naughty outdoor shenanigans they might get up to at the new place, she hung up and sighed. "You're going to get heat stroke."

"In October? I'm fine," Gillian insisted while the sweat rolled down her spine. "See if Bruce wants a cold drink, eh? And check my phone? I'm expecting a call. Forgot to bring it out."

"You're always 'forgetting' your phone," Frankie accused. "Convenient. It's almost like you don't want to talk to anyone."

Almost, Gillian thought, trimming the last edge of the mint and shuffling carefully to the left to take on the lemon balm. Warring scents were heady in the unseasonably hot afternoon air.

Frankie looked at her phone display. "Henry says you were right; it's a bear trap. He'll come take care of them. He says hi, and you need to make sure you've kept up your life insurance if you're really going to live somewhere booby-trapped. Ha!"

Gillian smirked; Henry had worked in insurance for decades and was often on her case about keeping her bills paid up and her policies current. "Tell him we'll get house insurance once the rest of the paperwork is sorted out," she promised.

Frankie laughed and swept in through the back door, which led into the kitchen, an extra-wide entrance compared to all the strangely narrow doorways in the big old home. Gillian heard her exclaim, "It's gorgeous. We have to leave this here. This is amazing. So intricate. Gills, come see!"

"What is it?" Gillian called, getting to her feet, dusting her knees off, and trundling inside to have a look. When she walked through the door and into the living room, she saw that under the worn, stained Berber carpet that Bruce had been pulling up was a scuffed hardwood floor painted with a room-sized circle. She was forced to repeat, "What is it?"

"What do you mean?" Frankie laughed. "It's nothing, it's just... Beauty. Randomness. It's perfect, look at it." She was down on her hands and knees, now, tracing the faded brush strokes. A merman. A centipede. A lock of hair tied in blue ribbon. "I can't believe she covered *this* up, and yet she kept those hideous black and white sketches just stabbed on nails on the wall in the hallway." Frankie shook her head and her earrings tinkled. "Gosh, just look at it. Have you ever seen something so striking?"

Bruce looked, but from a distance. "It's not random," he said. The old wood planks creaked pleasantly under his weight. "There's a pattern."

"You and your patterns," she teased, but she did give him the benefit of humoring him. She stared at it for a full minute, circling it, cocking her head, before shrugging. "I don't see it."

"Water creature," Bruce pointed out. "Earth creature, Fire, and Air."

"You're nuts," she said, but she stared still, feeling vaguely mesmerized.

"Maybe whoever painted this was nuts," Bruce allowed, "but not me. Look, dolphin-centaur-phoenix-storm. Water, Earth, Fire, and Air. First clockwise, then below that, curving counter-clockwise, over and over..."

"Deosil," Frankie whispered on an exhale, and her stare deepened. "Widdershins."

"What?" Gillian laughed in surprise.

Frankie jerked. "What-what?"

"What did you say? What's a deostill? Watershins?"

"Witchy stuff..." Frankie shook her head, frowning. "Never mind."

Bruce scowled, his nose wrinkling. Frankie was too lost in the painting to answer. The room felt uncomfortably silent for a moment. Abruptly, the fridge behind them began to hum loudly and Bruce, leaning nearby, started, and then swore at his own foolishness.

"Fancy words for clockwise and counter-clockwise, is all." Gillian swiped her forehead with the back of her hand, stepping into the kitchen and placing her gardening gloves on the butcher block counter top. She opened the fridge for a cold bottle of Pepsi. "All the furniture at the curb?" she asked him, handing him a bottle, too.

He nodded and grunted affirmatively. "Just got the last cabinet here to drag out and the rest of this carpeting, and then you're on your own, Boss."

Gillian smiled and tilted her pop bottle in thankful salute. She was in a junior supervisory role with the cemetery planting crew, owing to seniority, but it was not all that official. Still, the guys on the crew went to her first with their questions when the orders came in. "We've got to remember to bring a camp chair, Frankie, or something so we can sit for a rest."

"Feeling okay?" Frankie said, still distracted by the painted floor. "Overheated? It's so close in here. Have to get central air put in before we open for clients. There's no way anyone could sleep under those eaves in this kind of heat."

"It's almost winter. Give it a month. By the time we're ready to open in April, it'll still be cold as a witch's tit," Gill promised.

Bruce opened the freezer for a chunk of ice and plopped it in a glass, which he handed to Gillian. "Here, pour that Pepsi in here and drink up, missy. If I let you get heat stroke, your sister will never let me marry you."

Her smile tilted. "Oh, I'm marrying *you*, now? Since when?"

"I'm after your big money, honey," Bruce said with a smirk, and hauled his impressive bulk out back into the living room to finish yanking up carpet. He was a broad-shouldered bear of a man, heavily bearded, thick of neck and stern of face, with eyes that softened with humor quickly and easily. Bruce had been faux-proposing to her for seven years, even while she was married, pretty much on a daily basis; Gill was certain he was joking. Mostly.

"Seriously, Gill, it's like a hundred and eight degrees in the shade," Frankie said. "You know how you get."

"It's only eighty-two. I'll take it easy," she reassured, barely refraining from an eye-roll.

"Heat's gonna break soon, anyway," Bruce called back to them. "Check that storm front."

Frankie got up, her skirts jingling, and hurried ahead of Gillian to the living room window. Bruce was a formidable shape in the big bay window, the place where Gillian could picture pots and pots of trailing orchids and Frankie's colorful stained glass framing the wide view of Lake Ontario. A shadow had fallen across the west horizon, and the lake, which had been glaringly blue this morning, had gone grey and rough.

The bay window looked out on the massive covered porch that wrapped around both sides of the house. Wicker furniture was still strewn here and there, old but in fairly good condition. A porch swing that faced the lake had begun to sway erratically as the wind picked up.

"Sure you want to stay here tonight?" Bruce asked. "Might lose power."

"I've got a date," Frankie said, planting her hands on her hips. "You're on your own, Gill. Oh, that reminds me... a Nancy Shaw from Those Buns Dough called?"

Gillian glanced up at Bruce and they both burst out laughing.

"What?" Frankie said, cracking a smile. "That's what the bakery is called."

"I know," Gillian said, feeling like the heat might be getting to her. She giggled helplessly, struggling to pull it together. "They're going to supply our continental breakfast options. I'll call her as soon as I'm back from the grocery store." She washed her hands and arms, patted her neck with a cool washcloth, and gathered up her purse and phone. "Back soon."

Chapter Ten

Monday, October 27. 11:00 A.M.

Delia Slepsky of 226 Azure Lane leaned over the sink to look out her kitchen's bay window, the one George and his buddies had installed, brand-spanking new and crowded with potted herbs.

"There's that car again, third time gone by. Funny little thing. Stands out, don't it?"

George gave an affirmative murmur behind his newspaper. His coffee had gotten cold, but he wasn't about to get up in the middle of the international column.

"I don't know what kind it is," Delia mused. "Course, what I know about cars could fill a sow's ear—are you listening, dear? A sow's ear—but I bet you don't neither. If it ain't in the newspaper, you ain't seen it. Right, dear? If I had a dollar for every newspaper you bought." She shook her head. "I could probably afford to buy one of them zippy cars. Travis will know what it is. Even from a description by a dummy like me."

"You're no dummy, Delia," George Slepsky said, not about to let *that* opportunity get by him.

Delia cast him a little smile and came to fetch his cup. She dumped his cold coffee and rinsed the mug. "Yes sir, Travis knows all about cars. Even funny little foreign cars like that one."

George kept his teeth together when his wife got onto the subject of the man who lived in the brick bungalow across the road. Thirty years younger than Delia, Travis Freeman was, but she spoke like she had a real shot with him, if she could ever be rid of her simple, plodding husband. *Let her think it,* George thought, unperturbed. Delia asked for so little. He'd leave her to her smitten school-girl daydreams, and he would have his about the Channel Nine weather lady. Boy howdy, would he.

"You wouldn't know," she said. "You're not about cars. More like to know about vermin, you. Ain't that right dear? Yeah, shown a handful of droppings, no one picks up on a brand of vermin like my George. Don't I always say it at bridge, though? Don't I?"

George flipped the page. He had not the slightest idea what his wife said about him to the ladies at bridge, and he thought it was probably better that way.

"Travis can build a car from parts, did he ever tell you? Break one back down again, too. Handy skill for a man to have, I suppose. Real grease-monkey, a pro. Always so helpful, too. Saved us a fortune on the Ford, ain't he a doll?"

George kept quiet on that one, too, even though Delia likely expected a rant about the front yard or the junk cars in Travis Freeman's double-wide driveway. George had plenty to say on the state of his neighbor's yard, even in his less talkative moods. This time, he didn't take the bait. He said, "Is there more coffee?"

"Asked me to keep a look out," she said, touching the pot to see if it was still hot. It wasn't. She began a new brew, pulling the coffee maker closer to the sink so she could watch the street. She'd always loved a kitchen that faced the street. Every home she'd owned, George had made sure the kitchen, where Delia spent most of her time happily puttering, faced the street; besides baking cookies neither of them should eat, being the unofficial neighborhood watch was Delia's passion.

The coffee began to perk and drip, and Delia went back to the sink, folding both arms against the counter and leaning against it so she could keep one eye on the view, and one on her husband. The way she was standing popped one of her generous hips to the side. George remembered how those hips had driven him wild in their courting days; after four kids and forty years together, those hips still had the power to distract him mightily, boy, did they ever. He went back to his paper, smiling fondly.

"Asked me to tell him if any suspicious cars went by or stopped near his place," Delia said. "Weird thing to ask, right? Something's up. He said to watch for a red Fiat, but I don't think this is one of those. It's red, all right, but it doesn't look French. Looks like one of them little British deals. You know, he wouldn't say why he wanted me to watch."

"Probably as you're so good at it, darlin'."

"But then, he wouldn't want to involve us in his troubles, the doll."

George sighed and turned a page. Travis was a doll, all right. Everything about him was fake, plastic. Even his smiles weren't quite right, though George couldn't quite put a finger on why. Unnerving. Like it was just playacting. If he'd known the term *uncanny valley* existed, he'd have said Travis was at the bottom of it.

"He looked troubled, and why shouldn't he?" Delia huffed. "With that rat of an ex-wife nabbing his babies away, stealing all his money, slashing his tires, and now this horrible ex-girlfriend causing trouble, too."

That caused a corner of the newspaper to twitch down enough for George's bushy brow to show. "The little blonde piece?"

"That's her, the tramp. Cheating on him, stealing all his hard-earned money."

If his ex-wife stole it all, how could there be any money left for the ex-girlfriend to steal, that's what George wanted to know. It sounded like a load of horseshit to him. The young man just liked to play victim to sympathetic ears like Delia's, or any other sucker who'd buy his line of crap. Travis had tried it on George, too, but George didn't truck with sniveling baby-men. He'd grumbled that Travis should "man the fuck up," exactly his words, and that had put an end to the whining right quick.

When George didn't agree with her, Delia jumped to the man's defense. "Well, you can tell how hard he works for his money, works hard for every cent, just look at him." She flapped a hand at the street as though Travis were standing there. Delia always had appreciated the physique of a man who did hard physical labor for a living. Oh yes. George had shown off his own physique in his pest control uniform to catch Delia's eye decades before, snagged himself a chatty little redhead, a real firecracker. Now, her hair was dyed to keep the red up, and while baby-making had put a bit of weight on her frame, age hadn't slowed her mouth or her spirit one bit.

"Now this car, this weird foreign thing," she continued. "Parked down the street for only a minute, earlier, see? Now it's come again. A fourth time. Tinted windows, well, I ask you, who needs that, but tramps and drug dealers?"

George tried to keep the smile out of his voice. "*Your* windows are tinted, darlin'."

"So tramps and drug dealers don't see me with my diamonds." She clutched the necklace at her throat, ten karat gold with a genuine diamond chip in a heart, a gift from her coworkers upon retirement. "Can't be too careful."

"Of course not, muffin," George said good-naturedly, even if it was by rote.

"I thought I could make out a baseball hat on the driver," Delia said, leaning over the sink again so far that her large bosom grazed the bubbles from the washing up. "Worn low to cover her face, but definitely a girl."

"If the windows are tinted, how'd you see that?"

"Well the front one isn't *that* tinted or a body couldn't drive, George!" She poured him another coffee, bringing it to him grudgingly, like he hadn't quite earned her service. "Honestly! It would be nice not to have to explain every little thing, all day, every day!"

But then what would you run your ever-loving motor mouth about, darlin'? George was careful not to say it, smiling up at her as he sipped the coffee. She swiped with her tea towel at imaginary coffee drips all around him then flounced back to the sink in an exasperated manner. He watched her hips as she went, and said, "Yes, Delia."

"I'd better mark down the time," she said, turning her grocery shopping list over and checking her watch before making a note.

***

Delia thought Travis would like her report. He'd give her one of those big smiles that made the laugh lines on his cheeks, but never around his eyes. Nope, his smiles never quite touched his eyes, poor doll. And that's exactly what she'd tell the police detectives when they came to call just one week later.

Chapter Eleven

Monday, October 27. 12:30 P.M.

At twelve-thirty, when Gillian pulled into the parking lot at the grocery store, it wasn't raining yet, but the sky was lowering, growling warningly overhead, and a haze was sapping colors in every direction, lending the world a faded, muted facsimile of itself. The sun had slipped behind a battalion of clouds the color of a fresh bruise. At quarter to one, as she stood at the florist's counter picking out a potted African violet to cheer up Frankie, she glanced out the plate glass to see that the rain had started to speckle car windshields outside. *No more working in the herb garden today,* she thought.

Her phone buzzed in her back pocket. Thinking it was Nancy from Those Buns Dough calling back, she took her phone out and tried to answer. But it wasn't a call. Just a text. Blocked number.

Shopping, whore?

She blinked rapidly at it, taken aback. Her first instinct was to look around and see who might be watching her, but her pride stopped her. She did not like being toyed with or controlled. Pretending it didn't faze her one bit, she forwarded the message to Paul Langerbeins with a quick follow-up text that asked, *Level of one to ten, how worried should I be?*

Paul texted back, *Are you in a public place?* And then, *Do you need me to come?*

Feeling silly, she told him not to come. He, in turn, advised her to not delete any messages she might receive. Paul wanted to see each one, and their date and time, for his records. He suggested they might need to speak to the police.

Gillian felt her guts contract, and she nearly responded, knee-jerk, with a "no." She forced herself to put the phone away in her pocket, inhaled deeply, and pretended interest in the price of avocados.

She took her time, not eager to be out in the downpour, equally reluctant to leave the imagined safety of the store, where staff and customers provided something like cover. Gillian put kale, bananas, and apples into her cart. The cereal aisle came next, and when she reached for a box of cornflakes, something flashed in the corner of her eye; she nearly jumped out of her skin, her heart hammering hard.

It was just a kid darting away from his mother's cart. Gillian smiled at him and turned the corner. Dread told her she'd find Travis Freeman in the dairy section, waiting for her. *Why, dummy?* she chided. *What would he want with you?*

Brushing these fears away, she popped to the pharmacy section and added enough sleeping pills to her basket to see her through an apocalypse, shaking her head at her paranoia. This nonsense with Travis was really too much. Now she was losing sleep over this jerk? *He's not going to do anything. All jaw, no jab,* as her father used to say.

In the paper goods section, she selected a birthday card for her coworker, Aaron, thinking everyone on the cemetery crew could sign it before Friday. She browsed for a new paperback, a breezy romance with a beach scene on the cover; God, how it made her want to escape. And she would, for a little while, curled on the couch with herbal tea and a cookie and some reading. Tonight's big plans. It wouldn't be as relaxing as her and Frankie's recent trip to the Florida Keys, but it would have to do.

She lingered in the candy aisle, debating on whether or not to risk adding a small chocolate bar to her evening just this once, and decided against it, taking her groceries to the register. Her phone vibrated against her butt, or she thought it had, but when she dug it out to glance at it, there was neither a text nor a missed call. *Phantom buzz*, she thought. *Now you're jumping at ghosts.*

She queued behind two people in the express lane — an older man and a teenage girl — and chanced another glance at the parking lot while she waited. The storm hadn't fully rolled in yet, but tiny drops were hitting the broad front windows, building in intensity. The older man finished his purchase, and the line moved forward a few paces. Gillian scanned the parking lot for Travis's black truck, and an anxious little quiver began in her belly.

Stop it, she told herself. *It's not like he's everywhere. You can leave the fucking house without him being right behind you.*

But her nerves didn't want to take her word for it, and the nape of her neck prickled like she was being watched. She refused to look over her shoulder, stubbornly tallying up her purchases and calculating tax as a way to keep her mind busy. *And so what if he was?* she challenged herself. *What if he was standing right in front of you? So what? He's just some guy, not a monster or a bear. He hasn't got claws or fangs; he's just a man.*

Her nerves didn't buy that, either, though they had absolutely no proof that he was dangerous in the least. A pest, perhaps. Pushy, absolutely. *And you're overreacting like some silly flake, so get a grip*, she demanded, taking a quiet, deep inhale and letting it out slowly. The teenager paid for her Coke and Pringles, and Gillian put her things down for the cashier, declined the offer of a plastic bag, and pulled her cloth tote out of her jacket pocket. While the cashier rang her items through the till, Gillian's eyes strayed with almost helpless curiosity to the parking lot again, this time seeking out her Jeep.

There was something on the windshield. A little thing on any other day, but it made her guts freeze to slush. A piece of paper was tucked under the wiper blades. A brochure? A take-out menu? *Who does that kind of advertising in the rain?* She was sure it hadn't been there when she parked, and taking a quick look confirmed that no other cars had one.

"Ma'am?" the cashier was saying.

"Oh, I'm sorry," Gillian tried to focus on what the woman said, but her pulse was roaring in her ears. She opened her wallet and said, "Debit," hoping that answered her question. She had to plug in her PIN code twice, because her fingers had become stupidly clumsy. She gathered up her things, wishing she could linger, not wanting to go out there. Trying to seem nonchalant while her heart hammered, she pulled out her phone, pulled up Paul's number, her thumb hovering over the dial as she left the store.

The rain was coming down harder, and Gillian was torn between hurrying to the Jeep to keep from getting drenched, or drag her feet to stay close to the store in case of trouble. She kept her thumb over Paul's number as she approached her car, balancing the violet in one hand and the tote bag over her wrist, knowing she wasn't being nearly careful enough and hearing Greg in her head: *Always keep your dominant hand free, babe.*

For a moment, the memory of her husband steeled her, and she remembered who she was, remembered all she'd picked up from him. She put the grocery bag down on the wet asphalt next to the Jeep and did a quick spot check around her for people, movement, danger. Then she unlocked the car, set the violet inside, threw her purse in, and did another spot check before moving the grocery bag to the car. One hand still on the phone, she slid into the driver's seat, got in, and locked up.

Taking a long, deep breath, she put her phone down in the cup holder and stared at the piece of paper.

She heard herself say aloud, "I'm not even going to look at that," before she knew she was going to speak, and the decision made her feel in control, powerful. She admitted to herself that since Greg had died, she had felt alone and scared more often than not. She reached in the back seat for her box of tissues and snatched several up to pat her face dry. She was dripping wet and cold and tired from the jittery hyper-vigilance that seemed to ebb and flow every day now. She needed a hot bath and an escape into her new book.

She tried to start the car but nothing happened. She tried again.

Not a single thing. She didn't have a second of doubt that this was Travis's toying with her car. Somehow, he'd done something without her or anyone else noticing.

Was he watching for her reaction? Did he want to see tears? Fear? Anger? *He's not going to get any of that,* Gillian thought.

She called a cab, calmly, coolly, and then called Bruce. When he answered, she said calmly, "All done at the new place?"

"Got the last of the carpet in the dumpster just as the sky opened up," he said cheerfully. "I locked up. Frankie's off on her date. Sure you're gonna want to be here tonight?"

"Yeah," she said, soothed by the normalcy of the conversation. She felt herself smiling. "I want to get a feel for the place before Frankie and I make any decorating decisions. You know, where the light strikes at different times of the day, stuff like that."

"No sunlight now, lady," Bruce said with a chuckle. "Clouds. You're out of luck, there."

"Still," she said, watching for the taxi cab. "I got a card for Aaron's birthday. We'll pass it around, sign it tomorrow?"

"That creepy new guy?" Bruce said gruffly. "Better let him think it was my idea. I shouldn't like to give him too many ideas, you know?"

"He's creepy?" Gillian said, laughing with surprise. "Seems harmless to me."

"Then you ain't payin' attention, Gills. But then, you never do, eh?" he teased. "Gotta jet. Make sure you lock up tonight. I shoved your extra key through the mail slot. See you in the morning."

"Bright and early," she said in lieu of goodbye.

Gillian dropped her phone in her pocket, stared at the paper under her windshield wiper; it was becoming sodden and transparent, and she could now see words scrawled in blue ink. Two words, repeated over and over. *You'll pay. You'll pay. You'll pay. You'll pay.*

"I'll pay for someone to tow my car," she told the paper coolly in the quiet inside her Jeep as the rain drummed heavily on the roof, "and fix whatever stupid thing you did to it. That's all you're going to get out of me, asshole."

By the time the taxi cab pulled in front of the store and Gillian Hearth was safely inside with her violet and her groceries, she felt once again in control.

Chapter Twelve

Tuesday, October 28. 1:25 A.M.

Bobby McIntyre paused before walking into Frankie's house with a cardboard tray of drive-thru coffee cups balanced on one hand, a book of wallpaper samples clamped tightly under that arm, standing at the dark side door, and with a flash of irritation, she knocked. Heat rose in her belly. *Knocking,* she thought, *like a stranger has to. Have a few months apart reduced me to stranger status?* In truth, it had been three years since she'd last been in Frankie's social circle, though to Bobby, it felt more like last month. *I always let people treat me like dirt.* This was Bobby's burden, she figured, and in her quest to teach people how to treat her properly, she often lost them. Nonetheless, she couldn't bear being treated poorly; she had to teach this lesson over and over again, it seemed, with each person who entered her life.

There was no response to her knock, even though Frankie's cute little red Fiat was parked under the car port and a light was on in the bedroom.

In the bedroom. Her guts rolled unhappily. Maybe Frankie wasn't coming to the door because she was... being entertained. Bobby got a cruel mental image of Frankie sprawled across her bed, Frankie in a gauzy robe and little else, cheeks flushed, eyes sparkling, giggling at some bumbling, half-naked oaf of a man. She knocked again, this time more forcefully.

Half of Frankie's face appeared behind a twitching curtain on the door and then the locks tumbled and the hinge squeaked, and Bobby's belly relaxed; Frankie was wearing fluffy white pajamas and a bewildered expression.

"Bobby, it's almost one-thirty in the morning..."

"That's why I brought coffee, honey," Bobby laughed, advancing into the house, feeling embraced by the warmth of the place. "We're going to need rocket fuel to get through all these samples."

"You brought..." Frankie scratched her head. "Wallpaper samples?"

"You're redecorating," Bobby said, making a *duh* face and tapping her temple. "You thought I wouldn't help out? Come on, goof. What are you thinking? Of course I'd help out."

She went into the kitchen with the coffee, and left Frankie speechless in the hall, closing the door on the evening's drizzle.

***

Frankie stared in disbelief at the back of Bobby's head, her clipped-short, unnaturally red hair damp from the rain. She hadn't seen Bobby this often in years, not since all the trouble began, then Bobby's mother got sick and passed away, and Bobby went out west for a while, to Vancouver. Now, here she was, fishing around for a spoon in the kitchen drawers like she owned the place. It felt like a violation, but Frankie wondered if she was being oversensitive and prickly because of Travis. *It's hard to be objective when you're being bombarded with disrespect,* she thought. *But why is she here this late at night?*

Bobby put her hands in her pockets and rummaged, drawing out her sweetener packets, slapping them and ripping the paper and doctoring her own coffee first.

Frankie demanded, "Are you drunk?"

"Nah," Bobby said, shooting her a smile over her shoulder. "I've been sober as long as you have. Didn't you know?"

"Great," Frankie said, tired, relieved, confused. "That's great, really. Four months, huh?"

Bobby said, "Sixteen weeks and two days."

Frankie sensed she was lying, but didn't know why she'd bother, or why she should call Bobby out on it. Instead, she asked, "Did we make plans for tonight that I'm not remembering?"

"I'm sorry I didn't put anything in your coffee," Bobby said with her back turned. "I couldn't remember how you take it."

"Just a little almond milk," Frankie said. "It's awfully late."

"Almond milk? What are you drinking that shit for? Are you still a vegetarian, like, for real? Christ." Bobby laughed. "Don't know why I'm surprised. Maybe if we'd kept in touch, I'd remember how you take your coffee." Bobby opened the fridge to get the carton of vanilla almond milk. "I always brought you coffee, remember? Every Thursday before pottery class."

"I'm sorry we've drifted a little," Frankie began.

"A little? I didn't even know about your bedroom remodel." Bobby laughed, turning to her with the paper coffee cup, making sure the little plastic lid was on tight. "Almond milk, yuck."

"I've always taken almond milk in my coffee," Frankie said.

"It's kind of a funny color," Bobby remarked, looking into the coffee cup before putting the plastic lid back on. "The drive-thru must have made it too strong again. That place on the highway has really gone downhill. Does it taste okay?"

Frankie took the paper cup and smiled hesitantly. "I'm sure it's fine. Look, I don't think I have the stamina to look at wallpaper tonight, Bobby. I mean, it's after midnight."

"We used to party so hard, remember?" Bobby said, her eyes bright. "Late, late, late. You're getting old, honey, *jeeeeeezus*. Drink your turbo juice."

"I've had a hard few days, and I had a terrible date—"

"Is the coffee okay?" Bobby asked. "Hey, what date? Who was it this time? Another race car dude? I swear, you have the worst taste in men. Worse than your taste in coffee. Is it okay?"

Frankie sipped the coffee. "Yeah, it's good, thanks. Kind of sweet. Did you add sweetener to mine too by accident?"

"Nope, no sweetener, I promise," Bobby said, and though she gave a little laugh, her smile tightened. "Don't want to add too many calories. Not for my Frankie. Gotta watch that teensy little waistline."

Frankie relaxed and went to grab her purse. "Tell you what, let me pay you for the coffee, and tomorrow, I'll take you out as my treat, and we'll go over the wallpaper. Although, I gotta say, I don't remember saying anything about wallpaper. I don't think Gillian wants wallpaper at the new place."

Bobby looked like she didn't quite understand the language Frankie was speaking. "But you *love* wallpaper," she insisted.

Frankie shrugged one shoulder and tried to hand her five dollars. It hung there limply in her hand between them, but Bobby made no move to take it, so Frankie set it on the counter top. "Not really. I used to. Years ago. It's out of style, now. And this new place is Gillian's as much as it is mine, so we're making all the decisions together. I have to respect her input. Plus, it's got gorgeous wood paneling, it would be a crime to cover it up."

Bobby's forehead was one deep furrow. "You're the one with the artistic instincts, honey, don't let her steamroll over you like she always does."

"Gillian?" Frankie laughed. "She's the most supportive person I know."

She knew it wasn't the right thing to say by the instant chill in the air and the way Bobby stiffened as though she'd been struck. Bobby's head started bobbing, rapid nods, and her lips tucked inside her teeth like she was holding back words.

"Besides you, obviously," Frankie said sincerely. "All these years, you've always been there for me. Especially when I..." The words stuck, and she swallowed hard and tried again. "When I was so desperate for help. I didn't mean to invalidate that. God, I'm such a jerk when I'm tired. It's late. That's not an excuse, I'm sorry."

Bobby's smile returned, but it was wounded and wary. "Cut yourself some slack. You've been pushing yourself too hard. Finish your coffee, we'll curl up on the couch for just a half an hour and flip through some swatches."

I can't ask her to go now, Frankie thought, and even though her shoulders ached with fatigue and her eyes were dry, she nodded. *It's only half an hour.* "Sure."

"Don't look so excited," Bobby drawled. "You don't have to decide on any—hell, I don't fucking sell this shit. I just know how much you *ooh* and *ahhh* over flocked paisley and stuff. You deserve a little fun. I can help you chill out, relax."

Bobby lifted her own coffee cup and toasted in Frankie's direction. "Besides, I need to hear all about this horrendous date. See, this is what happens when you date men. Is Mr. Horrendous a vegetarian, too? Or, oh no... did he take you to a steakhouse?" Bobby gasped overdramatically and faux-swooned.

Frankie laughed exhaustedly, relieved that the awkward moment had passed and Bobby's humor was returning. "You're impossible, you know that?"

"Stuck like glue, me and you," Bobby promised. "No matter what."

Frankie sipped her coffee. It tasted too strong and far too sweet, but she didn't want to upset Bobby further by refusing to drink it. Especially after rushing her out last time, and asking for her key back. Frankie plunked her tired ass on the couch and Bobby brought the wallpaper sample book, and for the next hour and a half, they imagined papered walls that would never exist, and matched complementary shades and patterns, and finally, Frankie fessed up about her disappointing dinner with a poet named Daniel, a cute vegan whom she'd met at her new class at the community college. The poet had turned out to be a dreadful bore, droning on about himself without showing the least bit of curiosity in Frankie or her interests or opinions. Frankie imagined that he saw her as nothing more than a glossy mirror in which he could admire his reflection. But the poetry class itself, now, that made Frankie happy. Bobby matched her enthusiasm — about the class, at least — and vowed to sign up for the same one so that Frankie would have a friendly face in class.

Frankie felt it would be impolite to tell her not to, and finished her coffee.

Chapter Thirteen

Tuesday, October 28. 1:30 A.M.

There was a lull in the downpour by the time Gillian made her final sweep around the Blymhill house, but the thunder had picked up, rattling windows in their old wooden frames, echoing across the big lake ominously. Gillian barely noticed. She was dreamily picturing furniture, mentally adding a throw rug here or an art piece there. The rooms designated for writers would have to be soundproofed. *Or maybe not*, she thought as the soft sound of a train went by, the rumble of the tracks brought to life by high winds. She closed her eyes and could hear the waves crashing on the boulder-strewn coast of Higgins Point. Lake Ontario was rowdy under the pressure of the storm; the music it made was surprisingly soothing. Would it be distracting to a writer, or inspiring? That would require more thought.

She saw one of the central bedrooms as a sitting room, imagining big wing-back chairs clustered near the fireplace. The late hour finally softened her excitement and Gillian began to think of sleep. She took her purse from the hall table and checked the time. After one. No more messages since that afternoon's *Shopping, whore?*

She wondered, *why am I a whore, exactly?* She hadn't been with a man since Greg died, and before that, only with him. Oh, there had been the occasional boyfriend in high school and college, but once she'd met Greg, all other men seemed infinitely less interesting. She figured that, in this case, "whore" was a random accusation and not an educated one. Travis Freeman's ignorance was not a surprise.

When she hit the only bedroom with furniture — Mrs. Blymhill's bed frame topped with a brand new mattress — she pulled an emergency candle and a lighter from her purse and set them on the small, sound wicker table next to a lamp that looked like it might be older than she was. Her overnight bag was by the bed, and a plastic bag full of sheets and towels. She set about making the bed and got drowsy halfway through. A nice drowsy. An *at home* drowsy. Tomorrow, after her breakfast appointment with Frankie and Mr. Langerbeins, she'd get home and start boxing her things and finding a realtor. Living in her little home on Red Maple Drive was starting to depress her; it was hard to let go of her memories of Greg, imprinted in every room, but it was harder still to live with the ghost of him. She wasn't emotionally ready to let him go, to move on with life without him, but the opportunity had come up. It had been their one chance to snag this property, and she'd had to act fast.

She cracked one window a bit, and it thumped closed. She found a small chunk of wood on the sill and figured it was there to hold the window up. Wedging it under the heavy window frame, she managed to keep it open a crack for a cool breeze. Then she fluffed the blankets and crawled into bed. And instantly upon turning the lights off, she thought about Greg, and the day he'd died.

What she remembered most vividly were the dirty porch planks.

On the ride home from work, she'd been in a fog, cranky and sore, completely unaware that life was about to blow up in her face. A quick stop at the Food Mart for a pair of flank steaks and fresh asparagus and crusty Italian bread had taken ten minutes, and she was soon bouncing up and down the dusty back roads in her Jeep toward home. She turned the corner onto Red Maple Drive and the sight of three cop cars made her hit the brakes, her stomach dropping unpleasantly.

One hand turned down the volume on the radio by habit. They

were parked outside her and Greg's place; as a cop's wife, she lived with the daily knowledge that any day could be Greg's last. She hoped very much that her home alarm had just gone off, or they'd been burgled.

There were three men sitting in the wicker chairs on her front porch, waiting for her; two uniforms and one in plain clothes. The sergeant, Perkins, was the only one she knew, the only one who met her eye when she got out of the Jeep. She found her answers in his face before he could even speak.

She made it as far as the porch, still stupidly holding the bag of groceries, before grief punched her in the gut and she went down. She remembered how the sergeant had got down on the stairs beside her and told her when and how it had happened, how sorry he was, asking if he could call someone to come sit with her. She said the first name to come to her, the strongest person she knew, the only one as strong as Greg — Kenneth Koehler, Greg's partner, their dearest friend — but, of course, he was dead, too. The sergeant had to repeat this several times before it sank in. Both of them. Both gone.

The porch planks under her hands were gritty with dried garden soil. They'd spent the weekend gardening. She hadn't swept up yet. A pair of his dusty work boots still sat outside the front door, by the closest wicker chair, where he'd sat for a beer and kicked the boots off. The garden was only hers now, she'd thought. Who could possibly fill those boots? No one, not ever. She'd wept, then, staring at the dirty porch planks and wanting to die.

Both of them, gone. Just like that.

And now *she* was the strongest person she knew. Her alone. The sergeant had asked her if there was someone he could call. She'd asked the sergeant to call her sister to come, and sobbed into the grime on the stairs, not caring that the other officers, strangers to her, were watching, not listening to her sister's Fiat kick gravel as she spun into the driveway, not hearing the comforting words that people try to offer to those who grieve. Gillian knew she'd never be the same.

The dark part of her mind asked, *Would anyone mourn Travis*

Freeman with the same hopeless abandon? The same stunned devastation? Or would life in his absence go on very much as it was, perhaps a little easier, even a little brighter for some? Travis's ex-wife wouldn't mourn. No, Susan Freeman wouldn't fall to the floor as though she could sink right through it. Frankie? Would there be tears on her pillow? Gillian didn't think so.

But Frankie had cried for Mike Deacon.

And Frankie had cried for Gillian's neck. Cried in the hospital. Cried at the physiotherapist's office. Maybe Frankie *was* crying for Travis, or for the memory of their good times, or for the might-have-beens.

If so, she wouldn't confide that to Gillian.

Chapter Fourteen

Tuesday, October 28. 8:00 A.M.

Cold cases had a way of gnawing away Constable Dean Jagger's appetite, and this one was only different in that the victim didn't stir his sympathies: Mike Deacon, shady past of drugs, weapons charges, assault and battery. The last person to see him alive was his brother, Reggie, who was serving time at the SHU in Quebec for three counts of assault with a deadly weapon and attempted murder; both of them had pages of domestic violence calls, most made by their own mother. Classy brothers, the Deacons.

Dean sat at the booth in the far corner of the Sunnyside Up diner, pretending interest in a triple stack of buttermilk pancakes with blueberry sauce. The waitress brought his decaffeinated coffee; he sipped it black.

The Hearth sisters looked nothing alike at first glance. The younger one had a heart-shaped face, soft curves in all the movie-star places. A wild blonde mass of curls dusted her shoulders like a mantle. Her wide brown eyes blinked often, as though they were prone to filling with tears; her makeup was subtle but seductive, heavy on the mascara, nude lips, pale rose cheeks.

The elder sister was interesting to look at, too, but at first he couldn't pin down why. She was a bit too thin, a bit too plain. As an older sister (and surrogate mother for most of their life, as he understood), she'd been honed and hardened by the weight of early responsibility. Her fern green eyes were wary, guarded to the point of being unfriendly, under stern brows with an almost sinister arch. Freckles, the kind usually seen in natural red-heads, dusted her nose and cheeks and, he noticed on further examination, the length of her forearms. She wore a plain black t-shirt under a pale yellow cardigan with the sleeves pushed up, and worn-soft jeans.

The younger said something and the elder smiled down at her plate, laughed a little, and then shot a glance directly at him.

Dean's breath caught, and though he should have looked away, he didn't. Her smile dissolved, but not before completing its unexpected assault on his nerves. Caught staring, he feigned an embarrassed and apologetic half-smile and went back to his pancakes.

She wasn't fooled; when he glanced over a full ten minutes later, she was still monitoring him. Instead of flattering her ego, he'd set off this one's warning bells. In his peripheral vision, he could see the younger sister talking animatedly on and on, gesturing wildly with tiny hands, setting off crystalline tinkling he could hear from a charm bracelet under loose, chiffon blouse sleeves.

The elder was now perfectly still, staring straight ahead at her sister, a pose that gave away absolutely nothing. She appeared to be listening to her sister's monologue, but he was willing to bet that the bulk of her focus was still on him. Time to go. He would learn nothing else that morning.

But he was wrong about that. He wove through the tables, purposefully setting his path so he'd be sidelined by a waitress with a full tray, backtracking closer to the sisters' booth near the window. The elder turned her face only enough so that she could glance down at his ankle. On his way past, he heard the older sister's silken voice.

"Drive safe, officer."

He did not look back.

***

Frankie was gabbing excitedly. "You should let me paint you one. The irises. Hello?" She waved her hands some more. "I could do a big one. I need this. I need a project. The work will take my mind off things." Her hands told the same story, as Frankie's hands were wont to do. Busy, busy, busy, they never rested. "I'm only happy when I'm plunging into a new piece, you know that."

Gillian made an appeasing noise, which Frankie must have taken as agreement. She began excitedly planning the new piece. Frankie worked predominantly in stained glass and bronze these days, making windows, garden sculptures, lamp shades, and wind chimes. She ground to a halt during her talk about dimensions. "Gillian?"

"Roses," Gillian said. "Pink. Dark pink."

"But you said you wanted to paint your bedroom purple," Frankie said. "The irises would match your walls."

"*Rosa rugosa rubra*, if you need to look them up for reference."

"Those single, open ones with all the thorns?" Frankie's nose wrinkled with disapproval. "They're not even pretty."

Gillian shrugged with one shoulder, the bulk of her peripheral focus on the man who was watching her. "I like them."

"I know you do." Frankie sipped her diet Coke. "You already have tons of photos of them on your walls at the cottage."

"Yes I do." Gillian glanced down at the familiar standard-issue shoes of the man passing their table, spotted the telltale bulge of an ankle holster under his pant hem, and said under her breath, "Drive safe, officer…"

Frankie stopped gesticulating with her hands, which fell in a nested ball in her lap. Her lips barely moved. "A cop?"

Gillian smiled calmly behind her tea cup and nodded once, slowly. She knew she should have kept her teeth together and said nothing, but the temptation had been irresistible. He hadn't reacted, but he'd heard her. She knew the moment he dodged the waitress as an excuse to get closer to her table that he'd be listening extra closely. The whole act was mildly amusing, even as it stirred her concern.

Frankie asked, "He wasn't watching us?"

"Of course not," she lied easily. "He has no reason to. How are your fries?"

"I have no appetite," Frankie said. "Ugh, I had the worst dinner last night. That Devin guy—"

"Daniel?"

"Right, jeez, why did I think it was Devin? Where's my head today?" Frankie tapped her temple and her earrings tinkled prettily. "He insisted on Indian food, and it just didn't sit right. Then I had a late coffee, and I was sick all night."

"Food poisoning? Or just something a bit off?" Gillian shook her head with an exasperated smile that said *what-am-I-going-to-do-with-you.* "Why did you order fries and a diet Coke for breakfast if you threw up all night?"

Frankie dipped a fry in ketchup and chewed with mock rebellion at her sister, smiling around the potato. "Force of habit?"

"Junk food habit," Gillian teased. "I don't know how you're so skinny. I thought vegetarians were supposed to be healthy."

"Only the boring ones," Frankie said, sucking a French fry in mock fellatio.

Gillian accused, "Half the stuff you put in your mouth isn't even technically food."

"No, you misheard me," Frankie said mischievously. "My date *didn't* go well."

Gillian snort-laughed and shook her head. "Such a pig."

Frankie wiggled her eyebrows and then pointed behind Gillian to indicate their private investigator was here. Gillian finished her tea as Paul Langerbeins limped over to join them. The sisters fell into a quiet discussion about the weather forecast for the week as Paul got comfortable in the booth beside Gillian.

Gillian handed him a menu. When the waitress returned, she refilled Gillian's tea. Paul ordered coffee, black, and a bran muffin.

"Mr. Excitement," Frankie commented. "Settle down there, wild man."

Paul took out a pad and pencil, getting right down to business, though there was a softening around the corners of his eyes that might have been humor. "This is about as wild as I get," Paul promised them. "Got some more questions for you. Both of you." He jotted the date and time on his legal pad and then asked Gillian, "Any more communication?"

Frankie gave Gillian a stern *what-does-that-mean* glare which Gillian ignored. "No, not at all."

"And you, Frankie?" Paul asked, and when she pulled out a list and her phone to show him texts and emails and missed calls, he took all the information down. He asked to listen to the voice mails, and Frankie put in her password and handed him her phone. He listened, his long, serious face unhappy; since he always looked this way, Gillian found it difficult to gauge his reaction. His hand didn't stop as he recorded things in his notes. She was tempted to read them over his shoulder, but figured Frankie would share anything particularly worrisome with her later. As a rule, the sisters did not keep secrets.

"Tell me about how you met Travis Freeman," Paul asked.

Frankie said, "Online dating. I know, it's lame, but since I graduated school, I've been so busy with the boys and work that I don't get out to meet new people. Our profiles matched up and he seemed great."

"Isn't online dating dangerous?" Gillian asked.

Paul see-sawed his hand. "There are smart ways of going about it. Do you mind if I ask how your profiles matched up?"

"Well," Frankie said, squinting like she was trying to remember ancient history, "we both liked tribal drums, eclectic dining experiences, world travel, astrology and star gazing, studying art and architecture—"

Gillian choked on her green tea and grabbed a napkin to dab at the front of her sweater. "Travis Freeman likes that stuff?" she said, dripping disbelief. "He said that?"

Frankie looked like a deer in the headlights for a second, caught out like *she'd* been the one lying, and then threw her head back and laughed wildly. "Oh, for fuck's sake," she exploded merrily. "I totally bought that, too. He didn't like *any* of that while we were actually dating."

"He tailored his profile to attract you," Paul guessed.

Frankie used one forefinger to fish-hook her own cheek then rolled her eyes and sighed. "I feel like a dummy."

When the waitress came to check on Frankie's soda, Gillian decided she was hungrier than she'd estimated and ordered a carrot and raisin muffin.

Paul said, "You're certainly not dumb. Tell me about how the relationship progressed."

"I just wanted a casual dating situation," Frankie explained. "A movie on Friday night. Someone to have dinner with. Nothing serious."

"He got serious," Paul guessed.

"Fast," she said. "Within a few weeks, it felt like we were already married. He wanted to stay overnight every night. Sorry, dude, but I like having my bed to myself. Maybe that's not sexy or romantic—"

"That doesn't matter," Gillian said gently. "You have every right to sleep alone, if that's what you choose to do."

"He started leaving stuff behind at my house, which I'd throw in a grocery bag and return to him, and he would say 'just leave it in the closet,'" Frankie said.

"What sorts of things did he bring?" Paul asked.

The waitress brought Frankie another soda and Gillian's muffin. Once she disappeared, Frankie went on.

"At first, he'd leave his sweatshirt behind or a pair of gloves." She shrugged. "As you do. No big deal. But then, after he fixed the lock on my front door, he left one of his tool boxes behind. It was always in my way, because that's where the kids take their muddy boots off on the tray, there. I asked him a bunch of times to take it back home with him, but then I found it downstairs in my laundry area. I thought that was weird. And after that, I found his deodorant and a toothbrush in my bathroom and I never saw him bring those in." She gave an exhausted little huff. "They just appeared like magic. Did he smuggle them in, in his pockets? Every time I turned around, it was looking more and more like *our* house, but I wasn't sure how to tell him to slow down without hurting his feelings, and I figured there wasn't much harm in it." She nibbled a French fry, sipped her diet Coke, but her slim hand hovered over her belly and she pushed them away. "When I finally did try to gather up his things for him and left them by the back door, he got really upset. Like I was trying to break up. I just wanted my space back. I'm not looking for a new roommate."

Paul was nodding. "Fast-tracking a relationship like that is a red flag."

"Have you found something about him that we should be concerned about?" Gillian asked.

Paul was about to speak when Frankie's phone jingled.

"Speak of the devil," Frankie sighed.

Paul asked, "Have you changed your phone number yet?"

"I'll do it today," Frankie said with a nod. "Should have done it already."

Frankie's phone jingled again and then Gillian's vibrated at her hip. She drew her phone out and showed Paul the text. *If she doesn't need me, why would she let me keep the key to the garage and keep my tools there?*

Paul asked, "Is this true?"

Frankie said, "No. I asked for that key back ten times. I told him to put it in the mailbox. He said that wasn't safe to do that and he'd have to give it to me in person."

Gillian sighed. "Another attempt to manipulate and control."

Paul nodded. "From this point forward, zero contact from you, Frankie. You're going to change your number; landline, too. We're going to change the locks on your house and garage door. And if he does get any message through to you, you're to ignore it completely."

Frankie looked to Gillian, who nodded firmly.

Gillian texted to Travis. *She'd like the key back. Leave it in the mailbox. Your tools will be on my porch. Don't knock. No one wants to speak to you. You have until Wednesday to retrieve them. If you don't, I'll give them to charity.*

Frankie was peering across the table at her sister's phone. "I can't believe you said that."

"Why?" Gillian asked. "I'm not going to be afraid of him."

"Shouldn't you be?" Frankie said, her voice getting breathy again. Her fingers fluttered to the hollow of her throat.

Gillian frowned. "Don't be ridiculous. You think he'd try to hurt me just for suggesting he gives me the key to your garage?"

Paul made an uncertain noise. "You're taking control. He won't like that."

Gillian laughed bitterly. "Tough shit. I should care what he likes? He can go fuck himself." She felt her own eyebrows rise, and she glanced around at the suddenly curious looks from the other diner patrons. "Sorry." She smoothed the mother of pearl buttons on the front of her cardigan, tucked her hair behind her ear, and repeated to Paul, "Sorry. I'm just fed up."

"Understandable," Paul said. "But don't let your anger fog your judgment. I'm not sure I'm comfortable with this man coming to your house to get his tools."

"I won't be home," she promised. "I'm moving to the new place as soon as possible."

"You should get a dog, Gillian," Paul suggested.

"We have a dog," Gillian said. "Doogie can move in when Frankie does."

"Let's try *not* to make him focus his anger on you," Paul suggested.

Frankie nodded and pointed as though he'd taken the words right out of her mouth. "Yeah, he already thinks this whole break-up was your idea."

"Whoa," Paul said, "hold up. Why does he think it has anything to do with Gillian?"

Frankie shifted uncomfortably. "When I started feeling trapped in my relationship with Travis, I asked Gillian what she would do in my situation. And she gave me her honest opinion, that's all. I..." She wrapped a finger in her hair and snapped it. "I wrote this in my diary. I've always kept one, I write in it faithfully every night. Purging my thoughts on paper helps me sleep. Anyway, I wrote Gillian's words down, and my feelings, and weighed things."

Gillian's hand froze in the act of pulling the top off her muffin, and her tongue stuck to the roof of her mouth. "You write everything down?" Her eyes asked: *everything?*

Frankie nodded. "One night, I found him sitting up late on the couch, drinking a beer, reading my diary like it was just the most normal thing in the world to be snooping in someone's personal, private thoughts."

Gillian swallowed hard and tried to remember when she had bought Frankie's last gift of a pretty, new journal. Had it been Christmas of last year? Her birthday in June? *No,* she thought. *It had been a long time ago. An off-holiday thing. We'd been in that cute little shop in Ancaster, and we had seen those gorgeous leather diaries with the silk ties. I bought her the green one with the pattern stamped on the front. Was it two Novembers ago, now? No, three. Right after the first snow. We'd gone to see Webster's Falls, to see if it had ice on it yet, and to take pictures. Her painting from that trip sold at the winter fair in Toronto for five grand. She was so proud.* That would have been months before Mike Deacon proposed to Frankie, before Bobby's obsession with Frankie, before the accident and the fall, and months before Greg's death.

Surely, Frankie had filled the leather one long ago and was working on a new one? Gillian thought hopefully.

Paul was saying, "It's important that he is given no access to you whatsoever, Frankie. Complete radio silence, understood?"

"But that makes my sister the only available focus of his rage," Frankie said.

And that's a part I'm willing to play, Gillian thought. *As I have before.* "I'll be fine."

"You might be surprised at how wide a net he throws," Paul said. "New boyfriends might get calls, old friends, family, coworkers, clients, anyone he can reach with threats or attempts to embarrass you."

"Paul, is there anything specific about this guy we need to be worried about?"

Paul shook his head. "That depends. What did he learn from that diary?"

The green leather one, Gillian worried silently. *Would she still have it?* And then, though Gillian had never before considered violating her sister's personal property, *I need to get that diary. It needs to be in my possession so I can dispose of it properly.*

Frankie picked at her fries.

Paul studied them and advised, "If there were secrets in there, you might expect him to use them to punish either one of you. He may run a smear campaign. Are you both ready to withstand someone gossiping about you all over town? He's done this before, when his ex-wife Susan left him and took the kids. He started a website advertising her services as a prostitute, with her real phone number. She was getting calls from prospective johns for over a year, no matter how often she changed her number. A restraining order did almost nothing to stop him; Susan claims Travis started using his friends to harass her when he wanted to look like he was keeping his nose clean."

Gillian's world got very, very small, and though she felt she hid it well, her head swam dizzily and tiny stars danced before her eyes. *He* couldn't *know everything. He couldn't possibly know. Frankie wouldn't write* everything *down.* But when she searched her baby sister's face, she saw panic, a doe-eyed horror and so much regret that she thought Frankie might vomit.

Gillian didn't dare pick up her tea cup now for fear of her shaking hand giving her away. "All families have secrets, Mr. Langerbeins. But there shouldn't be anything in there that would cause a storm."

"Certainly no storm we can't handle," Frankie said with forced brightness, though the blush on her cheeks showed like a doll's painted circles on a face gone milk-pale.

Gillian didn't think Paul believed them, but he paid the check and left them to finish their lunch. They did so in perfect, stunned silence.

Chapter Fifteen

Tuesday, October 28. 3:05 P.M.

Gillian brought Aaron's birthday card to the back office of the greenhouse, popping her head in to say hi to Bruce and get him to sign. She was trying hard not to wonder where Frankie kept her old diaries, or if she didn't keep them at all. Maybe she threw them away when they were filled up.

Stop it. Just ask her, she chided herself. Gillian left the birthday card on the desk and went out with her clipboard to have a brief chat with the crew about what winter clean-up remained. They struck out through Pleasant Pines Cemetery, feeling the chill as October slid closer to November. It was still two days until Halloween, and, finally, autumn was beginning to feel less like summer. Focusing on work helped clear Gillian's head, and Bruce's sturdy presence at her side brought her back down to earth, grounded her, made her feel safe. She pointed out the left rear quadrant of the grounds, where two vehicles and a wood chipper were just visible through the old growth trees. They passed a crew on break for their lunches, eating hot dogs next to a particularly flat, table-like headstone.

"You guys are sick," Bruce joked as he passed them.

"Hey, the dead guy doesn't mind, why should we?" one of the

older workers said. He wiped mustard off his hand on the back of his bright orange safety vest and indicated behind them to the parking lot. "Someone's waving at you, Gillian."

She looked toward the lot by the funeral home, thinking it might be Frankie wanting to talk some more. What she saw was a familiar black truck, big wheels, chrome extensions on his mufflers, chick silhouettes on his mud flaps. *Travis. Here.* He was leaning against the truck, arms crossed, one leg crossed in front of the other at the ankle. Jeans. Baseball hat. She couldn't see his expression from where she stood, but she felt like he might be smirking at her.

Bruce was reading her face. "Friend of yours?"

"No," Gillian said.

"He's looking over here."

"Let him." She checked off a row on the list on her clipboard. "Doesn't bother me."

Bruce puffed up his chest and chewed the inside of his mouth. "Want me to speak to him? He doesn't need to be here."

"Absolutely not," Gillian said, imagining what Travis might tell her coworker, what things he had read in Frankie's diary, what secrets he might spill just to torture her. "He's not important. Don't make him feel important. Please."

"If you need backup," Bruce said, lowering his voice, "you know I'm here, right?"

"Thank you," Gillian said quietly, meaning it.

"Hey," Bruce said with a chuckle, "what are future husbands for?"

She pointed her pencil scoldingly at him but had to smile. "Scoring points, eh?"

Bruce laughed, a warm, booming laugh through a gruff voice, reminding Gillian of cigars and rotgut whiskey and nights by a campfire. They moved deeper into the cemetery, ignoring their guest; after an hour or so, he drove away.

There was a note on Gillian's windshield when she left work that day. She didn't read it. She didn't even touch it. It sat there for a day and half until the wind snatched it away.

She refused to think anything of it.

Chapter Sixteen

Tuesday, October 28. 9:00 P.M.

October was finally submitting to winter's heavy hand, and while Gillian would have preferred to have the sweet warm air blowing through the screens, she'd put the heat on to take the edge off the cold damp of the evening instead, leaving the windows locked tight. Now the furnace at the Red Maple Drive house clicked off. It was only after the white noise from the vents dissipated that she heard the low rumble of thunder outside. It was a lure she couldn't resist.

Turning off all the lights as she left each room, she checked the locks on the doors then moved to the back of the house, pausing at the dark *en suite* bathroom to start drawing a bath. She lit a single candle on the rim of the tub and sprinkled a bit of Epsom salts, and sweet basil and peppermint essential oils into the steaming water, then went to turn back her duvet and pull her nightgown from under her pillow.

Greg's pillow was knocked off center and she adjusted it, giving it a pat; the pillow case didn't match her current set of sheets, because she'd never changed it. After his death, she would often seek comfort in the smell of his hair, his cologne, in his pillow. His scent had long since disappeared, but she couldn't bring herself to remove the case yet. *Someday,* she thought, *but not yet.* Having already donated his clothing, shoes, and most of his tools, taking that pillow case would mean saying good-bye to the last thing she had of him, and she wasn't ready. She'd take it with her to the new house, and keep it on her new bed until she felt she could sleep without it. She cracked the bedroom window, and when the crisp smell of the oncoming storm reached her, the knot in her gut relaxed.

Greg always loved a good storm. He'd been the ultimate storm prepper, setting unscented candles and lighters in the kitchen, bathroom, and bedroom, and flashlights in the drawers. When a strong thunderstorm hit, he'd sit on the back porch with a coffee and watch it roll in over the lake. Gillian was momentarily certain that if she went out behind the house, Greg would be sitting in one of the Adirondack chairs, one ankle propped on his knee, elbows on the armrests, coffee mug cupped in his big, strong hands, his eyes on the distant cloud cover, as though he could keep danger away from his home and family simply by watching it. She had teased him about that often enough. They'd be out on the town and he'd get this look in his eye, an all-seeing and protective gaze.

That protective gaze is gone, the cruel corner of her mind taunted, *and you're all alone, now.*

"And that's the reason you're overreacting," she told herself quietly in the dark bedroom, feeling suddenly exhausted by her paranoia about Travis Freeman. *It's just a note. A couple of texts. It's a far cry from a direct threat. He's just a man. He's not a monster. Besides...* "I can take care of myself."

A soft scuffle alerted Gillian to activity on the back porch. Before Monday, before the note on her car, she might not have noticed the noise, or could have passed it off as a raccoon checking out her garbage can. Now, on high alert, she heard every sound and attributed it to danger.

She slipped into the bathroom, leaving the overhead light off, locked the door, and turned off the bathtub. Moving to crouch beside the window, she peeked through the blinds.

The back yard was full of shadows that swayed and danced in

the rising wind. She studied the familiar shape of him standing under the Japanese maple, shifting from one foot to the other. He hadn't knocked. He just stood there. *Travis is finally here, what's he going to do?* Gillian pushed away from the window, pressed her back against the bathroom wall and slid down further until she was sitting on her heels. Trying to relax, she slowed her breathing, in through the nose, holding it for a four-count, exhaling through the mouth. When she felt a bit calmer, she peeked again, holding the bottom-most blind slats open with trembling fingertips. He was standing close enough to the back door to have his nose and toes touching the door itself, and Gillian wondered what he could be doing. Was he trying to look past the blinds and curtains on the little window in the door? Was he trying the doorknob? *Neither of those will do him any good,* she told herself.

He wasn't there long. Before he left, he bent and picked up something near the garden. His figure moved into deeper shadow and she lost sight of him.

She couldn't get to the bedroom window fast enough. She quietly slid it shut and locked it tight, checking it several times before slipping into the hallway and pausing to listen for noises. All she could hear was the rising wind whistling through the trees and pushing on the tiny house. She hurried from one window to the next, double-checking the locks and the security of the doors. Peeking out the front door, she waited to see if she could pick him out of the gloom. Nothing moved except the rhythmic swaying of tree and bush and shadow. For the first time since Greg died, Gillian set the house alarm and flipped on the security cameras.

Her plans for the evening seemed derailed. Bath, TV, relaxing? How could she? *So you're going to let him change your life?* It was her Big Sister voice, the exact thing she'd tell Frankie, and she was using it on her own self. Determined not to be shifted by his behavior, she went back to her bathroom, locking the bedroom door as an extra precaution. She considered having a weapon next to the tub and then considered it ridiculous. *Maybe it wasn't even him.* She hadn't seen his face. Had she really recognized his shape? She didn't know him well enough to be sure it was him without a clearer view. Maybe it was a thief. Just some young punk looking to steal her electronics. But in her gut, she knew it was Travis. With that, the anger returned. *Stop thinking about him!*

Her enjoyment of her hot bath was more stubborn than soothing, and lasted half as long as her usual soaks. Climbing into bed afterward, bath-warmed and still damp, she switched on an old sitcom and tried to put him out of her mind. It was a difficult task, and she needed to text Frankie first, just to make sure she was okay. Frankie texted back that she had friends from poetry class over, and that a couple were sleeping there. Her younger sister had no reason to ask if Gillian was okay; why would Travis come to Gillian's house?

Why indeed? What was he trying to accomplish?

Stop thinking about him! She clenched a fist and demanded of herself that she would think about anything else. The hollow behind her right eye gave a warning, sickening throb, and she whispered a curse, and by the flickering blue light of her small TV, she opened her night stand and sought her Vicodin, shaking a few into her palm.

The pills would make her sleepy.

Is that smart? Is that what was best right now?

Stop thinking about him! Feeling obsessed and disgusted, she put the pills back in the bottle and slammed the drawer. The rest of the night, she tossed and turned, slipping in and out of a restless sleep. The sound of late night TV kept her company in her dark, sweaty bedroom with the laughter of live and canned audiences.

****

It was that same night that Frankie made the mistake of answering her phone without checking the caller ID first. Having passed out from a good amount of wine, her friends Nina and Amy were tucked on the couches with blankets and pillows Frankie had fetched from the kids' rooms, and she had just crawled into her most comfortable pajamas, her mind completely off her problems.

Now, the sound of his voice made something low in her belly flop over and turn to ice.

"Hey, baby, listen." His tone was soft, tentative. "I wanna apologize. I've been missing you so hard. I just wanna hear your voice so I know you're okay."

Frankie glared at her own reflection in the vanity mirror, applying cream to the spots on her skin where she'd nervously picked.

"I've apologized so many times," Travis insisted. "Punishing me with silence is immature. You've become vindictive and unfair."

Frankie opened her vanity dresser drawer and pulled out her retainer, toying with the blue container.

Travis purred, "I just need to hear you. I gotta hear your sweet voice, baby."

He always said her voice was like music to him. The memory of him saying that triggered something in her, and a jolt of fear went through her. *He wouldn't. That doesn't really happen. How could he have?* She cursed herself, wondering if it was natural to start suspecting the worst.

Frankie stood quietly and began a slow, methodical search of her bedroom, under and behind every piece of furniture, listening to him ramble on about how wonderful she sounded to him; she found the little extra wire beside the networking cable behind her TV and what she assumed was a listening device stuck to the back of her BluRay player. She stared at it while Travis breathed on the other end of the phone.

"This isn't the sweet Frankie I know and love," Travis said. "She's hardened you and you know it. Everything would be fine between us if you would stop listening to that cunt sister of yours. We'd still be together if it wasn't for her."

That's probably true, Frankie thought, *but it sure as hell isn't a good thing*. Thank the Sweet Lord for Gillian and her tenacity, her good, solid head.

Travis didn't seem to like the silence stretching between them. He was starting to breathe heavily and Frankie could sense he was on the verge of blowing up again. She grabbed the listening device and pulled hard until it came away from the wire, then tossed it on the floor and stomped it hard under her heel, feeling plastic crack and pieces grind into the carpet.

Travis bellowed in her ear, "You don't tell me when it's over. I tell you, you no-good whore. *I tell you!*"

Frankie inhaled deeply, held her breath for a long beat then let it slowly out, letting her stress drain away with it.

"I don't want you," she said quietly, and in the stunned silence, she added, "Nobody wants you. Drop dead."

She hung up feeling shaky and panicking over what she'd just said, knowing she'd pay for it, not knowing how but not really caring; it felt like victory, a terrifying sort of victory snatched from thin air at the final moment. Her mouth was dry and when she tried to swallow, her throat clicked but her heart soared.

She tiptoed back out of her bedroom and past her sleepy guests to double-check the locks on every door in the house, and then almost called Paul Langerbeins. Remembering that he'd told her *not* to speak to Travis at all, and he'd told her to change *all* her phone numbers, and realizing she hadn't obeyed either suggestion, she did not call.

Frankie checked her texts, ignoring the ones from Travis, reading Bobby's *Please answer me, Honey*, but not replying, and resolving that first thing in the morning, she would change her locks and phone numbers.

Chapter Seventeen

Wednesday, October 29. 7:00 A.M.

I'm not touching that, Gillian thought, staring in disgusted disbelief at her back door, the door where the man's shadow had been last night. *Travis did this.* She grimaced. *I'm not cleaning that up.*

Her mind whirled with doubts. *Maybe it's not what I think it is*, she told herself, but she knew very well what it was. In case he was watching, she locked up the house on Red Maple Drive quickly, pretending she hadn't seen the creamy splatter glistening by the door knob, and continued to her Jeep, pondering her next move.

Would he come back to check if she'd cleaned it? Would that satisfy him to know she'd had to do that, that he'd forced her to touch his semen? Should she report this? A wash of embarrassment rushed through her. She couldn't go into Greg's precinct and report that she'd had that pervert jack off on her back door. *They'd think I encouraged him. They'd think I'd invited this... that Greg's widow is out rutting like a pig all over town with the kind of guy who would do this.* She knew that she was blaming herself, now, but that didn't squelch the shame. Following close on the heels of that was a jolt of rage; how dare he make her feel like this. A second, more dangerous urge to lash back at him rolled through her as she aimed the key fob at her car, turning off the alarm and unlocking the door.

She noticed a clump of dirt and greenery at the end of her driveway that she didn't immediately understand. Yellow petals, mashed against the bricks under someone's boot. Her step did not pause, even as it registered in her mind that those were the chrysanthemums she had planted two days ago, sickly-looking leftovers from her autumn cemetery plantings that were going to be thrown out if she hadn't brought them home. Now they were crushed on her driveway. She turned the car on and backed over their remains, not reacting outwardly. *Plants are replaceable. They'd been free.* She breathed in deeply through her nose, filled her lungs with sweet peace, exhaled stress and anger until she felt better. *It was fine. Everything was going to be just fine.*

***

Dean Jagger hit the stairs leading up to Paul Langerbeins' office at a run, eager to find out just what he knew regarding the Hearth sisters. Unlikely suspects, a landscape designer and a stained glass artist, both with clean records. Mike Deacon, on the other hand, had a long history of drug dealing and violence; it was far more likely that he'd met his end near the canal with a shot to the back of the head as a result to a deal gone sour. Jagger had been poring over his case files and kept coming back to a couple of tiny discrepancies that bothered him.

An interview after the disappearance of Mike Deacon. The older sister, Gillian Hearth. When asked what she thought of her sister's missing fiancé, she'd admitted she wasn't too fond of him, thought he smelled like trouble, and was worried he might have opened his stupid mouth to the wrong person and that's why he was missing. She was a cop's wife at the time, married to Greg Ellis. Ray Sauffs, the detective who had taken down her words at the time, added that he thought Gillian had good instincts. When they'd interviewed the fiancée, Frankie Farmer, she'd said the exact opposite: that Gillian had been very close with Mike, that they'd had lots in common, that they would have gotten along great once they were all family. Gillian spoke of Mike in the present tense, like he was going to show up any second. Frankie did not.

It was a small thing, Dean admitted. But it stuck in his mind like a seed in a molar, and he kept picking away at it.

Frankie Farmer fully admitted she'd been the last to see Mike. The day of the disappearance, June twenty-first, he'd come over to drop off some flowers. Carnations. She'd confessed that she did not like carnations.

But a few days later, when Sauffs interviewed a Hearth family friend, Bobby McIntyre, she'd said that *she'd* brought Frankie the flowers the morning of the disappearance because Frankie and Mike had been arguing all week, and she wanted to cheer her up. Light red carnations, Bobby had said, because they represent admiration and affection.

After reading the case file, Jagger got the impression that it had seemed to Sauffs that the relationship between Ms. Farmer and Ms. McIntyre was hazy at best. Bobby claimed they were intimate. Frankie thought that idea was strange, when asked, and said that Bobby was a dear friend and a fellow artist whose talents she deeply admired and respected. He noted that McIntyre clung to her best friend far tighter, and that Farmer was less attached.

When asked about that, Gillian Hearth-Ellis had scoffed and rolled her eyes, and informed Sauffs that Bobby McIntyre was "mildly delusional" and her words should be taken with a grain of salt. She hurried to add that it would be unwise to repeat that opinion, because Bobby McIntyre was "mentally fragile" at the best of times, and speaking to police had her wound tighter than a spring.

Jagger opened the door to Paul Langerbeins' office and was met with a secretarial desk but no attendant. He waited there for a moment before moving to the inside door and giving it a few sharp raps.

Langerbeins opened the door and did a good job of hiding his surprise; Dean introduced himself and gave him one of his cards.

"I wish you'd made an appointment, constable," Langerbeins said, limping back to his desk.

Jagger had run a check on him, not surprised to find that

Langerbeins was a former cop, but intrigued to find that he'd been present at Constable Greg Ellis's shooting as a rookie, and had been wounded himself. After a year on administrative leave, he'd quit the force to work on his own. Now, he was working for the Hearth sisters. Jagger wondered what that was all about, and if there was any connection to his case.

"I won't take up more than a few minutes of your time, Mr. Langerbeins. May I call you Paul?"

"Sure thing," Paul said, easing into his chair with one leg stiff in front of him. "Have a seat."

"I'm looking into the disappearance of Mike Deacon," Jagger said. "Don't know if you ever met old Ray Sauffs, but he retired recently, and I inherited this one off his desk, so to speak."

"Never had the pleasure," Paul said. "And I'm afraid the name Mike Deacon doesn't mean anything to me, either. Should it?"

"He's been missing for over three years now," Dean said. "He was Frankie Farmer's fiancé at the time he disappeared. His car turned up at the bottom of the canal when they drained the locks for winter, but there was no body in it."

Paul ruminated, chewing the inside of his mouth, brow lowered, his extended foot tapping the edge of the desk rhythmically. "Strange. My client is a suspect?"

"I'm just doing my due diligence. You understand."

"Yeah, sure," Paul said lightly, though his eyes were dark with displeasure. "I'm sorry I don't have anything to offer you in the way of information, officer. Never heard anything about this missing fellow."

"But she has hired you," Dean said, not a question.

Paul smiled briefly, a mere flicker. "I can tell you that much, but my clients enjoy a certain amount of confidentiality. I can tell you she hasn't hired me in any way relating to this Mike fellow. What was his full name? I'd like to make a note."

Dean read him the information, including date of birth. "I hope if you come across anything that might be helpful to me, you'll not hesitate to call?"

"I'm not the sort to hinder an investigation, officer," Paul said.

"I've been in your shoes, however briefly. I'd be there still if I could. I have a feeling, though, that your time would be better spent elsewhere. Frankie Farmer is…"

Dean watched Paul's face patiently as Paul struggled to find just the right word.

He finally decided on, "Flighty." And then, "Delicate. I don't see her knockin' anyone off. I really don't. And if she had, I doubt she'd be terribly good at hiding it."

Dean nodded, biding his time, trying to put Paul at ease with a considerate look before he dropped his next question. "And the elder sister? Gillian?"

It was the slightest twitch, but Dean caught it; tightening around the lips, a micro-expression of doubt.

"She's a formidable woman," Paul said carefully, "but physically frail."

"How so?"

"Injuries," Paul said. "Before her husband died, she had a fall of some sort. Bad, I take it. Nerve damage. I've seen one of her headaches strike. It left her vulnerable, unable to take care of herself or anything else."

"Yet she works a physically demanding job, I understand?"

Paul made an uncertain noise. "I take it she has a lot of muscle on her crew, and that she's the design end of things. Ordering, delegating. I don't doubt she gets out there and gets her hands dirty, but…" He let out a soft chuckle. "The idea of that woman being able to make a full grown man disappear?"

Dean noted the language, Paul's avoidance of the word murder or corpse or anything of the sort. He nodded and took note of this. "Well, I've taken up enough of your time. Mind if I call, if I have any further questions?"

Paul handed him a card and said, "I'll help if I can." But he didn't look to sure.

Neither was Constable Jagger.

Chapter Eighteen

Wednesday, October 29. 10:00 A.M.

"Holy smokes," Gillian said, backing away from the linen closet next to the bathroom. "Mrs. Blymhill kept her urine."

"Oh god! Oh babe. No!" Frankie squealed with horror, opened one of the four unmarked jars, and sniffed it. "Well, it's not Listerine." She gagged and went into the bathroom with the cleaning caddy, leaving Gillian to deal with the pee jars. A minute later, she backed out of the room, laughing with playful horror.

"What is it now?" Gillian asked, using the clean back of her wrist to push back the hair band keeping her brunette bangs off her face.

"Do not open that," Frankie advised. "Ever." She *meep*ed and shut the bathroom door.

"What's in there?"

Frankie shook her head rapidly, lips crammed together, eyebrows high with surprise. "I say we nail this door shut, drywall over it, and pretend it was never here. I can erase it from my memory and everything will be fine."

"It can't be worse than mason jars full of old urine," Gillian stated, confident.

Frankie looked equally confident. "Wanna bet?"

Gillian strode forward and took the doorknob, and Frankie tried to hold the door shut. "Babe, trust me. Don't even."

Gillian muscled into the bathroom and went to check under the sink. "We have to clean this place u—" Her brain refused to comprehend what she was seeing for a moment, and then she finished, "up," and let her slam the door again. "Were those dead rats?"

"A lot." Frankie nodded, chin bobbing. "A lot of dead rats."

"Also in jars," Gillian said, mystified. "She must have been mentally ill. Who keeps dead rats?"

"No normal person." Frankie was rubbing her arms like she had caught a chill, looking at her sister with a concerned crease across her brow. "You wanna quit for the day?"

"I wonder why the family or the neighbors didn't say something to someone, get her some help?" Gillian wondered sadly.

Frankie said, "That Italian lady next door keeps saying something that sounds like 'striga' or 'stringy' at me. That must mean 'crazy lady's relative' or something."

Gillian gave a patient sigh. "Instead of calling her 'that Italian lady next door,' why don't you go introduce yourself and find out what her name is? Then she can see what a sweet girl you are. She might even tell you what she's saying."

"Uh huh," she made her *yeah-right* face.

"You feeling sick again?" Gillian asked. "Your color is off."

"Up late, too much coffee. Didn't sleep well. Don't be mad." She made puppy eyes. "I called Bobby."

Gillian blew out harshly. "Why in the world would you call Bobby?"

"She's my friend," Frankie said. "And she hooked us up with Paul. She's back in town for a bit taking care of her sister, remember Barb? Barb's been seriously ill. Bobby's just helping out, and she wanted to reconnect."

"Bobby can't help us," Gillian said, trying to stay calm. "Bobby is a mess, she can't even help herself. We don't need Bobby."

"*You* don't need Bobby. You don't need anyone." Frankie's voice rocketed to screechy suddenly.

Gillian's mouth popped open, but she remained quiet, waiting to see if this was the beginning of a full blown meltdown or if her baby sister would get it under control. "Sometimes, I need to check in with her," Frankie said. "It makes me feel better to see that she's got her shit back together."

Gillian flashed back on Bobby on hands and knees and the bottom of Frankie's stairs, sobbing and retching as she scrubbed the floor, the water and chlorine mixture spilling across concrete, the sponge stained red. "And does she? Have her shit together, I mean?"

Frankie hesitated long enough for Gillian to know the answer was *no*. Gillian moved into the kitchen to wash her hands thoroughly, open the blinds to let the afternoon sun warm the room, and put on the kettle for tea. Frankie got herself a soda from the fridge and glanced at the fruit and vegetables that Gillian had brought in before closing the fridge door, finding nothing of interest.

Gillian made tea, sipped her drink, and asked blandly, "Don't you owe Bobby some money?"

"Don't do that." Frankie sighed. "I owe Bobby a lot more than money. We both do."

"I don't owe anyone anything," Gillian said carefully, setting her mug down. "I never wanted Bobby involved. *You* did that." Gillian felt her temper stirring. "You involved her. The minute I was out cold, you called her. Knowing when someone can't handle something, that's an important call to make. She was unstable before this whole mess, and she sure as shit never got *less* unstable after the fact. You should have never expected Bobby McIntyre to help you."

"What should I have done instead? You tell me," Frankie said exasperatedly.

"I shouldn't have to tell you. Why do I have to tell you?" Gillian exploded. "Because you fuck up every choice you've ever made? You should have cleaned up after yourself. You don't call your unpredictable mine-field of a friend and get her to come over at midnight and clean-up a problem like that. That's not what you do. Dammit, Frankie, she was dented and bruised before you made that call. Thinking her best friend had been responsible for a death? Thinking the only person she trusted wasn't who she thought you were?"

"It wasn't me who pushed him," Frankie blurted; her eyes flew wide and it looked like she wished she could have gobbled her words right back up.

Gillian's voice dropped to barely a breath. "I came because you called me."

"I know, Gillian, I'm sorry."

"You *begged* me to come."

"I shouldn't have —"

"You were screaming into the phone."

"Gillian, I'm sorry."

"You were locked in that bathroom when I bust through the back door and I had no idea what I was facing. I had no idea he was armed. I had no idea he was going to turn on me. You didn't warn me." Gillian's hands shook with rage. "He had a knife. I had a split second to react. And I did." She stood up, needing to leave the kitchen as soon as humanly possible, no longer able to breathe in this place, no longer able to stand another second looking at her sister's haunted face.

"It was him or me, Frankie. And I'm still standing. You've got some nerve trying to make me feel guilty about that." Gillian's hands shook, her fists clenched, knuckles red going to white. "You practically threw me to him. You knew I'd come running. You knew he was dangerous."

"I should have called the police!" Frankie said, her voice breaking. "911, or Greg, anyone but you. But you were my first thought, you're always my first thought —"

"And here we are." Gillian felt the first warning throb of another wicked migraine behind her left eye and blinked rapidly. She turned to look at the nearest lamp, the one plugged in on the floor in an otherwise empty living room; the glow of the light seemed to swim and grow. It was going to be a bad one. "And when I came to, and there was an ambulance, and EMTs, I thought — silly me — that you'd done the logical thing and called police. The whole ride to the hospital, I figured there was another ambulance for Mike Deacon, and other EMTs helping him. After all, our tango down the stairs was self defense. I had nothing to hide, Frankie. I was fighting back to save my life. Calling the cops would have been the right thing. Instead, what did you and Bobby do?"

"I can't say sorry enough," Frankie barely breathed.

"You know what? Call Bobby if you want. I wash my hands of it," Gillian said. "You're a grown-up, you continue to make your own bad decisions. I can't keep saving you from yourself, Frankie. But don't discuss me with her. And if you know what's good for you, you won't discuss what's-his-face."

"Travis."

Gillian inhaled sharply, held her temper in check, and let her breath out slowly, pressing two fingers to her throbbing eyebrow. "Don't say that name to me. Don't say that name to Bobby. Don't speak it ever again, not to anyone."

"I won't, Gillian, I'm sorry." Frankie started to cry and crumpled so she could cover her face with her hands. "I'm sorry for everything, I'm sorry this happened, I'm sorry."

"We'll get through it," Gillian said, *But only if Bobby keeps her mouth shut. She can't leave town soon enough. Oh God, how do I get rid of her?* She patted the counter top until her hand landed on her purse, digging out the bottle of aspirin that contained not-aspirin, dry-swallowing two. The pain radiated from her spine, warmed her shoulder, arched up the back of her neck and settled behind her eye. She'd been gifted these headaches the night Mike attacked Frankie, the night he'd flown backwards down the basement steps, snatching at the last moment a handful of Gillian's sweater and pulling her down with him. The nerve damage from her fall would be with her forever, the surgeon warned, the headaches her new companion.

"I need to lie down," Gillian said softly. "Lock up front, side, and back if you're not sleeping here tonight, please."

"I will," Frankie said through her tears, but Gillian didn't hear it. She was blindly feeling her way down the hall to her new bedroom.

Chapter Nineteen

Thursday, October 30. 12:55 P.M.

It was a perfect site. A lonely site. The kind of place that human feet rarely tread. A leafy spot in the spring and summer, clogged by vines and rocks, teeming with insects. A place to sit and remember. Difficult to get to, but, to her, worth the hike. It was a ten minute walk from the last hydro pole marked with a splotch of blue spray paint; not her marking, but this, she had measured. It mattered, though she knew the path by heart, could find the site in the dark if she needed to.

She struck out from the car, boots crunching gravel in the morning quiet, adjusting the backpack until it rested evenly between both shoulders. Her camera swung around her neck as she walked; one hand steadied it against her chest as she took in her surroundings. Her stride was confident for the first half hour, and there was new power in her legs as she cleared the cemetery and hiked past the bright orange plastic snow fence and into the woods proper. The path worn into the earth between the trees was uneven and smelled pungently of loam and warm soil. At the first fork she took a left, towards shadier ground. At the next bend she ducked into a gulch and crossed a patch of long grass. The weeds tugged at her legs, but she plunged through and came out in another little-used path, this one grown-over and clogged with tree branches. Insects hummed in the air and clouds of gnats found the sunny spots where the tree canopy parted. She paused to swipe at the dark bangs clinging to her sweaty forehead with the back of her hand and looked around. A patch of birch indicated she was on the right track as she left the path behind completely.

Now, the walk became difficult and the terrain jagged. More than once, a jutting stone nearly turned her ankle. Though she had brought her cell phone as far as the car, she couldn't risk bringing it to the site; she'd turned it off and left it in the glove box. Getting lost or injured in the woods, even on an unseasonably warm, late October morning, could be very bad, but her need to be there, to see that the site remained undisturbed, drove her forward. Where the fallen leaves and dry pine needles from last fall weren't piled, her boots hit the root-bound earth with a hollow thump. She counted her steps past the last hydro line — twelve, twenty, forty — and then took a sharp right into deep cover.

The sprawling, ugly bush had a wintery collection of fat, red rosehips on bare branches already, and where there were leaves, they were yellow and dotted with black spot, but the rose stole her breath regardless. When she was clear of the buckthorn branches, she let her backpack slide off her shoulders and set it on the ground to unzip it. She got out the journal and a pen, and took a few notes that meant nothing: the date, the time, the weather, and a few local birds that she wasn't actually seeing. On this quiet morning, there was little bird activity in the trees, but no one else was here to know it. She got out the bird-watching manual, thumbed through it, folded a corner on a random page. Circled a random, common bird. It didn't matter. Her eyes never left the rose bush.

Rosa rugosa rubra, a wild rose. There were a few others that sprawled in this area, but *this* one hadn't grown wild. She'd planted it in the fall three years ago. It had advanced on the woods quite a bit despite the shade, nurtured by the perfect mix of fertilizer and forest compost. And, of course, the torso.

She put away her fake bird-watching journal and put the camera to her eye, aiming up into the trees. Nothing but a couple of squirrels, but she took some close-ups of these anyway. Nature photography and bird-watching, her two fake interests, though no one could prove that. She had dozens of books on both subjects, some well-worn, some close to her bed. Coffee table books that she flipped through without looking at the pictures, laying the book on her lap and turning pages while she watched TV. Even the closest observer would think her interest was real. Frankie surely did. The masquerade might never play out, the alibi never needed, but she was always prepared for anything.

Bird watching. That's why she was here.

For a moment, she allowed herself to stare at the rose bush. There were dry leaves impaled on several of the branches, and her fingers itched to tidy them away, but she dare not touch it. There was no valid reason to do so. Besides, the *rosa rugosa rubra* had wicked thorns, and not just here and there, but completely covering the branches. The last thing she needed was to bleed here. She knew that every time she came, she left a trace of herself behind; the trick was to limit those traces to things that could be explained.

The rat poison sprinkled over the torso had kept the wildlife from digging up and carrying away the bones. There were no signs of paw prints or scrounging, nor any signs of people having trekked this far into the wild brush, away from the paths. She took several pictures of the late blooming rose, admiring the plump red rose hips. She got one extreme close-up of the ground underneath, just to make sure the ground hadn't heaved and thrust up any secrets.

Then she collected her things, did a quick check for ticks, swiping at her pants tucked into long boots, and strode back in the direction she'd come from, feeling a thousand times lighter.

When she got back to her car, there wasn't another in sight.

Soon, the snow would fall. She resolved not to return until spring unless she had another unfortunate deposit to make under the forest floor.

Chapter Twenty

Thursday, October 30. 6:05 P.M.

Frankie was halfway home with a bag full of Halloween decorations — a jumbo pumpkin she planned to paint teal to let kids know she was a peanut-free home for trick or treating, some spooky spider webbing, and a plastic tombstone to replace the one the kids broke last October — when her phone started vibrating. She had only given a few people her new phone number so far: Gillian, Paul Langerbeins, the kid's after-school day care, and her ex-husband, since they were co-parenting the boys. Frankie had a list of clients to contact, and of course the nursing home where Dad was currently being cared for. And the school, she reminded herself, and the doctor's office, the dentist, the eye doctor for Kirk's check-up reminders. Frankie missed the boys with a sharp ache — little Matthew with his freckles just like Auntie Gillie, and sturdy Kirk who couldn't keep his nose out of a book long enough to get interested in anything else. She reminded herself that things were not entirely safe here right now, and that they'd be fine with Henry as long as they didn't develop a taste for gambling. This would be her first Halloween without them, but Henry had always loved the holiday and he'd make it a blast for the boys. He didn't have a lot of money, not with his heavy debts, but she knew he'd go the extra mile to make it work. Henry had a magic touch with holidays; the three of them were probably carving their jack o' lanterns right now.

The vibrations continued against one buttock, but she ignored them as she pulled her Fiat under the car port and swung out, her Halloween goodies and one bag of groceries, which was mostly just chocolates for her.

Her steps paused at the side door and she frowned at the concrete slab.

A single white rose lay there, wilting. It had clearly been there a while. She thought back to that morning, before she left. She'd gone out the front door so she could grab the mail, then gone right to the car. She hadn't seen the rose, but it may have been there. Now, she stepped over it, putting she shiny new key into her brand new lock, happy to hear her security system double-beep an entrance. She put the bags down to punch in her security code and disarm the alarm, locked the door, flipped on the lights, and bent to get her bags.

There was a damp, slightly moldy draft from the cellar, coming up the steps. To her right was the half-bathroom, ahead were the handful of steps up to her kitchen and living area, but to her left were the steep cellar stairs, hard painted wood with metal friction strips along each edge, and at the bottom of the twenty steps, a cement floor.

With vivid clarity, she remembered being locked in the bathroom. It had been another color, with a different set of curtains; she'd frantically redecorated the next week, her and Bobby, papering the walls as though that could somehow paper over her memories. Mike's big fists slamming the door. Calling Gillian. Heart hammering. Hands shaking. Throat tightening up around the words. Her sister's voice outside the bathroom door, first bellowing a demand and then screaming, a high-pitched, primal noise that seemed dragged out of her, a sound Frankie had never heard Gillian make, and hoped never to hear again.

Hearing the fall. She'd heard it through the door: knocking, bumping, and a sick, wet crunch. Being frozen with doubt, unable to face what might have happened. Forcing herself to move forward. Her shaking hand on the doorknob. The silence, that horrible silence, giving no clues about what could be waiting for her when she opened that door.

The phone vibrated once more and startled her out of her memory. Grateful for the distraction, she pulled it out and read it.

Blocked number. *Call me and there will be no more anonymous tips.*

Frankie felt a moment of dizziness and called her sister immediately, hoping Gillian's headache hadn't stolen an entire night of sleep. It didn't occur to her to deal with it herself, or to call Paul Langerbeins for advice. Gillian was always her first thought.

***

Gillian arrived less than an hour later to find Frankie pacing back and forth before the front windows, watching for her Jeep. She wasn't out of her boots before Frankie demanded, "Is he out of his fucking mind?"

Gillian read the text when Frankie's phone was shoved into her hand. "Blocked number. You're sure this is from him?"

"Who else?"

"You've been dealing with Bobby."

Flustered, Frankie huffed. "How would Bobby get my new number?"

"How would *he*?" Gillian retorted.

"I don't know!"

"What is he talking about, anyway? What tips?" Gillian asked, handing the phone back. "Tips to whom? Tips about what?"

Frankie started thumbing in a reply. "I'll ask—"

"No," Gillian said sharply. "Put the phone down. Do not respond. Whoever it is, they don't get rewarded for bad behavior. Remember what Paul said?"

Frankie nodded. "He must have called in a tip to the police."

"You said he knows nothing," Gillian said, her voice low and warning.

"He knows a little," Frankie admitted. "Just from casual conversation. And the diary. Not *details*. I mean, not many."

Gillian's temper flashed, but she controlled it, wrapped it tightly in a ball in her stomach as she was so accustomed to doing when speaking with her baby sister.

"What exactly did you tell him?" she asked calmly, sure that if Frankie could see what was going on in her head right now, she wouldn't dare answer that question.

"I told him he shouldn't mess with you. He thought that was pretty funny, and it was just so infuriating. You should have seen his smile. So smug. So I warned him you'd taken down worse than him."

Gillian chewed on her tongue for a full minute before saying crisply, "You said what?"

"He thought that was *hysterical*. You know, for your size. Said, 'Little miss florist, a stone cold killer, eh?' He busted a gut."

"You said *what*?"

"No, it was just… I warned him. Jokingly. I made it sound like it was *maybe* serious, *maybe* not." She hurried to add, "I didn't want him bugging you. He teased all the time, pestered and pestered. I thought it would get on your nerves. He doesn't have proof."

"Then what 'tip' is he calling in?"

"It's not like I came out and said you… y'know." Frankie continued pacing. "Besides, we were hammered at the time. The whole conversation was just a drunken blather session."

"He doesn't drink."

"Okay," she sighed. "*I* was hammered. We were joking around. It was nothing, I promise. He didn't believe me. He thinks I'm a fucking fruitcake like everyone else does."

"When did this happen?"

Frankie made like she was thinking hard, rolling her eyes up to the ceiling. "I dunno, let me check my journal." She charged down the hall on a mission, seemingly lightened by the conversation, though Gillian was sinking fast. Frankie returned with a leather journal the color of rust and flipped a few pages, scanning.

While she was looking, the blocked number texted. Gillian leaned over and read it aloud. "Call me or there will be trouble."

"More threats. *Idle* threats," Frankie assured Gillian, though it sounded like she was reassuring herself.

Stupid threats, Gillian thought. *If it's a blocked number, you can't call it back.*

"Fucking lunatic," Frankie muttered to herself, turning diary pages.

Gillian stared at the side of her sister's face while she read. "Who brought the booze to your house that night, him or you?"

"He treated," Frankie said, scanning pages.

Gillian felt her eyes narrow. "But he doesn't drink."

"No."

"So, he got you drunk," Gillian clarified, "and asked you questions about me."

"The conversation just kinda went in your direction."

"Keep looking. I need to know when."

"Uh, after we got back together that time?" She found the spot in her diary. "After the Victoria Day barbecue fiasco."

"Where he basically called me a frigid bitch in front of Dad and Bev and all the kids?" Gillian asked.

Frankie nodded. "But you stood up to him."

Gillian leaned forward. "I told him he had to play nice or he wouldn't be welcome at family events anymore. He tried to tell me I didn't make that call. Dad backed me up, told him I was right, and Bev agreed. Everyone took my side against him. So did you. So I won. And then after things settled…"

"Or I thought they'd settled," Frankie said, her eyes growing wide.

"He got you drunk and asked you questions about me," Gillian finished. "See the problem?"

"Maybe it's all a coincidence. We're reading too much into it. He's not that smart."

"I would have thought so too, at one time. But now?" She stared at Frankie's phone. "I don't know. It feels off."

The blocked number texted: *I miss you, baby.*

Gillian read the text and her poker face must have slipped. "It is him."

Frankie asked, "What did he say?"

Gillian showed her.

"What the hell? He's bat-shit fucking crazy," she barely breathed. "How can he threaten me one minute, and then..." Her confusion tipped toward anger. "For days, he's been mocking me, giving me orders—"

Gillian interrupted, "Like he has the right to call the shots."

"Right!" Frankie pounced on this, nostrils flaring. "Calling the shots in *my* house like he always did. *My* house, not his. Threatening me, insulting my parenting skills, insulting my body, my mental state, and now he 'misses' me? I'm his 'baby' again?"

Gillian took the phone back and stared down at the texts as they began to file in rapidly, one after another.

I love you.

I can't stand sleeping without you.

You know how restless I get.

I'm so hurt by your cruelty.

How can you be so heartless?

This isn't the Frankie I know.

You're not this cold.

And finally, *This is your sister's ice infecting you. Frosty, uptight cunt.*

Frankie shook her head. "I don't want to hear another text, not one."

They didn't stop, cast in like fish hooks wriggling with bait. *We should go to our spot by the lake. Don't tell your sister. Meet me there. It's a full moon tonight.*

"What's the moon phase tonight?" Gillian asked.

Frankie didn't even have to check. "Quarter waning, why?"

"Does the phase of the moon mean something between you?"

Full moon, baby.

"He always said he was more virile during the full moon. Is he trying to use that?" She pointed at the fridge calendar, when Gillian could see scribbled circles. "It's not even a full moon tonight. Does he think I wouldn't check? Does he think I'm an idiot?"

"I'm sorry, but yes, of course he does," Gillian said with a long exhale. "He's accustomed to getting his way, and getting away with all his lies and exaggerations."

"He's lying about the goddamn *moon* now?" Frankie laughed with disgust. "Like I can't just look the fuck up in the fucking sky?"

"Lower your voice, Frankie," she said, and went to take her sister away from the window. "And don't open these blinds."

"Think he's out there?"

"I think he's mentioned the moon to see if you'll come outside to look up at it."

"For what?"

"To prove that you're still thinking about his possible virility?"

Frankie's upper lip curled. "That's creepy. Seriously, you're starting to think like him."

"We have to," she said fiercely, using her phone to dial Paul. When he picked up, she asked, "Could you drive by Frankie's house and look for the black truck we discussed?"

"Do you one better," he said. "Cousin's on patrol at the end of his shift. How about I have him loop by in his patrol car and scan the firelanes on his way back to the precinct?"

Gillian let out a long breath and the knot that was slowly twisting in her gut loosened a bit. "Thank you. That would be great." She hung up and looked at her sister. "Who have you given your new phone number to?"

"Only trusted people!" Frankie didn't look so sure anymore. "Paul, you. Henry, because of the boys. The day care."

"Would they give the number out if they thought the caller was Henry? To contact you about the boys? Travis could have pretended to be Henry."

Frankie wilted. "I don't know. I want to say no, but... I didn't warn them not to give out my number."

"You'll have to change it again and warn them this time," Gillian suggested. "He can't keep reaching you like this. It's not healthy for your stress levels."

Frankie looked unsure. "Don't we need to know what he's up to, what he's trying to do?"

"He lies, so you'll never know for sure," Gillian assured her. "You'll only ever know what he *says* he's going to do."

"He left me a white rose," Frankie said. "Or somebody did. I just left it on the back porch. I don't even want to look at it."

"I'll get rid of it when I leave," Gillian offered.

"What should we do?"

We. Gillian sighed; already she was feeling another migraine beginning to build behind her right eyebrow. "Now we wait, and like Paul said, we ignore. Can you be trusted not to engage with him?"

"Oh, of course."

A lie, Gillian knew. *She'll text him back. Something threatening. Any attention he gets at this point will fuel his fire.* She put her cell phone down on the coffee table beside her sister's and coughed as though she had a sore throat. "Can we have the kettle on? Tea?"

Frankie nodded. "You know, all this stress is bad for your immune system. Have you been taking your Echinacea?"

"Yes, dear," Gillian said with a weak laugh.

"Are you getting enough sleep?" Frankie asked. "You know, you probably lost a lot of sleep last night with that headache."

"Mmmhmm," Gillian murmured, claiming a comfortable corner of Frankie's couch. "You need sleep, too, missy."

"Honey and lemon in your tea?" Frankie bundled her wild, blonde curls into a loose braid.

"Please," Gillian said. "Decaf green, if you have it."

Frankie's phone vibrated once more on the coffee table, rattling against the glass. Gillian waited until Frankie was out of the room and tinkering in the kitchen with the kettle and mugs and spoons before reading it.

I won't stop until you start seeing sense.

"You know who else gets wicked migraines?" Frankie called, and the kettle started creaking on the electric stovetop. "Bobby. Like, super-bad. They wipe her out for days."

"Is that right?" Gillian said, and listened to Frankie talk about some other folks she knew at school who also had bad headaches, and the remedies they used.

Gillian slipped her sister's phone with her own into her purse.

Chapter Twenty-One

Thursday, October 30. 12:00 A.M.

The texts continued to pour in, but they poured into Gillian's bedroom and wouldn't bother Frankie that night.

I know what she did, one text read. Gillian placed Frankie's cell phone on her bedside table face up beside her own. She walked away from it, padding barefoot to the kitchen to make one last decaf green tea for the night, this one jasmine-flavored. She took her time tidying the kitchen before bed, and taking care of her bedtime routine in the bathroom, removing her contacts and putting her glasses on. She released her dark brown hair from its loose braid and brushed it through, making it silky soft. She took Greg's old cologne bottle out of the cabinet and gave it a sniff, closed her eyes, let the memory of him make her smile. Tonight, the pain didn't come. Her head didn't hurt, her heart didn't hurt. She felt in control.

She stripped in her walk-in closet, chose her most comfortable nightgown, the one that Greg had teased made her look like an old lady. That Christmas, she had bought him a set of what he called "grandpa pajamas" so they could be old together, and he'd laughed. Joking aside, he'd worn them often that winter. She still had them in her drawer. When she packed to move to the Higgins Point house, she knew she'd bring them along. Maybe she'd have them taken in so she could wear them.

One of the phones on the night table dinged to indicate another text, but she took her time. Their effect was wearing off, she felt. Either that or she was numb. So far, he was all piss and wind. She couldn't pretend he hadn't given her a few scares, but now...

I know where the body is.

Gillian stared down at the phone and whispered, "You were saying, Gillian?"

Her logic kicked in immediately. *He doesn't know there's a body. He doesn't know any details.* He did read some things, she supposed, whatever Frankie was dumb enough to jot down in that old diary. And she had blabbed to him a bit. *He thinks he knows. He doesn't really know.* And even if he did know, he would have zero idea where the body is. No one did. Not Frankie. Not crazy Bobby. Certainly not that cop who had been sniffing around.

Gillian pulled back her quilt and flannel sheets, and slid in, nestling first on Greg's pillow, getting comfortable, then stacking her two pillows and sitting up to read a bit before turning out the light.

Frankie's phone kept buzzing. After a while, she could no longer resist the temptation to piss him off. She texted from that phone.

You have reached G. You may no longer have access to F.

Then she turned off both phones and drifted easily to sleep with a small, satisfied smile lingering on her lips, pressing her face into Greg's pillow.

Chapter Twenty-Two

Friday, October 31. 10:00 A.M.

Gillian stood looking up at Frankie's broken basement window, idly using the side of her work boot to shove shards of glass into a pile.

Frankie came down her basement stairs with a broom and dustpan. "I just put in a security system. I *know* I armed it. I'm very good at making sure."

"I'm sorry this happened to you," Gillian said, shaking her head. "Maybe Paul's right. Maybe it's time to get the police involved."

"God, no, Gills," Frankie said hoarsely. "What if—"

"Yes, think of the 'what if!' I can't bear the thought of him being in your house last night while you slept. How fucking creepy is that?"

Frankie made an uncertain noise and held the broom out at her. Gillian frowned but took it and began sweeping up the mess.

Frankie twisted a lock of hair around her fingers and snapped the ends. "I might not have noticed that anything was different right away, but the lamp beside the couch was left on. I always turn it off before bed. The wiring is funny and sometimes it flickers. I don't trust it on overnight."

"You should—" Gillian cut herself off before she sounded too much like Mom, and chose a different thought. "Is anything missing?"

She bent over with the dustpan to get as much glass in it as possible. When Frankie didn't reply, she glanced up. Frankie snapped her blond hair and little broken ends filtered down through the air to land on broken glass.

"I think he licked my bathroom mirror," she said.

Gillian grimaced. "Eww! He *what?*"

"And I'm fairly certain he turned my furnace up. It was eighty degrees when I woke up. I never set it that high." Frankie rubbed her own arms comfortingly. "Big old disgusting wet tongue mark across my bathroom mirror. While I'm sleeping in the next room. *Ugh.*"

"Is anything missing?"

Frankie shot Gillian a look and then, realizing she hadn't done the best job of hiding it, nodded rapidly. "Four of my old diaries. I had a whole box of them going back to my high school years in my bedroom closet. He came into my bedroom while I slept, Gillian. He took four."

Gillian straightened, forgetting the glass. "Which ones? What did you put it in them?"

"Private thoughts. Everything that was troubling me, everything I was feeling. Just..." She seemed at a loss, looked around the room for help, let out a sound that was half-sigh, half-laugh. "*Everything,* Gillian. All my worries and thoughts."

"The one with the night Mike fell?" Gillian froze.

"I'm so sorry, Gillian."

"Quiet," Gillian snapped, and went upstairs to the front window to watch the street for anything that might move. The bright morning revealed nothing. She checked the locks on the doors, and pulled all the blinds.

"This is all my fault," Frankie moaned behind her.

"What details did you write down and when?" Gillian demanded. "I need you to remember exactly."

"I know you did it for me, I needed you. You're my Pit Bull, my protector."

"I can't believe this. You wrote everything about Mike?" Gillian felt faint. "Do you mean to say he has all the *details* in your handwriting?"

"He won't do anything with it."

"How do you know that?"

Frankie laughed bitterly. "He can't do shit. What's he gonna do?"

"That's the problem! What's he going to do, Frankie?"

"He's not going to tell anyone," Frankie scoffed. "And even if he did, who's going to believe him? It's just bullshit written in a diary. It's ridiculous. Anyone who knows you—"

"Don't. Don't finish that." Gillian found herself pacing where just yesterday her sister had been doing so. "You put it in writing. I can't believe you could be so stupid."

Frankie's lips pinched together. "It's my own private writing. It's not for other people to snoop in."

"But they could and they did, and now we're both in deep shit, do you not get that?" She thought about the upcoming evening, all the kids in their costumes coming to the front door, and her sister opening it over and over. Frankie couldn't stay here. Halloween was canceled before the paint dried on the pumpkin. "What *exactly* did you write down?"

Frankie sighed. "I don't know, just feelings."

"Names?"

"What, you mean Mike's name?" She shrugged. "Of course. He was my fiancé. His name is everywhere; that whole year's entries."

"Incidents?"

"The first few. I was pretty specific. After that, I just referred to 'ongoing issues.'"

Gillian flashed back to Mike's snarling face up close, invading hers, smelling of sour beer, sweat, and sausage. *You sound like yer fucking slut sister!* And her calm, unblinking reply, *Maybe I should leave like she did.* The hate-filled blows that took her off guard. The sensation of falling. But just before that, the shove.

"Gillian?" Frankie was staring at her.

The shove.

Pressing her palms against the meat of his chest, and shoving. Hard.

The shock as his hand snatched the front of her cardigan and yanked.

The wet snap of bone.

The unnatural turn of his neck.

The shock of pain ripping through her shoulder, her head.

Seeing stars, then black.

Her sister's hand on her shoulder, tentative, a butterfly settling on a rotten apple.

Gillian blinked rapidly and stared at the clock. It was ten-thirty. She said, "Go pack your bag. You're staying with me at the new house tonight."

"What about Doogie?"

"Bring the pup," she said, looking at the sleeping old lump of golden fur. "He's no trouble. Still got that chocolate?"

Frankie exhaled softly and rose from the couch. "I think I do."

Gillian watched her go, and wondered if Travis Freeman had really fit through the window, if he could have been quiet enough to slink through the house without waking Frankie or the dog. Sure, the damn dog was deaf, but he'd hated most men and was very gruff around them. *The only other person who might want a look at Frankie's diaries is Bobby McIntyre.*

She was careful not to voice this suspicion when Frankie returned to the room with a handful of mini chocolate bars.

Chapter Twenty-Three

Friday, October 31. 2:45 P.M.

"Auntie Gillian. Happy Halloween!"

Colin Keller strode out of the playground and hovered under a well-trimmed weeping willow tree, choosing a shady spot in which to lean against the fence. The wiry young man watched her approach with a broad smile. From his finger dangled a black bag.

"Forgot your purse at my house again," he faux-scolded, watching a gaggle of middle-school kids rush by on the sidewalk.

Colin was not her nephew, nor any other sort of relative. He used to live with foster parents on Red Maple Drive when he was a young teen; Greg had busted him selling pot and let him off with a warning. He'd since expanded his wares, and after Greg died, Colin had approached her at the funeral to express his sympathies and remind her that he was "there for her." She remembered his hand on her bad shoulder. He'd shot up a good eight inches since she'd last seen him, all grown up in his black suit and tie. He'd noted the pain on her face, asked her if she was having one of her headaches, sympathized, spun her a nice tale about his dear old granny who suffered terribly with migraines (a story Gillian suspected was only true in his head). He'd put an envelope in her hand, told her he wanted to help, explained the difference between OxyContin and

Vicodin, and left her with his free samples, assuring her he'd "check in on her in a few weeks and see how she was doing."

That had been three years ago. Now he was a young father, waiting for his daughter to come charging out of kindergarten, selling Gillian Vicodin outside an elementary school. She hated herself for needing it, loathed him for selling it to her, and couldn't imagine life without it or him; her shoulder, neck, and head had not recovered from her fall, not with surgery and physiotherapy, and the pain meds the doctors offered never really cut it.

Gillian took Colin's beat-up backpack off her left shoulder. It was full of small purses. One contained several thousand dollars in cash. "And you left your school bag at my house."

"Aw, man, thanks," he said, comfortable with their routine. "I've got an exam next week."

"Math?" She knew the school part was true.

Colin's smile slid sideways; he was enjoying himself. "College level. Greg would be proud."

Gillian's lips tightened. "Please don't say that. Greg wouldn't be proud of any of this."

"I dunno," Colin glanced over his shoulder and smiled as his little blonde sweetheart flew out of the school and headed straight for the monkey bars. "I think he'd like Katie. Only thing I ever did right. Look, I could come by on Sunday morning if you need company."

Company was code for a refill, which they'd often fill quietly on her big covered porch over iced tea and cookies. Gillian wondered what his wife thought. Maybe the poor woman actually believed he went to Red Maple Drive to visit his Auntie Gillian. Colin had no family left, real or foster, no one to tell her differently.

She nodded, relieved but ashamed. "Don't bring Katie this time, please. It makes me feel—"

"I know," he said, slinging the backpack over his shoulder and pushing off of the fence in one smooth move. "Little kids make headaches worse. I understand. Talk to you soon."

"Colin?"

He paused in the grass. Katie had spotted her father and was waving like mad from the top of the monkey bars. He waved back and said, "Uh huh?"

"Might wanna talk about home security stuff. Think you could help me with that?"

He bobbed his head thoughtfully. "Woman living alone should be able to feel safe in her own home. I'm sure we can figure something out. Wait…" His eyes narrowed, and for a moment, Gillian saw the fox in sheep's clothing, the sharp teeth, the hungry focus. "Sure it can wait until Sunday? I could drop by later tonight."

"No, there's no immediate rush."

"It's not urgent?"

Gillian's belly fluttered but she mastered it with a single long exhale. "I'll make us some cookies for Sunday."

"You got my digits. Hit me up if you change your mind." She watched him go, flaxen hair like spun gold in the bright sun, slipping on his sunglasses and hurrying over to Katie as she clambered down for a hug. She squealed as he picked her up in the crook of one arm, then slapped him on the shoulder and lectured him on safety in the playground, her tiny, squeaky kid voice solemn and serious. He pretended to be humbled, apologized profusely, and set her on her feet, at which point she ran for the swings, pigtails slapping her shoulders.

Colin shot Auntie Gillian one last glance, and went to the swings.

Feeling vaguely like Pandora, Gillian walked home. On Sunday, she would ask Colin to sell her a gun.

Chapter Twenty-Four

Friday, October 31. 4:00 P.M.

Bobby McIntyre's sister Barb lived in a small village west of Derby Harbor called Sugarloaf, in an aggressively nondescript suburban brick bungalow at 84 Winthrop Lane. The streets had signs warning of children and pets in the neighborhood and plenty of crosswalks for schools. The trees were carefully maintained and the lawns raked mostly clear, though the afternoon's cold, damp wind had blown down many of the remaining leaves, scattering them into gutters, around car tires, and in scattered drifts.

Gillian slowed her Jeep to peer closely at the house numbers, pulling her glasses from her purse to slide them on. She'd only been to Barb's once, after her and Bobby's mother's funeral, to bring a casserole and a Bundt cake in freezer-ware, and to offer to tidy up if they needed help. Barb's home had been immaculate, even the small converted dining room that had served as her mother's bedroom, complete with hospital bed and monitors and all the paraphernalia dying required. There had been no tidying for Gillian to help with, but she'd held Barb's hand while she cried, made sure the tea and coffee was always brewing for the guests who dropped in to relay their sympathies, and did her best to fill in where Bobby was, in Gillian's opinion, falling short. Drunk by nine in the morning and slurring through the whole funeral, Bobby McIntyre was no help to anyone, and Barb was too deep in mourning to help herself or her sister. Frankie had been in Lisbon with the kids, and Gillian told her not to even consider cutting their trip short, picking up all the slack and taking care of things. At least, for that one day.

Now Barb was sick, if Frankie's gossip was to be believed, and showing a lot of the same symptoms that the doctors couldn't diagnose when her mother died. The illness was a weird one, surging forward and leveling off; Frankie said Bobby was mystified and worried that it was something in their genes, that she'd be next. At least this time, Gillian thought, Bobby was sober and able to help her sister. That was an improvement, she was forced to concede.

Gillian parked in front of the bungalow at the curb, noting that all the curtains and blinds were closed tight. She leaned into the back seat to retrieve a plastic bag, got out of the Jeep, and strode carefully around several large puddles to ring the doorbell.

Bobby answered the door, and it was clear she was shocked to see Gillian standing there. They stood blinking at each other through matching pairs of glasses.

"Bit early for trick or treat?" Gillian tried to joke, but Bobby's face didn't soften. "May I come in?"

"You shouldn't be here," Bobby said anxiously, looking both ways down the street. "What if…"

Gillian waited for the end of that sentence, shifting from one foot to the other on the porch. "What if what?"

"That creep Frankie dumped could have followed you here," Bobby scolded. "Think I need the hassle? Think I want on that guy's hit list?"

"I'm fairly certain I wasn't followed, but I understand," Gillian said. "And I should have called first, I'm sorry. This is rude."

"You can't just show up unannounced," Bobby agreed.

Gillian bit her tongue so she wouldn't point out the irony of Bobby McIntyre of all people saying those words. "I just brought Barb a care package," she said instead. "I can leave it with you if it's a bad time."

Barb called out from inside the house, "Is that Gillian Ellis?"

"Gillian Hearth now," Bobby bellowed over her shoulder. "God, keep up. Don't remind her she's a *widow*. That's cruel, even for you,

Barb! Her husband is *dead*. Have some goddamn sensitivity."

Gillian tried to hide her surprise and shook her head. "No, it's fine. Either name is fine. I only went back to my maiden name because..." She stopped dead. The Ellis family had blamed Gillian for Greg's death. According to them, she'd encouraged him to stay on the police force instead of suggesting a safer line of work, and once he'd been shot and killed, Gillian no longer deserved to wear the Ellis name. Insulted, and disgusted with her in-laws, she'd quickly and quietly agreed to reclaim her maiden name. She knew Greg would have understood.

Bobby, on the other hand, would take that morsel and run with it God knows where, she knew. So she finished, "For business purposes. May I give this to Barb?"

"Just be quick about it," Bobby said with a put-upon sigh. "I still have all this laundry to do and cooking and cleaning and nobody's around to help out so don't expect it to be a frickin' show-home or anything."

Gillian smiled to disarm. "Of course not, this is a very difficult time for both of you," she said, but nothing could have prepared her for the hoarder-level mess just inside the door.

The living room was piled with dirty clothes, dishes covered with food in varying levels of decay, garbage, empty cans, papers, and tools. There were four interior doors with the hinges still attached leaning against the far wall. Gillian dragged her attention away from that to the room to the right, from which Barb's voice emanated. The sick room was in equal disarray, and the smell of vomit in a bucket on the floor was nearly overwhelming. Gillian breathed through her mouth, plastered on another smile, and approached the cranked-up hospital bed, where a paler, skinnier version of Barb McIntyre laid.

"Brought you some crosswords and number puzzles," Gillian said. "And chocolate, though you might not want it today."

Barb chuckled sadly. "Won't stay down, so I'll save it for a better day."

Bobby took the bag before Barb could touch it and said, "I'll check this stuff out and make sure it's okay for you. Gotta be careful. You're very sick."

Barb drawled, "Thank God I have you to tell me, I'd never have figured it out on my own." She rolled her eyes at Gillian. "Just put me out of my misery already. I think a crossword puzzle book isn't going to be too stimulating for my poor heart. See how she worries about me? She's been an angel, I admit it. But *such* a pain in the ass. I'd kill for something to do. I'm stir-crazy in this room. All I do is sleep and puke."

"Gosh, Barb, do the doctors know anything yet?" Gillian asked, looking for a chair she could pull up beside the bed, but finding nothing she could use without picking through soiled, mildew-smelling clothes and garbage.

Barb shook her head. "It's just like with mum. Better for a while and then *whammo*, the vomiting comes back, I can barely walk to the bathroom. I feel like a burden, I swear."

"When did it start?" Gillian wanted to know.

Bobby cleared her throat. "Should I make coffee or anything?"

"No, thanks, I try to steer away from caffeine," Gillian told her, and turned to Barb. "I get headaches, and I save my caffeine intake for those days, to help with my remedy."

Barb's eyebrows went up. "Hear that, Bobs? Maybe you should try Gillian's remedy. Bobby gets the *worst* migraines," she confided. "It's terrible. Nothing works. They can last for days and days. We used to think it was eye strain because they happened a lot when she didn't wear her glasses, but the glasses haven't helped. Right Bobby?"

Bobby left the room without answering, and Gillian heard noises from the direction of the kitchen at the end of the hall, what sounded like cardboard boxes falling. She dreaded seeing that room, and wouldn't be touching a single edible thing that came out of it.

Gillian asked, "So, um, when did all this start? You seemed healthy the last time I saw you. Granted, it's been years…"

"Three months or so," Barb said, and squeezed her eyes shut as though that might clear fog from her mind. "Sometimes, it seems like yesterday that I was out at the museum, or shopping, or at the bar." Barb had been a bartender at the local Irish pub, The Nimble Fiddler, for as long as Gillian had known her. "I know it'll get better, but it just feels like it's been forever."

"Maybe being in this sick room isn't the best idea," Gillian suggested. "Would you like me to take you out somewhere? I could help you to the Jeep and take you to the library, maybe? Stock you up on a few dozen books and then you can read and recuperate?"

Barb smiled widely and her eyes glistened. "I'm not sure I'm well enough today, but please offer again. God, that sounds great."

"We should plan it before the snow starts," Gillian agreed, reaching for Barb's hand, dismayed to find it shaky and skeletal. She swallowed hard. "Is there anything else I could bring you? I notice you don't have a TV in here. Did you want me to help Bobby move one into the room? Get you some DVD seasons of a favorite sitcom or some stand-up comedy?"

"Oh, Gillian," Barb said, tearing up. "You really are too much." Then she looked over Gillian's shoulder. "Hear that? She's going to help you move my TV in. Now, you've got no excuse to complain about it."

Bobby stood there with a mug of coffee in each hand, and a blank look on her face, her lashes fluttering rapidly behind her glasses. "Oh, good. That's great. We can do that, sure." She moved to shove one mug on the raised, rolling bedside table among the dirty dishes, which Gillian moved to take. "Sure you don't want some coffee? It's maple dark roast, a really good new kind."

"Maybe next time," she said, stacking filthy plates one atop the other, loading cutlery on tip. "If they have a decaf version."

"Just put those anywhere," Bobby told her.

Gillian fought to keep the grimace off her face and said smoothly, "I'll just put them in the kitchen sink, and these," as she picked up a bunch of other food-encrusted dishes from around the room.

"Oh, Gillian, you don't have to clean up after me," Barb objected. "Bobby was going to hire someone to come in, but we're low on funds since I'm off work."

And Bobby can't clean? "Don't be silly," Gillian said. "I'm just moving them from one spot to another, no big deal. Be right back."

Gillian picked her way down the hall without making it look like she was trying to avoid the piles of garbage and mess, ignoring it politely like it was the most normal thing in the world. The smell in the kitchen was astounding, sour milk and spoiled food and human waste, even with a cold breeze slithering through a small window cracked open over the sink. She deposited her load of dishes nearby, though there was no way they'd fit in the sink with all the moldy ones.

She wasn't sure why the small yellowish ring of liquid caught her eye on the countertop among everything else that was unclean in the room. Perhaps because it seemed fresh. She bent over a little and sniffed at it. It smelled like maple syrup, though it didn't look like it. Much too watery. ("*Maple dark roast, a really good new kind.*") She glanced around for the coffee maker and dented tin of Maxwell House sitting open beside it. Ground coffee. Unable to help herself, she peeked into the coffee machine and stared in horror at the mold clinging to the edges of an old, overused coffee filter and a mound of wet coffee grounds. The recent percolation had rinsed most of it away, into the coffee pot below. She could see a film of floating bits on top, complete with foam. She sniffed at the filter basket. It did not smell like maple, the way the coffee had in Barb's sick room.

"Thought you didn't want any," Bobby said, directly over her right shoulder.

Gillian started, and laughed guiltily. "It smelled so good," she lied quickly. "I changed my mind. Is it okay if I help myself?"

Bobby's eyes had taken on a cold, lizard-like quality that Gillian found deeply alarming, but her words were light, and if you didn't look directly at her, they sounded comforting. "Of course, no problem," Bobby said with a wry chuckle. "I wanted you to have some. My home is your home, such as it is. Here, let me make it. I do it up real good."

Gillian nodded gratefully and watched as Bobby took down a fresh cup, poured the coffee, dug in the front pocket of her jeans for yellow sweetener packets, and slapped two before ripping the paper and pouring the crystals in. Then she leaned into a small bar fridge beside the counter to get a carton of cream. Noting Gillian's' glance toward the big fridge nearby, Bobby explained, "Barb had trouble after mum passed. She couldn't get rid of any of mum's things, see. All mum's medications are in the big fridge. I tried to take them away, but Barb wouldn't allow it. Then I tried to clean out mum's closet. I made a special trip back here in June to do it, remember?"

Gillian hadn't known that Bobby was back in town in June, but she thought it would upset Bobby to know that, and Bobby wasn't someone you wanted to upset, in Gillian's opinion. So she nodded, as though perhaps Frankie had known and mentioned.

"You came to help clean out your mom's place," Gillian repeated, nodding. "Barb has had trouble letting go of things?"

"Look at this place," Bobby whispered. "It's a fucking dump. She went from not being able to throw out mum's stuff, to not being able to get rid of anything. Seriously. I'm not allowed to put out garbage at the curb. Sometimes, I sneak things out. Like her broken TV, by the way. Thing hasn't worked in over a year. She won't let me spend money on a new one, and now she wants us to move the old one into her room? Seriously?"

"I'm sorry, Bobby," Gillian said.

"You can't take her *out,*" Bobby said scornfully. "The library, what a fucking joke. She's having seizures, she shits her pants. She can't leave that room, never mind the house." She shoved the coffee cup at Gillian's waiting hands, and Gillian took it, regretting not only her polite request but her assumptions about Bobby.

"I'm sorry," Gillian repeated sincerely. "This must be so hard for you to deal with. I had no idea. How can I help, Bobby?"

"Well, first of all, you can stop telling Frankie not to see me," Bobby snapped. "Don't pretend you didn't."

"Frankie is headstrong," Gillian replied immediately. "I've never been able to tell her not to do something. Honestly, Bobby, she's a free bird."

"She's been dodging me since I returned to town."

Gillian raised her mug to her mouth and pretended to test the temperature. It did not smell like maple, which surprised her at first. She paused in the act of mock-sipping to ask, "When was that, Bobby? When did you know Barb was sick?"

"June," she said frankly, "when I got a look at this place and what's become of it. I told her I'd hired someone to come give it a good clean-out, you know, maybe those people who help hoarders. She told me to leave. She didn't need me, she said. Well," Bobby smirked, and it was oddly smug as she cast a look around the room. "Who needs who now, eh? Yeah, *suuuuuure* she doesn't need me. *Noooooobody* needs me." She rolled her eyes dramatically, and her hands flew in the air. "Nobody needs Bobby until they do, and then look at all the fucking messes Bobby has to clean up."

Gillian felt gooseflesh crawl up the back of her scalp at that, recognizing the reminder and feeling threatened. Her reply was carefully crafted. "Barb's sure lucky to have you right now," she said, and the words felt like poison on her tongue.

There was a retching noise from the other room, and Bobby sighed. "Gee, ya think?" She opened the cabinet under the sink and grabbed a pair of rubber gloves and a roll of paper towels.

Gillian got a glimpse of a square yellow bottle before the doors slapped shut, and put her coffee mug down on the countertop, untouched. "I'd better get out of your hair," she said to Bobby's retreating form. As soon as Bobby disappeared into the sick room, she grabbed the under-sink cabinet door and yanked it open to make sure she'd seen what she thought she'd seen.

Antifreeze. In the kitchen. Casting a nervous glance over her shoulder to make sure Bobby was still busy in Barb's room, she grabbed the bottle and spun the top off as quickly as possible, her heart suddenly racing. She brought it to her nose.

Syrup. Sickly sweet maple syrup. For a split second, she felt faint, and tiny stars danced across her vision. *Fainting right now would be very bad*, she thought, followed quickly by, *Is Bobby poisoning her sister's fucking coffee? Is that actually fucking happening?*

She replaced the bottle exactly where it was, noting the ring on the countertop one more time. *What do I do now?* Gillian wondered frantically. *Do I confront her? Is there antifreeze in Barb's coffee right this second? What if I accuse her and I'm wrong? What if she blows up and tells everyone what happened after Mike...* Gillian's tongue was glued to the roof of her mouth, and as she walked down the hall toward the front door, she felt numb, like a zombie shuffling through debris. *I can't let Barb die because I'm afraid to face my own demons.* She looked into the sickroom to say a quiet goodbye, and promised to return soon.

How much of what Bobby had said about the hoarding had been true? How much of *anything* that Bobby said was true? She had to assume most of it was bullshit, and trust only what she saw with her own two eyes.

Once out in the fading sunshine and the freedom outside the McIntyre house, her sanity roared back to life and she only barely resisted the urge to stand right there on the front porch and call 911. She went to the Jeep, keys shaking in her nervous, clumsy hands, feeling dazed with shock and sick to her stomach. Once buckled into the driver's seat, she did some deep breathing before driving to the nearest public parking lot, blocking her phone number, and dialing the police with an anonymous tip. She told the dispatcher as much information as she could, and while she was talking, heard herself put together their mother's odd illness and death, too.

And hadn't Frankie been violently ill the other night, Gillian wondered? After confessing everything she suspected about Bobby McIntyre to the police, she hung up, opened the car door, threw up on the asphalt, and closed the door again. *Why, why, why would she do this?* She sat there shaking for a long time, collecting herself. She thought about how Bobby had fixated on being needed, pretending to be burdened but seeming oddly smug about it. Wasn't she always eager to jump into Frankie's life at the worst moments, too? A martyr, preferring people around her to be broken down enough to cling to the help she conveniently offered just at the right moment. How much of that suffering had she caused, just so she could be the hero? Gillian sat breathing slowly through her nostrils, hoping that she'd caught it in time, worried about Frankie, before turning on the Jeep and heading home.

She never did ask Bobby about the missing diaries.

Chapter Twenty-Five

Friday, October 31. 4:10 P.M.

Constable Dean Jagger strolled through Pleasant Pines cemetery, his six-foot-six frame not easy to miss, his broad shadow sweeping the old graves at the far north side of the graveyard, sticking to the pathway. He'd never been entirely comfortable in cemeteries, having a superstitious streak a mile wide, and he couldn't imagine why anyone would choose to work in one, spending day after day with the dead. *Isn't that what you're doing now?* the gloomy side of his brain teased. *Spending day after day with the ghost of a mother-beating drug dealer, looking for justice for him? What a joke.*

He didn't like it. He was honest enough with himself to admit that he'd be much happier when he passed this particular torch to a new officer; cold case files made his already grim life even more so. He envied Ray Sauffs his retirement. Hell, lately he envied Paul Langerbeins his injury and his new job; though that was morbid, it was in total keeping with the deepest, truest part of Dean's personality, the part he kept carefully hidden from girlfriends and lovers. No one needed to know just how dark his morose streak ran.

The asphalt was well maintained in the back corner, something that struck him as incongruous; surely, the relatives of soldiers from the War of 1812 weren't swinging by to visit their ancestors nearly as often as those in the more recent graves, and he'd seen some terrible potholes on those pathways. This one had been patched. He paused to admire the stand of pines and oak and maple rising up from the gully just beyond a war memorial fountain. The deciduous trees had lost most of their leaves to a cold, October wind, but the pines stood sentinel over a deep ditch full of vines and fallen trees and boulders and secrets.

Secrets? Dean smirked at his own funny mood. *Is that all it is, a mood?* A flurry of nervous activity raced through his belly, always a sign that his intuition had struck something. Probably the same thing that brought him back to Pleasant Pines for the third time that week. There was something here, but it was just out of reach. *The body of Mike Deacon?* No. If the Hearth sisters had anything to do with the disappearance of Mike Deacon, Gillian would know better than to try and dispose of a body here, where she was known to work. TV and movie murderers buried the bodies of their victims in open graves; real people didn't get away with that without a conspiracy of multiple helpers, diggers and movers and people willing to look the other way. Not impossible, but very unlikely. Not nearly as easy as a crematorium *two-bodies-one-box* deal, and still requiring helpers. Loose lips. Jagger didn't think that Gillian Hearth would tolerate loose lips.

Gillian. Why was he focused on that one? Again, his gut shuddered. Despite there being no evidence to support this feeling, he had begun to suspect … *No.* He chuckled softly at his own thoughts. *Just… How would she? Why would she?*

What had the private investigator said on the tail end of a chuckle? (*"The idea of that woman being able to make a full grown man disappear?"*) Even Langerbeins, who knew the woman, thought it was unlikely.

She's got access to light earth-moving equipment, he thought. Maybe she knew how to drive the CAT. Definitely the ATV. She could transport. But lift a man like Mike Deacon, dead weight, who went about 5'11, two hundred thirty pounds? *A cop's widow,* Dean reminded himself, shaking his head. At the time of Mike Deacon's disappearance, Greg Ellis had been alive. A cop's wife. *You think a cop's wife is a murderer? Really grasping at straws, there, Jagger,* he chided.

But when he turned away, his belly trembled once more. There were answers here of some sort. He altered his path to stroll across the rows, something he had never done and which made fingers of discomfort creep up his spine. He mentally apologized to the dead for walking on their sacred plots, painfully aware of their presence under the green-falling-to-brown grass. He only barely resisted the urge to tiptoe or dodge where he thought their feet might reach. Goose flesh crawled across his scalp, and he hurried to make his journey shorter.

He arrived at the next paved pathway and approached a memorial bench beside the fountain. The plantings here had been trimmed for winter, the roses cut right back and the bushes wrapped in burlap to protect them from the sometimes brutal lake-effect snows they received in that part of the peninsula. The soil had been heavily mulched. He wondered if the crew had planted spring bulbs, tulips and hyacinths and daffodils. The little bronze name plate on the bench read "Ellis," with no other information.

He felt his eyebrows shoot up and he looked around for any headstones that read Ellis, but didn't see any. Had Gillian paid for this bench in memory of her husband? If so, why put it here, and not closer to his grave? Was he even buried here? Maybe this was the only available place for it. The fountain, according to a plaque, was created in memory of the firemen who died fighting a warehouse blaze in the late nineties. Overnight frosts warned that winter was inbound, and the fountain's water had been shut off for the season.

The gully behind the bench was protected not by a fence but by several dead trees piled up and some brush piles that no one had gotten around to mulching yet. He walked closer to the edge and peered into what occurred to Dean Jagger to be a rather promising darkness. For a good acre or so in all directions, the ditch was piled high with rocks and vines, uneven crevices that disappeared below, deadfall tangled with secondary growth, a veritable maze of impassable vegetation and drop-offs. From somewhere below, he could hear the trickle of water. Someone had tossed a pair of old tires and half a broken bathroom sink, which had made a nice home for a green coating of algae. One tire was almost completely wrapped in vigorous evergreen ivy, which also had a stranglehold on a dozen nearby trees.

Dean dug into his jacket pockets and found a handful of receipts, an elastic band, his pocket knife, and an individually wrapped zinc lozenge still lingering from his last sore throat. Searching the ground around him, he came upon a goodish sized stick with fair girth. He wrapped a receipt around the stick with the elastic band, eased a bit closer to the edge of the chasm, testing his footing before he settled his not inconsiderable weight there fully, and dropped the stick.

It tumbled end over end, bounced off a boulder, and came to rest against a flat, metal object with a clang. He squinted, jogging his head into the shade to remove the late sun's glare from his eyes, to see better, but he couldn't tell what the metal thing was. It had a sharply defined edge where the stick was propped, but was too covered by shadow and foliage for him to make out what it was.

He took out his phone and snapped twenty or so pictures of the area, and that settled some of the furious churning in is guts. Jagger flipped through the pictures to make sure he got at least a dozen clear ones then returned to the parking lot just as a young custodian was emptying one of the green metal garbage cans on the property. Jagger paused, considered him for a long beat, then decided it wasn't quite time to question the staff yet. If the Hearth sisters were hiding a something here, he didn't want to raise their alarm. *Any more than you already have*, he thought, remembering Gillian Hearth's almost smug, "Drive safe, officer."

Knowing he'd be back soon, Jagger drove away, planning to be home in time to order himself a pizza and Buffalo wings and settle in to watch that night's baseball game.

***

Aaron Fletcher watched the last visitor of the evening drive away as he swung the cemetery gates closed for the night and locked up; a huge man, big shoulders, stony face. *Probably a crook*, Aaron thought. *Everyone's a crook these days*. Aaron had never had a chance to be a happy idealist; he'd been raised a pessimist and he'd embraced that side of himself as he came into adulthood, pitying the starry-eyed optimists, thinking them naïve at best, bordering on stupid.

That guy wasn't stupid, Aaron noted. *He's not blissfully unaware of how shitty this planet is, and how shitty everyone on it is. That guy knows too much. Probably why he became a crook. This place is dog-eat-dog. And he looks like he's not about to get eaten anytime soon.*

Pleased with his assessment and feeling wise beyond his years, Aaron finished collecting the garbage, locked up the shed, and hung the key ring in the office. He checked the time and made sure he was really alone before sidling up to Gillian Hearth's locker and nudging it open.

Never locks it, he thought sadly. *Optimist. Trusting.* He didn't go as far as thinking her stupid. He liked her perky tits and her sweet, round ass far too much to think too far past them. She was All Right in Aaron's books. A real catch. Maybe a bit old for him, though that wouldn't matter much if she was on her hands and knees, now, would it? Fuck, no. And he thought he had a real shot with her, down the road. Not like that hairy moron, Bruce, with his pit stains and his ill-fitting shirts, clomping around with one boot's laces untied, stinking of the outdoors. She may confide in a guy like Bruce, she may even accept his help more readily than she had accepted any of Aaron's early offerings, but she wouldn't spread her legs for a caveman like that, not his Gillian. She was a class act. She deserved someone a tad more cultured than big, dumb Bruce Wertheimer.

Aaron fantasized often about the day Gillian when would finally notice that cultured young man standing right in front of her, how grateful she'd be for all the pleasures he'd give her. He was patient. He could wait. She better not make him wait too long, but he thought that wouldn't be a problem. Already, she was warming to him. After all, she'd been the first to sign his birthday card, her big, looping feminine script plastered diagonally across one side with a smiley face beneath it. *A smiley face, really, love?* he'd thought at the time, but then corrected himself. *Nobody is perfect.* And they were at work, he allowed. She had to maintain some semblance of professionalism. But cutesy little symbols were the mark of emotional immaturity, he thought. It was something they could work on together when the time came. That and her name. "Gillian" was so boring compared to her actual first name, the full name he'd seen on her employee records, the one on her pay stubs: Lacey G. Hearth. Why she was going by her middle name, Aaron couldn't fathom. Lacey was a sexy name, a Hollywood starlet name, a fuck-me-now name.

Shuffling through her locker, he was disappointed again. She didn't keep much at work. Papers. Junk, as far as he could tell. A personalized pair of gardening gloves which didn't look like they'd been worn, crammed next to a dirty pair that often had been. Bird-watching binoculars and a worn notebook — just like his dear Lacey to be enchanted by the delicate, flighty, small-boned creatures, so much like herself, a sign of self-obsession but something else they could train out of her in time. A pack of Dentyne gum. An open box of latex gloves; he'd seen her wear those when dealing with fertilizers, though that wasn't really her job. He imagined her wearing them and stroking his cock, closed his eyes as a dizzying wave of hot lust rolled through him. Continuing his search, he found a baseball hat, faded and frayed along the brim. Chicago Cubs. *She won't be celebrating them anytime soon,* he thought, though they were having a pretty good year so far.

Aaron stole a single piece of peppermint gum and closed her locker.

He spent the rest of his short shift jerking off in the bathroom, after which he cleaned up his mess, washed his hands, and went outside to wait for his ride.

Chapter Twenty-Six

Friday, October 31. 8:10 P.M.

Six and a half miles from Constable Jagger's bachelor apartment, there was a homemade vegetarian pizza in the Hearth sisters' new special-delivery four-oven AGA stove, cheese bubbling, almost ready to come out. The stove was something Gillian had always wanted, had saved a significant portion of Greg's insurance payout for, an extravagant luxury that she'd never dreamed she'd actually own someday. A big bag of paper plates waited on the kitchen counter with a pack of napkins. There was a checkered picnic blanket on the floor in the dining room, several large faux-fur throw cushions, and a bottle of root beer with two red plastic cups. Gillian had planned on telling Frankie about Bobby immediately, but when she arrived at the Higgins Point house, Frankie had been humming and pink-cheeked and happy. The serenity on her sister's face had made her breath catch; she hadn't seen Frankie this content in ages. And she looked well, not the least bit sick, not at all like poor Barb McIntyre.

Maybe it can wait one night. I'll let her have tonight, and break the news in the morning, she'd thought, listening to Frankie recount all the work she did this evening. Actual, physical labor — raking leaves, preparing for Halloween trick or treaters, building a fire in the fireplace, carrying in more wood for later that night — and Gillian gave her the "atta-girl" she was looking for. *It can definitely wait.*

Now, settling in for a quiet night, Gillian knew she'd made the right choice. Frankie's hands didn't pick nervously at her skin or twist and snap her hair. The dog lay beside her chair and sometimes thumped his heavy tail on the floor when she shifted; mostly, he just slept. Frankie lounged, relaxed, staring at the fire, no doubt thinking of future artwork the way she often did when she got that far-away look on her face. Gillian had seen that look many times just before Frankie would light up and announce a new idea. She waited for it to come, but for now, there was just the dreamy look.

"Our first official fire at the new place," Frankie said, curled up in a wide rattan Papasan chair beside the hearth. The wood crackled pleasantly. "Too bad I don't drink anymore. We could have had a toast to celebrate."

Gillian brought the big salad bowl full of leftover treats for trick or treating kids. "Celebrate with candy. Looks like we only got those two kids, and they were the neighbor's grandchildren."

"More for me," Frankie gloated, grabbing a handful of mini chocolate bars. She unwrapped one, said, "At least she stopped calling me names in Italian. Allowing the kids to come here for candy is a good sign, too, right? Cheers," and popped it in her mouth, smiling as she chewed.

"I guess we're too far out for parents to think to bring them out here. Maybe we'd attract more if we decorated?" Gillian pictured the Halloween nights of her childhood, romping through the streets ahead of Dad, who hung back at the ends of people's driveways and puffed on his cigar as she and Frankie flew from house to house. Blissful, carefree moments, excitedly chattering to one another about a full-sized chocolate bar or, better still, one of Mrs. Mason's caramel apples with the jaunty little address tag on it so parents could track the treat and know it was safe. She smiled at the memory of Frankie's every-year costume: the old crone. A long, white wig, a pointy black hat, a flowing black dress, a long fake nose held on by an elastic band that inevitably snapped half way into the night. "Or had an open house? Maybe a fog machine?"

"You and Henry," Frankie said with a fond half-smirk. "You guys always did love this holiday. Give me Thanksgiving any day."

"You don't even eat the turkey," Gillian reminded her.

"Tofurkey isn't bad," Frankie said through a mouthful of chocolate. "And I still make a mean mashed turnip casserole."

"Blech," Gillian teased, winking. "Don't fill up on chocolate, your dinner is—" Gillian caught herself and sighed, shoulders slumping. "Sorry, I sound like Mom again."

"You do," Frankie said, rolling her eyes over at the front window, where night was a heavy blanket pricked with distant stars. "When do the curtains come?"

"A couple weeks after we order them," Gillian said, going to check the pizza. "Two slices?"

"Three, please!" Frankie called.

No lack of appetite, that's got to be a good sign, right? Gillian put on her oven mitts and took out the pizza, delighted with the smell of crust and sauce and cheese and olives and pineapple, Frankie's favorite. She heard a soft tapping in the dining room followed by more firm thumps. "What the hell are you doing in there?" she called.

Frankie's reply was mumbled and lost under more thumping.

Gillian slid the pizza stone onto the stovetop and grabbed the pizza cutter and two plates. Usually, she would let the cheese set before cutting, but after the day's stresses and at this late hour, she was starving. Hacking off two messy slices for herself and three for her sister, she took off the oven mitts and carried their dinner plates back into the dining room.

Frankie had nailed the picnic blanket to the wide, bay window. It fit almost the entire width. Gillian nodded in approval. "Good plan."

"Didn't like the night staring in at us," Frankie said.

"Well, it's not the pattern I would have chosen for this room, but it'll do for now." She wanted to say *Travis doesn't know where this house is*, but it sounded like a promise she couldn't make, and besides, she didn't want to bring him up. "We've got lots of time to decide on curtains. Won't be opening for customers until spring."

"I kinda like that plaid, actually," Frankie said, admiring it with a cocked head as she took her plate from Gillian. "Looks good with the original color of this room."

"This boring tan?" Gillian gasped, choosing a pillow to sit on next to the big stone hearth. "You? *Beige?*"

Frankie blew on the steam billowing off the pizza where the melted cheese had slid off. "I could live without every room being wildly dramatic, I suppose. It's a soothing color."

"Will wonders never cease," Gillian said, promptly burning her tongue on pizza sauce. She hissed and poured herself some root beer. "Ouch. Dammit."

"Dork," Frankie said, and then made the exact same mistake with the cheese. She squeaked and her lips formed a perfect, surprised O.

They shared a long laugh, which got them into a contagious loop of stress-busting giggles. When that wound down to dry titters and the occasional snort, Gillian said softly, "We can't live like this much longer. I don't know about you, but the anxiety is killing me."

Frankie nodded. "It's my fault."

"Don't go down that road," Gillian said, though she didn't entirely disagree. "You had no idea Travis would take the break up this badly. He wasn't an out-and-out nut when you met him or you never would have dated him."

Frankie rocked forward in the Papasan chair. "Let's go away for a while. We'll pick up the kids at Henry's and head down to Cape Hatteras, take up windsurfing."

"It's almost November!" Gillian cried, though Frankie had a tempting idea, there. "It's probably about sixty degrees there today."

"Okay, so we'll go somewhere warm," Frankie said. "Portugal. Madrid. You've got money. Where do you wanna take me?"

Gillian fired a free pillow at her and her sister laughed. "How come *I* have to pay?"

"I don't have anything," Frankie said, the *duh* heavily implied.

They tentatively ate their pizza, their burnt tongues wary, and stared into the fire in companionable silence. Gillian thought she heard a knock at the door, but when she listened for a bit, there wasn't any other noise until she recognized the rumbling of a distance train, quieter this evening, but this time with a whistle. Frankie poured herself some root beer and sighed.

"Will you think I'm a bad person if I tell you I haven't told Bobby about the new place and kinda don't want to?" Frankie asked. "That part of me wants to just pack and move all my stuff here and not give her my forwarding address?"

Sounds perfect, Gillian thought but bit her tongue. "Don't see her for a while."

"How can I avoid it when she shows up at my house?" Frankie stared down at her plate and picked an olive off the cheese to pop it in her mouth. "Crouch down and not answer the door?"

Gillian finished a slice so that her mouth would be too busy to say what she really wanted to say, and then swallowed and shrugged. "If you have to. Consider it a break for your sanity."

"At least no one has called or messaged in a while," Frankie said. "I think. Honestly, I've stopped checking. I called Henry to check on the boys yesterday, and he said they're doing great. I just left my phone in my purse. I think." She frowned, and Gillian thought she'd get up and go searching for it, but she apparently thought better of it and leaned back, nestling into the round cushion of the Papasan chair. "Anyways, it's been a relief to have the silence."

"Good," Gillian said, genuinely pleased. "Leave it until morning. We'll get a solid night's rest, and tomorrow, we'll treat ourselves to a cone before the Humboldt Dairy Bar closes up for the season. I heard a rumor they're already out of Moose Tracks and aren't making more until April."

"Dis-*ahhh*-stah," Frankie expressed in her finest faux-posh accent, puckering her lips, and when she sipped her root beer from the red plastic cup, she flicked up her pinky finger. "I say, whatevah will one *dooooooo* all wintah in these deplorable conditions?"

"Stay in and pet the dog?" Gillian suggested, doing just that.

"Is that a coy euphemism for masturbation?"

"No," Gillian murmured. "If it were, I'd have said 'pet the cat.'"

"We don't have a cat," Frankie pointed out.

"Then we'd better fucking get one," popped out of Gill's mouth before she could stop it and Frankie's mouth made that surprised O again before she collapsed into giggles.

"You don't need to pet the cat, missy," Frankie said when she'd collected herself. Her lips curled into a sly grin. "You've got your admirer."

Gillian propped an extra pillow against the stone hearth so she could lean back against it comfortably. She rolled her eyes grandly. "I have a *what?*"

"Uh huh," Frankie tossed her hair over her shoulder then whispered, "The married man. *Tsk tsk*, you naughty girl."

Gillian laughed. "Sounds scandalous."

"Do you deny it?"

"I'm forced to deny it," Gillian said helplessly, "because I have no idea what the hell you're talking about, kid."

"Paul!" Frankie said, sitting up straight and flailing her hands with exasperation. "Good gawd, Gillian, how dense are you?"

Gillian's jaw fell open and then she laughed so hard that she nearly knocked her root beer over and dropped her pizza plate. "Francine! I'm not sleeping with Paul Langerbeins."

"Bull," Frankie said crisply, "shit."

That started Gillian off again; she hadn't laughed this much without alcohol being involved in a very long time. Tickled by her sister's matter-of-fact expression and her eyes glowing with a mixture of lewd amusement and suspicion, she laughed until she had to dab her eyes with her napkin. "For crying in the sink, Frankie, why would you think I'm sleeping with Mr. Langerbeins?"

"Oh, is that what you're calling him?" Frankie teased, eyes twinkling. "Is that what he likes you to call him in bed?" She lifted her voice to falsetto. "'Oh, *MISTER* Langerbeins, how you do make me swoon!'"

"Oh, you totally nailed it; that is exactly how I talk in the sack. Swoons galore."

"That should be the title of your autobiography. Swoons Galore:

The Gillian Hearth Story."

"You are a ridiculous woman," Gillian told her sister with a swell of affection.

"So if you're not sleeping with Paul, how come he's always springing to your rescue, huh?" Frankie looked smug. "See? I can be a detective, too. Y'all aren't smarter than me. Running around just the two of you in your little detective's club."

"There's no running around," Gillian said, "and no detective club. He's not springing to my rescue. The man can barely walk, he's not springing anywhere."

"Do the bullet wounds in his hip make it hard for him to have sex?" Frankie chewed her bottom lip and looked thoughtfully at the ceiling. "Is that why he's not doing his wife?"

"You don't know he's not having sex with his wife."

Frankie smirked. "Yes, I do."

"And just how do you know that?" Gillian challenged.

"The hungry way he looks at you," Frankie said. "He either wants to fuck you or eat you like a turkey drumstick, caveman-style."

"Oh, lordy, now I'm wishing we had booze," Gillian said.

"If it's any comfort, he probably doesn't want to fuck you caveman-style. Probably, with his wound, he needs you to be on top. Am I right?" Frankie's eyes sparkled. "Does he like it when you're on top?"

"Stop it," Gillian insisted through a lopsided grin. "I'm not now, nor will I ever be, sleeping with Paul Langerbeins. He's a married man."

"Uh huh."

"That *does* matter, Frankie."

"Uh huh." She didn't sound convinced.

Gillian fired a second throw pillow at her sister's head, which startled the old dog into a rattling, claws-on-hardwood departure from the room. "Incorrigible."

"You just need to get some, lady," Frankie told her. "I'm just saying. Been a while. You could use a little."

Gillian listened to her sister go on a pretend rant about her lack of sex life, finishing her pizza and feeling, for the moment, as though all the worry of their past week, all the threats and the deception and the danger was just slipping away. Like nothing could pop this bubble.

Like for the night, they were truly safe.

Chapter Twenty-Seven

Saturday, November 1. 9:50 A.M.

Frankie licked her ice cream cone and looked at the wrought iron gate as they drove through it. "Why are we stopping here?"

Gillian parked beside the custodian's spot, turned off the Jeep, and glanced in the rear view mirror at the other car that pulled in further away. She didn't recognize it, but she had seen the driver once before, in the Sunnyside Up Diner last Tuesday, the plain clothes police officer checking her out. She was not at all concerned about his second appearance in her life. If anything, she felt safer; a cop's widow, she saw the law as being on her side, even when that wasn't black and white. Regardless of what he might be up to, sniffing around her tail, it was good to have him nearby. Travis Freeman would be sorry if he threatened them physically if he was witnessed by a cop. Gillian almost hoped he would. Almost. *If not for that stupid missing diary.* She fought her temper, cast an outwardly calm smile at her sister, and shrugged.

"We need a nice, quiet place to talk where we won't be disturbed," Gillian said, "but it's nothing disastrous. Enjoy your ice cream."

"Sorbet," Frankie corrected.

"Whatever," Gillian said with a smile, and rolled her eyes.

They got out, and Gillian zipped her coat against the fresh November chill, while Frankie adjusted a vintage cream knit shawl over her peasant blouse. She stepped over a few small puddles along the walk, and headed into the cemetery. The late autumn foliage drop was scattering red and gold leaves across their path. Frankie's tan, high heeled boots — vegan leather, she'd crowed, upon flashing them this morning — struck hard against the pavement. Gillian's black work boots were relatively silent except for the crunch where the damp gravel was beginning to frost over. Frankie's untamed blonde curls tossed in the wind and bounced against her shoulders, turning to gold silk where the sun caught a thin lock or two. Gillian buried her bare hands in her pockets and cast a quick glance over her shoulder. The cop wasn't following them, but he'd been joined by a familiar silver Audi, two other cars, and a big black truck. *Well, well,* Gillian thought. *Isn't this perfect.*

Frankie was oblivious, finishing her sorbet and munching the cone. "So this is Pleasant Pines. Isn't Great-Aunt Willa buried here?"

"No, that's over in Pleasant Fields," Gillian said.

Frankie admired the landscaping. "Everything's pleasant when you're dead, huh? At least it's peaceful. And pretty. Did you plant here?"

"Some, yes." Gillian pointed to a swath of graves on a little sun dappled rise. "This family up here, for one. Their relatives are in Ottawa; can't make it down to plant. The usual. We haven't done the winter clean-up yet."

"Those are beautiful, what are they?"

"They're just a fancy kind of begonia." The wind picked up and the sisters flinched against it, ducking their heads into the gust. "They wanted pinks, but I couldn't get them from my usual supplier, so I planted white."

Frankie murmured thoughtfully, content to wander. "Surprised you didn't go with red. That's closer to pink."

Gillian faked a mild smile and shrugged. "Let's take this path."

They ended up at the top of a rise overlooking a small fountain surrounded with willow trees. Near it, there was a bench with a plaque that read "Ellis." Gillian had bought it in memory of Greg. Behind the bench was a large area for plantings, and behind that was a drop-off into a gully full of tangled trees and bushes and vines that teemed with insect life and small scurrying creatures during the warmer months. There was still some shade from the taller trees, oaks and maples mostly, that hadn't yet lost all their leaves. An ATV with a flat bed was parked there; the driver had presumably wandered off to take a break. She recognized Aaron's jacket slung over one of the seats and a fabric tote he used to carry drinks and snacks at work, and wondered where the new guy was.

"Wanna sit?" Frankie asked, and the wind shook her earrings, adding a fine, silvery tinkle to the sounds of rustling leaves around them. She didn't wait for her sister's agreement, and swept some fallen twigs off the bench for them. Gillian remained standing before her for the moment, cautiously not looking at the gully behind her sister.

Frankie seemed less anxious today, and Gillian supposed that it was defeat that she was seeing on her sister's bright face, a resignation to whatever punishment was coming. With the diaries missing, especially the one she'd written in during the Mike Deacon fiasco, their secrets were vulnerable to someone who clearly wished them both harm. There wasn't much left to do but wait for the axe to fall, if it was going to.

Gillian was not so willing to roll over and accept her fate. "I have something to tell you about Bobby," she started carefully. "You're not going to like it. And you must keep it very quiet. If she ever finds out it was *me* who told…"

Frankie blinked rapidly but didn't move another muscle. She stared straight ahead, dread momentarily brushing the defeated serenity aside, and her large brown eyes, that Gillian thought were the most beautiful of her sister's many lovely features, gained the glossy sheen of tears. Frankie wrestled with words.

"Okay?" Frankie finally got out.

Gillian glanced behind her to make sure neither their new cop shadow, or Paul Langerbeins, or Travis Freeman was anywhere nearby to hear her. "Bobby has been poisoning Barb. Maybe her mother, too. With antifreeze."

Frankie deflated, shoulders slumping, the remainder of her sorbet falling from her hand to drop on the grass. "The coffee."

Gillian's stomach lurched to have it confirmed. "The other night when you thought you had food poisoning? Was Bobby with you that night?"

"Bobby came over late with coffee from the drive thru," Frankie confessed.

"Oh, shit," Gillian said, though "shit" did not go nearly far enough to describe her anger.

"And it was *way* too sweet. I didn't want it, but it was such an awkward night. I felt I should be careful not to piss her off." Frankie shook her head. "Why me? Why would she do this? Are you sure about this?"

"I think her motives with Barb are twofold. One, she's after Barb's money," Gillian said. "She had to share her mom's inheritance. Barb says she doesn't have anything left, but she has the house. That's got to be worth a fair chunk of change. Two, I think she's making Barb sick so she can gripe about being burdened, to gain attention and pity for herself. As for you... she seems to have a problem with feeling used and unappreciated, but at the same time she thrives on being needed. I wonder if you're being punished for not keeping in touch, for not being as close as she wants you to be. If you were to fall sick, she could swoop in and take care of you, and then you'd owe her. Need her. Appreciate her. Love her."

"Maybe you're wrong?" Frankie said faintly.

"Frankie, we always knew she wasn't quite right. The good news is, you're not dead," Gillian said wryly. "If she dosed you, it was obviously not lethal. And you seem fine. Do you feel fine?"

Frankie nodded mutely. "I do now."

"But that's the only good news. I phoned in an anonymous tip and begged the dispatcher to send someone over for a wellness check, have them get in there with some excuse to look. It's in the police's hands."

"Can't they just arrest her?"

"Honey, they can't even look in her cabinets without a warrant, you know this," Gillian said. "I told them as much as I knew. I hope it was enough."

Frankie stared at the dregs of her cone on the ground, kicked at it with the tip of one pretty new tan boot. "What if the cops go in, don't find anything, and leave Barb at Bobby's mercy?"

Gillian nodded. "Then I'll have to go back and tell Barb what I suspect. Which means I'll need *you* to get Bobby out of the house."

"Oh my *gawwwwd*," Frankie whispered, hugging herself and rocking back and forth on the bench. "Gillian, if she's killed her mother and is killing her sister and maybe tried it on me, I *caaaaaan't* spend time alone with her. How? How can I?"

"By playing stupid," Gillian said. "This is Barb's life we're talking about, here. Suck it up, Francine. We cannot be responsible for another death. I won't allow it."

Frankie opened her mouth to object to that then snapped her jaws shut. "You're right, of course you're right. Should we tell Paul?"

Gillian blinked with surprise. She hadn't even considered that. "We should tell Paul that we suspect it was Bobby who's been coming to your house to mess with you."

"Wait, what?" Frankie shook her head. "No, I know Travis was there. I saw his stupid, big, ugly truck cruising up the firelane. The firelanes are for local traffic only, they're not through roads. Most of them are dead ends. There's no reason for him to be there."

"Who left the rose?" Gillian asked. "Bobby or Travis?"

"Travis," Frankie said, knee-jerk. "I think. Bobby's too cheap. She buys carnations."

"Who broke in through your basement window and stole your diary?"

Frankie thought about it. "Either one of them could have fit through that window. It's larger, an emergency exit for fire safety. But Travis read my diary without permission before, and he was furious about things I said about him in there. It *feels* like something he'd do."

"And would either of them have been able to guess your pass

code for the new security system?"

Frankie squirmed. "I used my birthday."

Gillian's lips tightened unhappily but she didn't scold; there was no point in that now. "You've since changed it, right?"

"Yes," Frankie said, nodding rapidly.

"And not to some other obvious anniversary?"

"Random number, wrote it down, it's hidden in a zipper pocket in my wallet."

Gillian sighed. "Throw that out as soon as you've memorized it, please." Then she thought about what Paul had said about stalkers stealing your garbage and going through it. "Better yet, flush it."

Frankie agreed. "Is Travis still calling you?"

Gillian nodded, and glanced toward the parking lot. She hoped very much that he would be stupid enough to vandalize her car again, this time in front of the cop and Paul. It would be worth the repair bill just to see him punished. "He tries. I don't listen to voice mail from blocked numbers. I don't read his texts, I just *select-all-delete-all* and turn my phone off at night."

Frankie nodded. "I haven't even glanced at my phone. If Henry and the boys have an emergency, they'll try both of us. I can't bear to look at the phone right now. I haven't touched it."

Gillian knew as much; Frankie's phone was still in *her* purse, not Frankie's. She pulled her scarf up to cover the hollow of her throat against a frigid finger of wind and zipped her coat up even tighter. She looked down at Frankie's slim legs in pale woolen leggings, the peasant blouse and shawl, no gloves, no hat. "You must be freezing."

"Do I need to go to the doctor?" Frankie wondered aloud, staring into the distance.

"Might be a good idea to get blood tests," Gillian suggested, "to make sure everything is okay? I can take you."

Frankie stood. "Maybe we should do that now, just in case."

Considering Gillian knew little about antifreeze poisoning, she thought this was a good idea. She hooked her arm around Frankie's and they started back to the car, mostly silent.

Gillian cast a last glance over her shoulder at the gully behind the bench, where impassable vines and brush choked the whole deep ditch and trees grew so closely together that they sometimes became intertwined. It looked untouched, but of course it was; who would bother with such an overgrown, steep drop-off? The saw that rested there was very likely safe.

"We need to get that diary back," Frankie whispered, and her words were mostly snatched away by wind. "Before someone uses it."

Gillian nodded. And she knew just where she *wouldn't* dispose of it.

***

Paul Langerbeins watched as Travis Freemans' truck pulled away. He noted the officer in his personal vehicle was taking notes. He did not make eye contact with Paul, but Paul didn't doubt he'd been spotted. He watched his clients get back in Gillian's Jeep. Something new was wrong. He could tell by the way Frankie's usual vivacious nature had been nearly extinguished. She was walking like she was exhausted, wilting. Gillian was supporting her right up until she set her inside the passenger seat of the Jeep.

He didn't follow them when they drove away. He made some notes of his own. Then he turned on the scanner that tracked the GPS device he'd hidden in the undercarriage of Travis Freeman's truck on Wednesday night, watched on the display as the truck did a few circles in a nearby suburb and head in the direction of Frankie's house. So far, the truck had not once gone to the Hearth sisters' new home at Higgins Point. Paul was convinced that Travis wasn't aware of the purchase or the address of the new house. That was good. He also didn't think Bobby McIntyre had been invited to the new place, though he'd seen her at Frankie's home twice.

He slapped his notebook shut and headed off to get some greasy fast food, needing to fortify with calories and carbonation. Something ugly was brewing with the Hearth sisters, and Paul didn't like the way it felt. He was missing a puzzle piece. The big picture was unclear. He felt like he was watching a train rushing down the tracks to hit something, and if he could warn them, if he could flag them down…

Paul didn't realize it yet, but the Ugly being brewed was only a day away.

He wouldn't be able to warn them in time.

Chapter Twenty-Eight

Sunday, November 2. 12:20 A.M.

Gillian set the mug of herbal tea beside the bed and listened. She thought she'd heard a knock at the door. If she'd considered Paul's suggestion to get a dog, she'd know for sure. She checked the time: after midnight.

There was another knock, and this one was certain. She checked the time again, exhausted and disoriented, wishing she'd decided to stay at the new house again. Maybe it was Paul or Frankie at the door. She grabbed her robe and slipped it over her tank top and boxers, cinching the belt tightly. Maybe it was Colin, far too early for their meeting. He shouldn't be at her house so late at night, but he'd never been one for rules.

She didn't put on the overhead light because she didn't want to immediately announce her presence. She peered through the curtain at the unfamiliar shadow standing there; big, male, shifting uncomfortably on the porch. Too big to be Travis Freeman. Who and why? Her pulse started drumming hard, but she told herself to settle down; not everything was a goddamn disaster. Maybe a neighbor needed help. *At twelve-thirty? Sure. We don't choose when trouble strikes.*

She turned on the overhead light, and it illuminated a stranger's face; she noted details as she'd been taught. Then she slid the security chain on, and eased the door open.

"Something wrong, sir?"

He glanced back at the firelane and then made hurry-up motions with his hands. "We doin' this or what?"

"What is it we're doing?" Gillian asked.

"Your ad said—"

"My ad? What ad? I'll stop you there," she said, curious but no longer afraid. "Sir, I don't know what you read, and I'm sorry if it gave you the wrong impression, but I don't have an ad. Anywhere. Where did you see it?"

He showed her his phone. The ad had her photo, her goddamn wedding photo with Greg cropped out, and her current address and cell phone number. It read: *I'm all alone now. Come anytime. I like to be "convinced." Hard. I get so wet when a man just takes what he wants.*

She blinked rapidly and the fear returned; the man standing in front of her had showed up to "convince her hard," but luck had been on her side, and this was no fool. He had believed her initial confusion, hadn't bought it as part of some role playing act, and he wasn't about to go to prison for pussy. Genuine force wasn't his thing. Role playing was. If this had been another type of man, Gillian could be having a very bad night.

She met his eyes to judge his reaction, to make sure she was still reading the situation right, while half her mind searched the area around her for possible weapons she might use if she saw him make a move.

"Not your ad?" he said quietly. No anger. Mild disappointment. By the look of him, he probably had plenty of ladies crawling into his lap, just perhaps not in the way he'd prefer. Judging by his reaction to the ad, showing up at a strange woman's home at twelve-thirty to "take what he wants," maybe easy wasn't what he craved.

"Someone else placed this," she told him, "trying to get me hurt."

"Not your idea of fun," he confirmed, and he was already moving off the porch, a subtle shift in body weight, but enough to make Gillian's shoulders ease down a bit. He said, "Better lock up when I go."

"I'm sorry someone did this," she said, genuinely horrified not just for herself but for this man who came for aggressive role play with a stranger and could have ended up in prison for rape.

"Yeah, you should probably report that. I'm not the worst who'll show," he advised, which she found surprising enough to shock a laugh from her.

The tension of the night spilled out of her belly and she slapped a hand over her mouth to stop the nervous giggles. Tears prickled her vision.

He paused, clearly debating offering some form of comfort, but that was ridiculous in the space between them, and in the end, he turned, boots crunching down the driveway.

What do you say to a dude who likes to role-play rape but not actually cross that line? Thank you for not being a full-on asshole? Thank you for hearing the word "no" when it's truly meant? Thank you for recognizing I wasn't playing? Maybe he had well-honed instincts for that. But Gillian found herself speechless as he went back to his car. He'd parked in her driveway. Yep, he'd been confident that this scenario was wanted by the lady placing the ad, not a crime, no need to hide his identity. *But what about the next guy who reads this and shows up to "convince you hard"?* She locked the door, leaving the light on, and stood there with her hands covering her face, shaking. When she finally threw herself into action, it was to call Frankie's landline and make sure she was okay, but her thumb stalled on the phone.

Wake your sister to scare the shit out of her? Again? She dialed Paul instead. He answered on the second ring, sounding wide awake. "Gillian."

"A man. A m—" She lost her voice to a squeak, which turned into a sob that she tried to choke back. "There's an ad. Paul, he's taken out an ad."

"Call the police if it's an emergency," he reminded. "I'm getting dressed. I'll be right over."

Not feeling like the police were immediately needed, and embarrassed enough to not want them here, she paced until Paul arrived, afraid to sit down, troubled by her own temper. *This was Travis's doing.* The darkness, hot, familiar, and frightening, spilled into her veins. *Dad's rage, not mine,* she told herself, an old mantra that had helped her cool down in the past. *Helped? Not enough.* She chewed her thumbnail viciously, tearing at the nail with her teeth. *In the end, you're just like him, aren't you? And is that really so bad?*

"Dangerous line of thinking, Gillian," she whispered in the quiet house. "We won't go there again."

When headlights lit the front of the house, she made sure it was Paul's Audi before she unlocked the door. She'd had no plans to hug the man, but when he approached, his arms opened, and she fell gratefully into them, not caring if Travis Freeman was out there somewhere watching the fallout of his prank. After a moment, the embrace was comforting enough to make Gillian self-conscious, bringing her back to the ground hard enough to remind her that she was in her robe, and this was a married man, and not *her* married man. Trembling, she let go of him and stepped back to let him into the house.

She let out a shaky breath and wiped her face with one hand. "I guess this is a bad sign."

"It's not an improvement," Paul agreed grimly, his normally serious face gone stone hard and angular with displeasure. "Tell me what's happened."

She explained the encounter with the strange man on her porch, grateful that Paul did not feel the need to say "told you so" about not having a dog yet or getting a security system like Frankie's installed. Still, feeling defensive about the distress in his cool blue eyes, she capped her recounting with, "I'm not going to be in the house much longer. A few days, tops. I'll book a moving van."

"No," Paul said. "This situation has moved beyond you moving your own shit in a marked van that anyone can follow to your new place, Gillian. If he doesn't already know where you and Frankie will move, we need to keep it that way."

Gillian blinked rapidly, feeling stupid. "I don't understand. What do you suggest we do instead? It's not safe here for me, and it's sure as hell not safe at Frankie's. She's already had to ask Henry to keep the boys longer."

"That's smart," Paul said, moving past a pile of packed boxes to move into the small pocket kitchen. He pointed at the countertop, seeking permission to start the coffee maker, and she nodded. He got down the few mugs she'd left out of boxes. "For you, too?"

She was going to say no, but after a moment of checking in with her body and finding a warning dullness behind her right eyebrow, she nodded in resignation.

Paul put a fresh coffee filter in the basket, filled the water reservoir, and looked around for coffee grounds. She stepped past him to get them from the freezer. "New bag," she explained. "Sugar is in the cupboard above your left shoulder."

He got everything ready, and Gillian flashed back on the disgusting coffee maker in the McIntyre house. "Paul, I need to tell you some things. You deserve that. I haven't been completely honest with you."

Paul didn't turn around. "I know. You will when you're ready, if you choose to. Gillian, you're not obligated to tell me the whole truth and nothing but the truth. I'm not a jury of your peers. I work for you."

He added four heaping spoons of sugar to his mug and then glanced at her. "One, please."

"That being said," he continued, adding a bit of sugar to her cup, "I can probably work a lot more efficiently for you if I have all the information I need. You can trust me. You pay me to have your back. Gillian, I've got your back."

"You have to understand. They're not just my secrets." She pulled out a chair from her tiny dining table and sat. She caught herself cupping the right side of her neck, and dropped her hand guiltily. "And none of this is the way I'd have done it, if I'd had the choice."

"How serious is it?" he asked. A spoon clinked in the mug while the heady fragrance of brewed coffee began to fill the small room. He did not look back at her.

Gillian recognized this tactic. It was easier to confess if you didn't have to look into someone's eyes; Greg had used this method when trying to extract sensitive information. Even seeing the method, Gillian admitted she felt safer saying it to his back. "I anonymously reported Bobby McIntyre to the police for poisoning her sister with antifreeze. I suspect she's done the same to Frankie on a smaller scale. Just a tiny bit, to make her sick. The hospital has taken samples of blood tests and urine for a toxicology screen, but they weren't able to do it on site, and had to send it out to a different lab for results. The immediate antidote was medical-grade ethanol. They *were* able to report that her electrolytes were balanced and that's a good sign. Likely, the tests will come back okay, which means it was a tiny dose, not large enough to do lasting damage to her kidneys. This time."

Paul turned now, handed her coffee with the milk, and then leaned his hip on the counter, taking the pressure off his bad leg. He measured his next question. "Why would Bobby do this to her supposed best friend?"

"Whenever Frankie has pulled away from her in the past, Bobby has melted down. I was there once when Frankie had told Bobby their friendship wasn't working anymore," Gillian said. "Bobby showed up sobbing and wailing, throwing things, snot running down her face, crawling on the porch, clinging to Frankie's skirt, shaking and begging. It was such a scene that the neighbors came out to see what was happening. I was surprised no one called the police."

"And this was *just* a friendship?" Paul asked.

Gillian hesitated and see-sawed one hand. "In Frankie's eyes, yes. They met in art class, did a few projects as partners. Bobby gets... attached. Neurotically so. Frankie was so mortified by Bobby's extreme reaction that day, she back-pedaled and convinced Bobby that she hadn't meant to break up their relationship, that she was just having a bad day and that everything was going to be fine. I was alarmed. I'd never seen anything like it. It was..." She wrapped both hands now around her hot cup, and sipped her coffee tentatively. "Like a tsunami of emotion. Bobby came completely undone. According to Frankie, they hadn't even been all that close. Bobby has always taken the friendship much more seriously than Frankie did. Bobby clung to Frankie like her life depended on it. That made it more alarming, in my opinion."

"Forgive me," Paul said, "but your sister does collect some rather strange people around her. And I in no way mean this is her doing. What I mean is, strange people are drawn to her."

"Everyone is drawn to my sister. My father always said she was the pretty one and I was the smart one. You know, when he first said it, it had stung. That wound was deep." Gillian stared into her coffee. "What thirteen-year-old girl wants to hear she's the *plain* sister and always will be? Dad said looks were a burden, though. That brains would get me farther in the long run. Not at first, no. The beautiful ones tend to float through youth where doors are opened to them, where jobs, drinks, and love are freely offered. That was never easy to watch, Mr. Langerbeins. It took me a long time to find a man who loved my brains. Had my share of disappointments, while Frankie seemed to flounce from love affair to love affair, juggling men without a care. I was envious. But I'm finally wondering if Dad was right. Frankie loves to be the flame that moths flutter around, I assure you," Gillian said, smiling a little, "but it does cause her a certain amount of grief."

Paul said nothing, just watched his client speculatively and sipped his coffee.

The seriousness of the night rushed back in to wipe her smile away. "I'm just glad that asshole isn't sending strange men to *Frankie's* house. She's softer than I am, you understand. I can't bear the thought of some pervert throwing his body in her back door, forcing himself on her. Or me, of course. I suppose it could be worse. It could be Travis himself. God, what if he *does* show up here? What do I do then?"

"Travis Freeman is a coward," Paul said. "That's what this advertisement means, Gillian. He'll convince other men to try it. But he's not going to hurt you. He's not going to do it himself."

He's not going to hurt you. This was amazing to her, and she clung to it. *He's a coward, face to face. He needs other men to do his dirty work.* And suddenly, she knew she had the upper hand. *Because you* can *hurt him. You won't need anyone else to do it.* And on the heels of this:

You've already gotten away with it once.

Paul looked like he was watching the gears click in her head and the furrow in his forehead deepened. "You let me handle this, Gillian."

"Of course," she lied coolly. "There will be other ads. This is just the first we've found."

"Lucky the guy who showed up was merely kinky and not a rapist."

"Probably a real rapist doesn't wait for permission via a sex ad," she reasoned.

"There's a lot of grey area, there. Don't count on that," he warned. "And don't for a second think the guy who showed up wasn't dangerous at all. He has a predilection you won't enjoy. Don't open the door for him again."

"I won't."

"Or anyone else you don't know."

"I won't."

"I'll put a man outside Frankie's place for a bit from second shift onward, just to see what crawls out of the woodwork." He paused. "Any idea why he'd send these creeps to your place and not hers?"

"Doesn't want Frankie ruined for him by some random rapist?"

Paul nodded. "Maybe."

"Wants me punished? He does think his break-up was my fault."

"Wants to scare you into backing off and letting him get back into Frankie's life."

"If Frankie knew he'd sent someone to rape *her*," she said, "she'd never take him back."

"But sending someone to rape her sister would be excusable?"

"In his brain, maybe. He's delusional. He thinks he can convince her I'm some horrible influence in her life; maybe he thinks he can convince her I made this ad myself. That this is some indication I'm secretly kinky?" Gillian gave a sad sort of titter and shook her head. "She wouldn't shun me if I had a kink. And Frankie knows I have no secrets from her. Sisters tell each other everything. Travis Freeman should know that about us by now."

Paul finished his coffee and put the mug in the sink. "You gonna be okay here tonight?"

"I don't think I'm," she admitted. "I want to go to a hotel."

"Grab an overnight bag and I'll drive behind you to make sure you're not followed there," he said. "You'll use my credit card and register under my surname."

"What for?" Gillian asked. "You don't think he can check things like that, do you?"

"I have no idea what he's capable of, and I'd rather not have him pull a fast one on some overtired front desk clerk," Paul replied. "Bag, bedtime stuff, maybe a few things in case you decide to stay another night."

"How can I ever repay you for all this?" she asked tiredly.

"It'll be on my invoice," Paul said quietly, and she went to pack a bag.

Chapter Twenty-Nine

Sunday, November 2. 6:00 A.M.

It was only upon waking in a strange bed — floundering for her glasses in the dim room with a beam of sun slashing through the poorly designed curtains that did not keep out nearly enough light — that Gillian considered the possibility that Bobby had set up the advertisement. Maybe it wasn't that Travis Freeman wouldn't rape her, it was that Bobby McIntyre physically *couldn't*, and needed a male surrogate for her crime.

And if Bobby did it, Gillian thought, *that meant she knew I called the police about Barb and the poison. Or suspected that I'd cause a bigger rift between her and Frankie. Either way...*

She wondered how to safely check on Barb without further fanning the flames. She didn't dare go over, not until she was sure Travis had sent the midnight mystery man. She rolled over in the hotel bed, burying herself under the too-many pillows piled all around her.

All she wanted was to run a cute little bed and breakfast at Higgins Point, a retreat for artists and writers, a quiet place near Derby Harbor where she could stare out at the vague shape of Toronto across the water through the fog on the horizon. On a clear day, you could see the CN Tower and the bright skyscrapers on the other side of the lake. She just wanted to share that peace with other artists. How had things gotten so complicated again?

She checked her messages. Text from a blocked number. *Did you enjoy your date, whore?*

Travis was her first thought, but again, suspicions about Bobby snuck into her mind. And the darkness pushed it out, the rage. She was under one of their thumbs, and she was not accustomed to being made to feel small and intimidated.

There was also a message from Paul. *Frankie thinks you may have picked up her phone by accident?*

She texted back, *Let me check my purse*, though she knew the answer. Not an accident. A few seconds later, she thumbed in, *Dammit, yes I did. Tell her not to worry. I'll come by the new place today and bring it.*

Paul replied, *When I got here last night, there were pages of a diary taped to the front door. I photographed it in case we need evidence of harassment then removed them before Frankie could see them.*

Gillian's heart nearly stopped in her chest. "He's got your back," she told herself aloud. "It's okay. You can trust him." Her heart didn't believe her, and panic clawed at the back of her throat. *Did he read it?* She called him, sitting bolt upright in the sheets, wrapping them around her tightly for comfort. When he answered curtly with just her name, she asked, "Did you put them somewhere safe?"

"Yes," he said. "I'm assuming they are something we want concealed?"

We. Gillian felt her breath rush out. "They're Frankie's. I meant to tell you last night, I really did. I was just so tired and frazzled… He—*someone* broke into Frankie's house Thursday night, early Friday morning, and stole several diaries."

Paul was quiet for a long beat. "That's something I should have known about immediately," he finally said, and Gillian didn't feel chided, but rather validated. It was as serious as her gut told her. She was not overreacting.

"Was she home when this happened?" Paul sounded winded. "Was there a confrontation?"

"She slept right through it," Gillian barely breathed, horror constricting her chest. "Whoever it was came into her bedroom and took them from a box under her bed."

"Goddammit," he swore. "I really wish you would both just tell me everything. You can't go home, she can't go home, her kids *must* stay with their father for now. We need to consider contacting the police."

"There's one who has been tailing me around," Gillian admitted slowly. "Tall guy, broad through the shoulders..."

"Constable Dean Jagger," Paul supplied. "He spoke with me about you. Wednesday."

"Now who's keeping secrets?" Gillian said tightly. "You might have mentioned."

"It wasn't anything to worry you about," Paul said. "He's just clearing an old cold case, you're not serious suspects. Had some questions, is all. I told him nothing he didn't already know. You and your sister had hired me, that it had nothing to do with his case, and that neither of you were capable of shady shit. Though frankly, the way you Hearth sisters keep secrets, maybe I spoke too quickly." She heard the frustration in his voice and grimaced as he continued, "Jesus, Gillian, he broke into her house while she was sleeping, and you didn't think it was important that I know?"

Gillian felt the beginning of a throb, the warning weight of a brewing headache in its infancy, behind her right eyebrow. She agreed with Paul, placating, submitting, saying whatever she needed to in order to end the conversation. He wasn't fooled, but he let her off the hook after suggesting that she not come directly to the new house; he would pick her up in a new car and talk about his plan for moving her things. She negotiated and they agreed that she'd be fine to drive to her home to box up the last few things, and he would meet her there. She promised to only go in the house if she was sure it was secure, that she was alone, that the house was empty, that *at least* her single neighbor to the west was home.

Gillian hung up and dragged her purse into her lap to find her pills. She shifted things — pocketbook, hairbrush, lipstick, notepad, contact solution, glasses case — and didn't find the bottles. There was no way she'd have left them at home.

On the kitchen counter. She groaned. She could picture them beside the coffee maker. It had been late last night when Paul told her to throw together a bag, and she'd forgotten to toss them in her purse. *Fuck, fuck, fuck*. There was no time to waste. She had twenty minutes before the migraine hit; in her experience, an unchecked migraine would blossom into a raging monster if she didn't stop it early. It was bad enough that she'd have to drive home in the bright sun.

"Why couldn't it be a cloudy day?" she moaned at the universe, as if it were out to get her personally. Crawling out of bed quickly in a shuffle of sheets, she pulled her nightgown off her head and crammed her legs into the yoga pants and t-shirt she'd shoved in a backpack. She ignored her usual morning routine, skipping the shower and the make-up, simply rubbing on some deodorant and brushing her teeth quickly, wrapping her hair into a high, loose bun, being careful not to tighten it too much and pull on her scalp. She did take the time to put in her contact lenses, so that she could wear her dark sunglasses on the drive. Ramming the rest of her things into her backpack and purse in a rush, she grabbed her room key, phone, and sunglasses and went to the door.

And stopped. Her hand shook in midair in front of the doorknob. *What if he's out there? Could he be?* She opened the door with the chain lock still on, moving her head to peer one way and then the other as best she could through the little crack in the door. When she was sure the hushed, carpeted hallway was empty, she unchained the hook and left the room, pulling her backpack on her shoulder.

She pressed the elevator button, and her mind teased, *This is where he'll be waiting. In the elevator.* She told her brain to shut up, but it warned her over and over like a broken record. *Or the stairwell. Neither is safe.* She tried to swallow but her mouth was too dry. By the time the bell dinged and the doors slid softly open, she was keyed up and ready to run or fight.

The elevator was empty and polished to a high shine. The mirrors reflected a worn-out, beaten-down woman with eyes too wide and dark circles underneath them. She got in, pressed the button for the lobby, and forced herself to calm down. This constant state of hyper-vigilance was not going to help her migraine. If anything, it would feed the pain. She knew she had slept funny on her injured neck; her own pillow was just right to support her head, but these had propped her at a funny angle. The nerve damage in her shoulder, neck, and spine were likely permanent, the doctors had warned; she should do whatever she could to live comfortably. That did not include sleeping on strange pillows or having tension ratchet her shoulders up to her ears for days on end.

Had it only been days? The elevator doors opened and released her into the lobby, empty except for two female desk clerks, one checking Facebook on her phone, the other smiling at her expectantly. Gillian checked out as Mrs. Jane Langerbeins, which was only slightly better than Jane Doe, but had been the most creative thing she could come up with at nearly two o'clock in the morning.

She slipped her sunglasses on and went out into the bright morning, wincing as her eyes adjusted. Praying for clouds on her drive home, she made it halfway there before the first sickening pulse of pain rolled up into her brain. Her day would be lost, she knew. She was about to be kneecapped by agony and she was too late to stave it off.

She kept her focus on checking that she wasn't followed, making sure she didn't pass the black truck on her way, and upon pulling onto Red Maple Drive, that she didn't see a single unfamiliar car. By the time she parked, backing the Jeep in as close as possible to the rear door of the house, her headache was a four-alarm emergency. Barely squinting through her left eye only, she flung herself out of the Jeep, stumbled to the back porch, her keys gripped tightly in her hand. A wave of nausea doubled her there and she vomited in the dried up hydrangea bush, panting and clutching the porch rail with one hand. She breathed through her teeth until she was sure she could walk without throwing up again, then lurched up the porch steps and stopped short.

A torn page of diary was tapped to her back door. Across the tidy, flowing script that was Frankie's cursive handwriting, "MURDERER" was written in black marker, all capitals, huge letters. Gillian grit her teeth, snarled, and grabbed the paper roughly, glaring at the words her sister had written. It was a retelling of a lovely day of apple picking with a friend from poetry class, some Aaron guy. It was a recent event that Gillian remembered. Weeks ago. And underneath, some musings on the friend's "hotness quotient" in Frankie's joking words. He'd rated a full six and a half out of ten. Not too shabby.

Gillian's mind piped up, *Don't you know an Aaron who's Frankie's age? From the cemetery crew? The new guy that Bruce thinks is a creep? He just had a birthday.*

What did any of that matter, Gillian wondered, but it sat in her belly and quaked. *Now I'm being paranoid, suspecting everyone of wrong-doings. And why would taking my sister apple picking be a wrong-doing? It's probably not the same guy, but so what if it is?* she thought, with another moan of pain as her head throbbed. It was too much. It was all too much. She'd reached her breaking point. She stuffed the diary page in her purse. Unlocking the back door, she hurried into the relative darkness and imagined safety of the house.

The house was blessedly quiet and empty but for heaps of boxes. She grabbed her pill bottles, desperately reheated some of last night's coffee in the microwave, then wove through the maze to her bedroom, bringing her purse with her.

She set the coffee and pills on her night table, pulled her phone out, and put her purse on the floor. Her phone was dinging with messages as she crawled into bed, her sore head sinking to her pillow. She cracked her left eyelid to peer down at the message display and her vision blurred warningly as the glow of the backlight hit her. Paul, wanting to know if she got home. She replied *yes, but headache.* He said he'd head over as soon as Frankie's girlfriend had picked her up for a day of shopping. Gillian wondered if that was wise, but then figured they'd be in a mall, surrounded by shoppers, staff, and security guards.

She popped the lid on the Tylenol jar and shook out a single pill, expecting OxyContin. Instead, the pill was a blue, white, and red-striped capsule stamped with TR and 500. *What the—* real Tylenol pills. She threw them on the floor and groped for her Aspirin bottle, whipping the lid off with a whimper, looking for her Vicodin. Looking inside, she saw to her horror dozens of round, white tablets marked "Aspirin."

She stared at them for a long minute, reaching one trembling hand up to pull her hair out of the bun and stroke her aching scalp. *Someone switched them* turned over to *someone's been in here* and then *they might still be here.*

Just then, there was a rap on the front door, a jaunty shave-and-a-haircut. She didn't think Paul would administer such a cheerful knock, but beyond that, her brain refused to function clearly enough to offer an alternative. *If it's Travis*, she thought through a wave of pain, *I'm just going to fucking stab him in the throat and be done with it.* To that end, she grabbed a pair of scissors on her way past her writing desk and held them in her fist. *I'm done. Let's do this*, she thought, and whipped open the door.

Colin blinked in surprise and a wry smile burst out across his face. "Auntie Gillian, you gonna cut me?"

"My head," she managed, and dropped the scissors.

Colin sprang into action, stepping in and closing the door behind him. He threw the backpack off his shoulder, smoothly lowering into a crouch, and fishing out one of the empty purses she'd given him.

"You left your purse at my house," he scolded, his voice sing-song.

"Please," she croaked. "You don't have to do that while we're inside alone."

"Right, sure," Colin said with a casual one-shouldered shrug. "Dr. Keller is in the *hizzouse!*"

"Please don't play with me right now," she pleaded.

"Okay, okay, okay, right, sorry," he said, and shook out her pills into the palm of his hand. "You're paid up for the meds, but you wanted to talk about security? I got a guy who's got some nice pieces. Feeling clear enough to discuss that now?"

"Just get me something," she said, dry-swallowing a double

dose. "I don't care about the cost."

"Sure, sure," he said, still squatting by his backpack. "Preferences...?"

"No." She rethought that, sitting on the edge of a wingback chair and closing her eyes, willing the pain to recede just enough so she could think in a straight line. "Is it possible to get, um, untraceable? Is that a real thing?"

Colin chuckled at her. "It's a real thing. Just to be clear, we're talking about a gun, yes?"

She nodded silently, waiting for the painkillers to start filling her with a pleasant, blurry brand of relief.

"May I ask... why?" he said. "Not that I need to know, I'm just a curious son of a bitch. I can't imagine why you, of all people, would need a gun."

"Home and personal protection," she said.

He made an affirmative *mmhmm* noise, and added, "But you can get that with non-lethal options. And you wouldn't need an untraceable option if you weren't planning on using it. C'mon, Gillian. Level with me, here."

"It's best you don't know," she said, opening just the left eyelid, raising her hand to massage the right eyebrow. Relief was coming; she could almost sense the lightening in her head. The nausea was returning, though, riding a wave of self-loathing and regret.

Colin stood with the easily physicality of youth and scrubbed his face with both hands like he was washing without water. "Look, if there's someone bothering you..." He let that hang.

It opened her eyes. "If there is..." She had no choice but to let that hang, too. Then she carefully finished, "I should let the police handle it."

"*Riiiiiight,*" Colin drawled. "Sure. They're real good at making someone stop harassing you. Have you ever reported that kind of shit? Do you know how hard it is to get a restraining order? And even then, it's just a piece of paper. Dangerous guys don't give two shits about paper."

"I can handle my own problems," she said, hearing the uncertainty in her own voice. Was she really considering what she thought she was considering?

"A few words of advice, then," Colin said. "When I deliver it. Weapons accountability. Keep your weapon on you, yes?"

She nodded mutely.

He continued, "Situational awareness. Three-sixty degrees at all times, even when your head is pounding."

"Yes, sir." Gillian couldn't help but smile weakly.

"Not kidding." Colin was blank-faced. "A little recon wouldn't hurt, either. An early heads-up to know what you're dealing with would be helpful. Don't go anywhere alone, either. Buddy system. If all else fails, you call me. I'm your buddy. Got it?" After she nodded obediently, Colin pulled the empty backpack onto one shoulder. "How soon do you need the piece?"

"As soon as humanly possible," she said.

He frowned. "Maybe you want me to stay for a while. I mean, are you okay alone here?"

That made Gillian's lips curl up wryly despite her pain. "Drug dealer to the rescue?"

"I'm a complex man with many fine layers, m'lady. A gentleman and an entrepreneur," he told her in an uppity accent that might have been an attempt at posh British. "No, but seriously..."

"Tonight?"

He nodded once. "It'll be about fifteen hundred."

"That's fine," Gillian said, and felt the calm of a final decision purl through her veins, pushing out doubt and fear. "I'll have it."

Colin opened the door, said, "See ya, Auntie Gillian." Then, "Oh! excuse me, pardon me, coming through!" to someone, after which he left the door open.

There were boot sounds, and her heart contracted. *He's here, he's here, oh God, it's him.* Gillian opened her mouth to scream at Colin to come back, but the man that took his place in the doorway did so with a badge and a professionally measured smile, and asked,

"Okay if I ask you a few questions, Mrs. Ellis?"

Gillian felt the badge cure her fear at approximately the same rate as the Vicodin cured her headache, and she sank deeper into her chair with relief. Much to her embarrassment, she began to tiredly weep.

The policeman waited at the door without comment.

Chapter Thirty

Sunday, November 2. 12:00 P.M.

Constable Dean Jagger sat in Gillian Hearth's small kitchen on Red Maple Drive at a dining table built for two, wedged between boxed kitchen supplies and a small half-wall. The kitchen was north facing with a broad window that faced the lake; a canvas-covered pergola blocked most of the sunlight. The kitchen was not merely dim; he could barely see, but Gillian moved with cat-like surety, and he saw she was in her element, a nocturnal creature, not hindered by the lack of light, though she *did* seem to be in pain. He watched her fuss about the stove without turning on that light, either. She turned on the kettle for tea, nimble in the dark, after which she excused herself to wash her face; when she returned, she looked more composed but much drowsier. She repeatedly stroked above her right eyebrow, sometimes pinching the bridge of her nose before returning to the brow. Her right eyelid drooped ever so slightly, twitched a bit under her ministrations.

Dean noted the boxes and asked, "Moving out?"

"What can I help you with, officer?" Gillian asked, and set out two cups with a sugar bowl and a little carton of milk. "Have you had complaints from the neighbors about my wild partying late into the night?"

"I sense sarcasm," he said amicably.

"Nothing gets by you, detective," she said, answering the kettle's whistle. She poured boiling water in a floral teapot, tossed in two teabags, and brought the pot to steep on the table between them. When she sat, she offered up nothing else to the silence.

He said, "That boy who called you 'Auntie' looks a bit old to be your sister's son."

"He's not really my nephew," she said. "He used to live on this street. Friends of the family. I'm that sort of auntie."

"Ah, that makes more sense," he said, opening a little notebook. "Nice photographs. They yours?"

Gillian didn't look behind her at the framed, enlarged pictures of the roses; she nodded and said, "One of my hobbies. I'm not terribly good at it but I enjoy it. You didn't come to judge my photography skills."

"I just have a few final questions about a missing person. Mike Deacon."

"I spoke to Officer... Sauffs, was it? Many times," she said wearily.

"Well, I'm wrapping it up," he assured her, "and it sure would help me to clarify one or two things that I've got you on record as saying."

"Sure, fine," she said. "It's been a few years. My memory might not be the freshest."

"I realize that, of course," he said. "This is just closure, you understand."

Gillian poured tea for both of them; her hands were steady. She sipped hers immediately but slowly, not nervously. Dean noted these things; she was exhausted but seemed in pain. At the same time, she didn't look like she wanted to rush him out. She seemed comfortable having him in her home. *Nothing to hide? Or just accustomed to being in the company of cops?* he wondered.

"When you got to Frankie Farmer's house on June twenty-first at three o'clock, do you recall seeing flowers in her kitchen?"

Gillian shook her head. "I don't remember going in her kitchen."

"Well, you said you visited and sat on her couch talking before going home?"

"Correct."

"Did you come in through the front door," he asked, reading *Gillian enters through side door* on his notepad, "or the side door?"

"Side door."

"So you would have passed through her kitchen to get to the living room."

Gillian frowned. "Of course, you're right. I don't recall seeing flowers, but I don't remember looking around the kitchen for details like that. If I was briefly in the kitchen, it was to breeze through it. I fail to see the significance…"

"Was Bobby McIntyre there that day?"

He saw a flinch, unmistakable, ripple through her, so quickly that if he hadn't been looking for a reaction, he may have missed it. It told him more than words could.

She said, "I'm sorry, I'm not sure about all of Frankie's visitors that day. Maybe. Not while I was there."

"You don't like Bobby McIntyre much, do you, Gillian?"

Gillian sighed. "Off the record? I don't trust Bobby McIntyre as far as I could throw her, and with my bad shoulder, that's zero feet."

"Oh right, you had a bad accident a while back," Dean said, frowning. "I'm sorry, is that what's giving you a headache today? Maybe I've come at a bad time. I can come back."

"No, it's fine. I've taken some Tylenol."

"I see," Dean said. "You let me know if you need to cut the conversation short, though, will you, please?"

Gillian put her teacup down and rested her chin in her palm, staring at him with no small amount of amusement showing, before she said, "Your *aw-shucks* Good Cop routine is very good, constable. You must realize I've seen it a million times. It's how Greg got me to say yes, after all."

Dean had enough grace to smile down at the table and nod. "I don't have much of a Bad Cop routine anymore," he told her. "I'm old. I'm tired. And I just want to get through this paperwork before it swallows me whole."

That made her chuckle, and the smile that accompanied it brightened her green eyes. It almost made his next question stick in his throat. "Your accident, it was a fall, wasn't it?"

"Mmmhmm," was all she said. The smile disappeared.

He made a show of checking his notes, though this wasn't written in the book, it was back in his files at the station. "Fell down your sister's stairs." He grimaced. "Ouch."

"It was no joyride," she acknowledged, and resumed sipping her tea.

"Did that on your way out?" he asked.

"Yes."

"Hit the landing wrong and just..." He made a whistling noise. "Sailed down those stairs and hit the concrete, huh? Says you dislocated your right shoulder, tore your rotator cuff, nerve damage, multiple bruises and contusions, minor skull fracture?"

"A lot of stairs," she said. "I hit a few on the way down."

"Your sister called an ambulance," he said.

"Of course. Wouldn't you?"

He sensed her stiffening towards defensive, so he nodded and backed off, sipping his tea and taking a moment to let her relax. When he saw her shoulders release, he said, "You and your sister seem to have a very close relationship. I envy that. My sister and I don't get along." He rolled his eyes. "Can't even be in the same room for Thanksgiving, Christmas. We visit my mother on separate days."

Gillian's flat gaze said she wasn't buying what he was trying to sell. She sipped in silence. He cut it.

"Gillian, do you know where Mike Deacon is?"

"As I told Detective Sauffs, I think one of his criminal friends probably did something to him," she said. "I don't hang out with criminals, so I have no idea who they are or what they might have done."

"Would you say you got along with your sister's new fiancé?"

"Not hardly," she admitted, much as she had to Ray Sauffs years ago, "but I kept the peace for Frankie."

"Why would your sister tell the detective that you and Mike got along well?"

"Frankie sees the world through rose colored glasses," Gillian answered easily, and he heard the truth. "Her world is butterflies and flowers blooming, and even when her sunny days turn to storms, those storms are beautiful. That's why..." She choked off whatever she'd been about to say, then continued, "Truly ugly things hit her hard. She never expects the worst. She just can't see them coming."

Like you do, Dean finished mentally. "How do ugly things hit you, Gillian?"

"Like a flight of stairs." She left that hang as the air chilled between them. "They very rarely surprise me," she said, and a knowing look told him that she knew damn well he was the same in that respect; a loud and clear *let's-get-real* tilted the side of her mouth.

"If I get a search warrant for your sister's house," he said, lowering his voice to *serious*, "am I going to find anything that implicates either of you in his disappearance?"

"Would you like to search *my* house, constable?"

"I think it's odd that you hurt yourself the same day this man disappeared," Dean told her honestly. "I think it looks bad."

"It didn't feel good, I assure you."

"Did you have company on your fall, Gillian?"

"If I did," she fired back, "then surely the ambulance guys would have taken us both to the hospital, doesn't that make sense?"

"If they saw a second body, yes," he agreed. "If that second body had been dragged off into another place..."

"You think my tiny sister dragged a two hundred pound man up all those stairs by herself and hid him?" She gave a derisive snort. "Apparently, you don't know my sister. She doesn't do physical labor. There's no way she would have thought of such a thing, never mind managed it."

"Maybe she had help."

"Yes, I got off the floor with my dislocated shoulder and torn muscles and skull fracture to help her hide a body," she said, dripping sarcasm. "Instead of just calling my husband, *a police officer*, to report an accident and get help."

"I have no doubt, that if you had been conscious, you'd have done it the right way," he said, feeling like he was definitely onto something. "But you weren't conscious. And she panicked. And he was dead. But you needed help. So she dragged him off somewhere, and hid his body, and then called you an ambulance. And then she tried to wake you so she could tell you not to say anything about Mike Deacon and the fall. There's a nurse on record saying you didn't speak to anyone the entire time you were in hospital. They were concerned that might be the effects of a head injury, but I think you were clenching your jaws around a secret, a secret you could tell me right now."

"Sorry, it's a stretch," she said. Her hand went up to that right eyebrow again to knead it. "There's no space for nefarious acts in your timeline. My sister's *first* instinct in a panic would be to call *me*. Since I was the one who was hurt, she called an ambulance. Frankie wouldn't leave me writhing in agony or bleeding on the floor to focus on him. Also, there's no place to drag a man's body. A tiny furnace room barely big enough for the furnace, hot water heater, and a big water softener. A storage room full of boxes. Your scenario just doesn't work."

"Where was your sister when you fell?" he asked.

"She had popped into the bathroom at the top of the stairs after saying goodbye."

"Mike Deacon hit you, is that it?"

Gillian let out a harsh *ha!* "If I killed every man who hit me, officer, there would be a pile of dead bodies in my wake."

Goosebumps prickled on his scalp and crawled over the back of Dean's skull. "He threw you down the stairs and then came down to finish you off," he tossed out. "You had no choice but to defend yourself."

"With what?" she asked. "One arm and no weapon, and I took out a big man like that? Can you actually picture that?"

"If it was an accident," he pushed, keeping his voice insistent but warm and friendly, "and you took Mike Deacon down those stairs with you, I may be able to help you. But you have to come clean. You've got to help me out here."

"There was no accident," she said.

About that, he thought she was being completely truthful, and it threw him off his stride for a moment. He recovered while she refilled his teacup from the pot, his gears turning. "If it was self-defense, if he attacked you, I can also help…"

"I don't need any help," she said.

Again, he felt she was being truthful, and his hope of solving the case started to rattle a bit like the teacup on his saucer when he tried to pick it up. "You're telling me that Mike Deacon was not in Frankie's house when you fell?"

"I don't know when Mike Deacon arrived at my sister's house, but I know I wasn't there when he came or left," she said.

More truth, Jagger thought miserably, though he did not miss the specific, exacting way she had phrased things.

"Whether he's gone, or not gone, or here, or somewhere else, I just don't give a shit anymore. Life goes on, constable. Mike Deacon is not my problem." She went to one of the boxes near the cupboards and took out a box of cookies, brought them back to the table. "Now, if you're finished accusing my baby sister of hiding corpses, I can offer you an oatmeal cookie, but beware: they're raisin, not chocolate chip. I bought the wrong ones."

She swung the open end of the pack at him and he selected one, careful not to drop too many crumbs on her table. "Raisins. That might be an indictable offense."

"You caught me. *Mea culpa*."

He answered her switch of a smile with a wary one of his own. "Can you think of anything else I might not have asked that could be helpful in finding Mike Deacon?"

She looked down at the table, tracing the pattern in the polished pine for a few moments. He thought she was thinking about saying something helpful, finally, and found himself holding his breath. She had just lifted her fern green eyes to meet his when the kitchen window exploded loudly and a brick slammed into the drywall next to her head.

Chapter Thirty-One

Sunday, November 2. 1:00 P.M.

Gillian Hearth had the worst self-defense instincts of any person under attack he'd ever seen. She didn't duck, she didn't flee, she didn't scream. Frozen in place with her unblinking eyes wide and her hand clutching her teacup like she could use the dainty porcelain as a weapon, she just sat there as the second brick whipped into the window, missing her head by centimeters. Jagger dove out of his chair and tackled her to the floor, no time to be gentle with her injured shoulder, wanting her out of the firing range.

Once she was under the table, he barked, "Stay down," and sprang to his feet to bolt out the front door.

He was in time to see a fleeing figure — baseball hat, jeans, old white running shoes, blue t-shirt, five-ten, one-sixty or less — cutting through a neighbor's yard on the diagonal to jump in a dark grey sedan with the engine running. Dean pelted down the street to see if he could catch sight of the license plate as the brick-thrower sped away, but he only got make and model. Digging out his phone, he called it in as he jogged back to the house to check on Gillian.

He found her with a broom in her hand, silently sweeping up

chunks of drywall, brick bits, broken glass, and a shattered teacup — she'd dropped hers when he grabbed her, Dean supposed, though he noticed then that his was also broken, having toppled from the table. He took the broom and told her softly, "Let's leave that for the moment so we can get some pictures for the report, okay?"

"Of course," she said, blinking at him with a stunned expression. "I should know better."

"Why?" he asked. "Do bricks come flying through your windows often enough that you know the routine?"

Gillian looked at him for a long beat and then started to laugh tiredly. "No, this is a first for me. Hopefully, it's the last."

"We need to teach you how to duck and cover," Jagger said seriously. "He could have caved your head in."

"He?" Those green eyes sharpened. "You saw him? It was definitely a guy?"

"Yes," he said, thinking the suspect was either male or a very boxy-shaped female. "Do you know who it might be?"

She did. He saw that in her face. She wasn't going to say his name. He saw that, too. To his own surprise, he heard himself asking, "It wasn't Mike Deacon, was it?"

"You just spent the last hour suggesting that my sister had something to do with concealing that guy's body," Gillian said, her gaze incredulous. "Is he back from the dead to chuck rocks at my head, constable? Make up your mind."

"Help me make up your mind, Gillian," he replied. "Who broke your window?"

"Just some asshole," she said.

"Which asshole?" Dean demanded. "Give me a name."

"An asshole by any other name--"

"Yes, you're very clever," Dean interrupted. "You're quick and witty, and you're avoiding my question. Drop the verbal sleight-of-hand and level with me. Let me help you."

The way she looked away from him, like she was trapped and desperate for escape, troubled him. He knew that look; she *wanted* to say more. This was a frightened woman, but a proud one, too, a tough nut to crack, as his mother would say; proud women only get tougher when the stress piles on, she'd tell him. The woman before him had a stubborn streak, even as she cradled her right arm. He might not have realized that he'd hurt her when he'd put her on the floor if he hadn't looked specifically for it. She was very good at keeping this pain off her face.

"After we get this reported, I'm going to run you into the ER so someone can have a look at your shoulder," he said. He fully expected her to refuse him, so when she nodded quietly, her eyes filling with tears for the second time since he'd got there today, he knew how badly she must be hurting.

"Do you want me to call someone for you?" he asked. "Someone to sit in the waiting room with you? Your sister?"

"No," she said. "Not Frankie. She's been through so much lately and she'll only freak out."

"I could sit with you," he offered.

"Constable Jagger, I doubt we're destined to be the best of friends, you and I," she said with a sad flicker of a smile.

"I dunno," he said, "I can hold up my end of a conversation without being crass or indecent. I'm a relatively inoffensive fellow."

"An inoffensive fellow who accuses me of murder," she added. He opened his mouth to point out he'd never gone that far, but she was talking over his attempt. "You could call Paul Langerbeins for me, if you'd be so kind? His card is in my wallet; it should be in my purse in the living room."

He turned to step into the room to grab the closest purse he saw, a slim black patent leather clutch. Inside, he didn't find a wallet, just a jar of Tylenol and a jar of Aspirin, and in a rush, he understood the young man he'd passed on his way in; if there really was Aspirin and acetaminophen in those jars, he'd eat his shorts. Gillian Hearth had a painkiller dependency. After a quick glance, he saw a bigger purse on a pile of boxes near the front door, hanging open to display its guts — wallet, eyeglass case, pencils, assorted make-up. He brought her wallet to her and she fished out Paul's card, though he had one of those in his own wallet.

A patrol car rolled up to the curb and Jagger flagged the

uniform, waved her in the front door while he dialed Langerbeins. Gillian was staring at the mess, still looking pale and tired. The officer took her details as Jagger recounted what happened to Langerbeins, and Paul said he'd meet them at the ER. He hung up, and after a minute's consideration, he made another call, this time to his brother-in-law, Ed.

"Yo, dickface," Ed answered. "Get that nose job yet?"

"Hey, thanks," Dean said. "Wish I could reply freely."

"Sucks to be you, copper."

Dean could picture Ed's smug grin. "Uh huh. Look, you got a couple of extra sheets of plywood lying around?"

"Stupid question," Ed grumbled. "When do I not?"

"Mind throwing a couple in the back of your truck and heading up the north end to seventeen Red Maple Drive? It's one of the firelanes past the old church, there."

"Can't get there until after four," Ed said, "but yeah, sure."

"Could I trouble you to screw them up over a broken window for me? No one will be here. Doesn't have to be fancy, just temporary until tomorrow so the homeowner can call someone in? She's on her way to the hospital."

"Fuck, sure." Ed hacked, a heavy smoker's cough. "Hope everything's okay. Let me know if you need more than two."

"Two should do it," Dean said. "Appreciate it, Ed. I owe you."

He hung up and noticed Gillian Hearth staring at him from around the uniformed officer's side, considering him intensely as though she was noticing something important. In the years to come, he would look back on that intense look and wonder what Gillian might have said if she'd felt safe enough in that moment to have spoken her mind.

Their drive to the hospital was done in silence.

Chapter Thirty-Two

Sunday, November 2. 3:55 P.M.

Paul returned from the Tim Hortons coffee stand near the hospital cafeteria with a green tea for Gillian just in time for the porter to roll her bed back from the X-Ray department into the curtained cubby. He stood aside, leaning heavily on his good leg, nodding at a passing nurse before turning into Gillian's room and easing into the chair next to her.

Someone groaned in the next cubby and retched, and Paul did his best to ignore it.

"Everything go okay?" he asked, handing her the tea.

"I think it's fine," Gillian said, blowing on the steam. "Frankie's going to be irritated that I didn't call her."

"She's got her hands full right now," Paul told her. "Her ex-husband brought the kids down to see the new house. They're both wearing big rubber boots they found in the sun porch off the garden, and when I left, they were playing a noisy, clomping version of hide and seek, tracking mud all over your floors."

That made Gillian smile and relax back into her pillows, minding her shoulder. She sipped tea and then put it down on the rolling tray table. "But filling the house with laughter. That's a fair trade-off, in my books."

Paul watched her pale eyelids flutter closed and remembered the days when his wife would say things like this, things that caught him off guard and made his heart happy; Julia hadn't spoken a word to him in eight months, lost in her own little world since their only child, Simon, had been killed in a car accident that had left Julia blaming him, though Paul hadn't even been in the car.

He agreed, "We could all use a little laughter these days. Your sister especially." *It would do you good, too,* he thought at Gillian as though she could hear him.

Her smile remained, and she did not open her eyes again until the curtain parted about an hour later. Paul thought she was sleeping, was flattered by her trust in him, glad that she felt comfortable enough to rest in his presence. She stirred easily when the young ER doctor came in to discuss the results of her ultrasound and X-Rays.

"Good news," he said simply, "I see no damage. Very likely just jolted the old injury. I can give you a prescription for a few days of pain medication…"

"No, that's fine," Gillian said, already swinging her feet out of bed. She reached for her clothing, flinched a bit, and tried it with the left hand instead. "As long as there isn't anything broken or torn, I'll manage on my own. Paul, would you be able to drive me home?"

"Of course," he said, turning his head to face the curtain as she removed her hospital gown. The doctor smiled at him, said something about a nurse and discharge papers before disappearing, and whisked off to deal with the next patient. For a minute, Paul stood with his eyes politely averted, until the sounds of cloth slipping over skin stopped. "Safe to turn around?"

"Uh, could you help me with this sleeve? I can't slide my arm up and in this way."

Carefully, he confirmed, "Eyes open or closed?"

She chuckled to acknowledge the discomfort. "I'm sorry. It doesn't matter, I'm mostly dressed. I just can't get this one arm to…"

He turned around and found she'd put the left arm in and her head through the neck hole of her black sweater, but the right shoulder did not want to cooperate and the sleeve dangled across her pale biceps like a panther's tail. He ignored a flash of a plain, beige bra strap under that arm to yank the sleeve down low enough for her hand to slip in, and then eased it along her arm. Her lips crumpled inward to be pinched by her teeth, but she did not complain; the ripple of agony across her forehead did that for her. When things were settled, she adjusted the sweater at her waist with her left hand and used her right to pick up the brown paper cup of tea.

"Invoice me for that, too, would ya?" she joked, her smile full of gratitude.

Paul promised to do so, and together, they walked out of the hospital and into the parking lot under a lowering sky on dismal grey November afternoon. The bright morning had been swallowed by a dark, heavy bank of clouds moving in from the southwest. The air had a fragile quality to it, as if you spoke too loud, it might shatter into frigid shards of ice. They got to his Audi and Gillian set her tea in the cup holder. He made sure the radio wasn't too loud, paid the parking fee at the kiosk, and headed out.

He wasn't thinking about Travis Freeman.

He wasn't thinking about Bobby McIntyre.

He wasn't thinking about that constable, Dean Jagger.

He wasn't thinking about anyone else in the world, if he was honest with himself.

He was trying hard *not* to think about Gillian's chestnut hair, the way it fell across the black cashmere of her sweater in a thick wave nearly as dark and rich as the fabric. He was trying to put the sight of her pale bra strap against soft skin out of his mind. Frustrated with his inability to do so, Paul did not notice that they were being watched all the way from the hospital doors, through the massive parking lot, to his car, and he did not notice that they were followed most of the way to the old house on Higgins Point.

***

Gillian was overjoyed to see that Henry's SUV was still parked in front of Mrs. Blymhill's house — *your house, now, you goofball*, she chided, still not able to believe that it was really hers — and that her nephews were running in circles on the front lawn which faced the lake. They were stuffed into puffy parkas and snow pants; though no snow had fallen yet, it felt imminent. Henry was standing in a too-thin khaki jacket with his shoulders hunched and arms crossed, rocking back on his heels, talking to Frankie; she was laughing at something he said, flailing her thin arms and gesturing wildly the way she did when she was keyed up about a new project or event. The wind snatched at the multiple layers of gauzy fabric that made up her blue striped skirt, pushing and pulling and stirring the hem. She wore a heavy, cream cowl-neck sweater pulled up around her chin but it wasn't enough to keep her warm, and she was hugging herself when she wasn't waving her arms to and fro. The wind coming off the lake blew her hair back from her face. The two turned to watch Paul's car pull in behind Henry's, and Frankie gathered her boys with a sharp whistle and an energized point.

"Uh oh, here come the hugs," Gillian said, beaming. "Better brace myself."

She got out of the car and was promptly besieged by little boys crashing into her legs and twittering excitedly about their news and their games and what happened at the horse races when a pony fell down. She couldn't hope to follow the conversation, not from knee level and still fairly high on the morphine they'd given her at the hospital. She looked back at Paul with a helpless laugh and said, "Help, help, munchkin overload!"

"Hey, you rotten, no-good pile of bones," Henry greeted Gillian fondly, strolling over, gravel crunching under his sneakers. They'd always maintained a playful sibling relationship, even while the divorce was contentious; Frankie and Henry's troubles were money-based and Gillian tried to stay out of it as much as possible.

"And hello to you, ya big rat fink," Gillian said, offering a one-armed hug, keeping her right arm crooked up protectively close to her side. "So glad you could come see the place and visit a bit.

Staying long?"

His eyes flicked to Frankie and he stuck a hand out in Paul's direction. "Hey, Henry Farmer, Frankie's awesome ex."

Paul shook his hand. "Paul Langerbeins, Frankie's awesome private investigator."

Henry shot a finger at him and wagged it. "Ah, see? This guy, I like this guy."

Frankie spoke up, "Gills, I was thinking… I mean, Henry offered me the guest room at his place. For a little while. Just to get a break from the craziness."

"Oh!" Gillian blinked, surprised; she wasn't sure at first how she felt about that, and then realized there was likely no better place for her. "Great. Yes. That's a fantastic idea. For how long?"

"Couple of weeks?" Frankie said, as though she was asking permission. "You sure you don't mind doing some clean up on your own?"

"I'll save you some," Gillian assured her with a chuckle. "I'll save you lots, I promise."

"And choosing the paint and all that?"

"We'll Skype about it. I'll link you ideas on Pinterest. Seriously, Frankie, go. It's only two weeks. This is the best thing for you and the kids right now." She smiled up at her ex-brother-in-law gratefully. "Thank you, this is very generous. Trust me, I know how annoying she is to live with."

"Yeah, I thought I'd ditched her for good, totally scot-free," Henry teased. "Now you're saddling me with her again, Gills, Jesus Christ."

"I'm going to get my bag," Frankie said, aiming an accusing eye at Gillian and then at Paul. "Don't let them bad-mouth me too much while I'm gone." Tossing her hair over her shoulder, she hurried back inside, skirt layers whipping in the wild wind.

Henry's smile dropped the minute she was inside and the kids had torn off to run in circles again. "Seriously, how's she doing with all this?"

"Her nerves are frayed," Gillian said. "And I'm not exaggerating when I say she's in danger. If you see any signs that someone's snooping around your place, grab the kids and Frankie and head up north to your mom's for a while."

"That bad, eh?" Henry said thoughtfully, looking to Paul for confirmation. When Paul nodded grimly, he exhaled hard. "Okay, good to know. Quebec is nice this time of year. I could go moose hunting, bring you some meat to serve your customers at the bed and breakfast. Got a big freezer?"

"I don't have a freezer yet," she said, "and I'm not serving my customers spaghetti and mooseballs, goof."

"Hey, mooseloaf would be good," Henry teased. "I'll keep an eye out for trouble. Who exactly am I looking for?"

Gillian and Paul exchanged looks, and Gillian wasn't quite sure what to say. A man, a woman, maybe any number of men, based on her midnight kinky caller. The conflicted look on her face must have told enough of the story because Henry swore again.

"Are *you* going to be all right here without her?" Henry asked. "Seriously, have you got a security system installed? This place is kind of quiet..."

Gillian's shoulders relaxed. "Leave me the dog for company."

"Who, Doogie? He's practically deaf, and his big offensive strike is to lick you to death," Henry said.

"I'll be fine," she insisted.

Henry looked at Paul speculatively. "Is she just talking tough, here? Is she going to be fine?"

Gillian used her left fist to give Henry a gentle punch in the belly. "Hey, you don't need his word for it. Besides, he's on my payroll. He'll say I'm fine if I tell him to say I'm fine."

Paul's eyebrows quirked a bit at this but he didn't argue. "I've got people. If need be, I can have someone shadow her sun-up to sun-down."

Frankie yelled from the front door, "I heard that! I vote bodyguard!"

"Yeah, I vote bodyguard, too," Henry said, stuffing his hands in his coat pockets for warmth. "Alarms! Guns! A cannon on the rooftop! Hey, boys? Two minute warning."

"A bodyguard ain't cheap. Neither am I, yet here I stand," Paul said.

Frankie joined them, swinging her overnight bag and her big turquoise purse over one shoulder. She was still not wearing a coat over her sweater, but Gillian bit her tongue about it. Frankie balled her fists and started chanting, "Body. Guard. Body Guard."

Henry joined her and Gillian laughed.

"I think we'll wait and see, all right?" Gillian said. "Kids? Come give Auntie Gillian smooches before you go!"

Matthew and Kirk ran squealing at the sight of Gillian crouching to receive love, and she grit her teeth and bore the pain in her shoulder so that she could grab and cuddle and kiss each rowdy child in turn. Matthew nearly toppled her off her feet but she used his sturdy body to hold herself upright. Kirk danced around chanting snippets from a cartoon theme song he loved, and wiggled to escape her last attempt at a smooch. She let him go with a chuckle. "All right, weirdos, be good for your mother," she told them.

"No, you're a weirdo!" Kirk said, grinning.

"You're a weirdo!" Matthew told Kirk as they pushed and shoved on their way into the SUV.

"No, you are!" Kirk said.

Frankie rolled her eyes and hugged her tight, smelling of citrus. "Thanks for that. I'm going to hear about who's *really* a weirdo all the way to Henry's."

"A serious issue for our times, but I can think of no finer minds to put the question to rest once and for all," Gillian said into her sister's hair. "Look on the bright side: they probably have no idea that *you're* the weirdo."

"Ha!" Frankie said, and her body jostled in Gillian's arms.

Gillian rested her temple against her sister's. "Be safe. Watch for both of them. Watch for anyone."

"You watch out here," Frankie said. "Mrs. Blymhill put a damn curse on this house. You know that, right? The weird drawing on the floor. The jars of rats and urine. It's a spell. This place is cursed."

"Please." Gillian rolled her eyes. "Don't get complacent. It's only a twenty minute drive."

Frankie dropped her voice. "Live a little, eh?" When she drew back, she dropped Gillian a wink and then her eyes widened slightly, knowingly.

Gillian knew she was hinting about lascivious dealings with Paul and shot her a *you-be-quiet* look. But she couldn't help answering, "Life's short."

The Hearth sisters' motto. Gillian only hoped it wouldn't be a self-fulfilling prophecy.

Paul said his good-bye, off to a meeting with another client. The Audi pulled out, then the SUV containing the four Farmers followed, and Gillian watched alone but for her trepidation as the sky darkened quickly toward evening. She puttered around on the front porch, straightening a couple of the wicker chairs that had been blown around. She picked up the metal snow shovel that had fallen. Gathering some extra wood for the fireplace, she found her right shoulder throbbed fiercely. She was glad she hadn't had to tell Frankie about her injury or the brick through her window, and that Paul had thought to keep it to himself.

Locking up, she called Bruce to ask if he wouldn't mind taking her to Red Maple Drive so she could get her Jeep, and if he could help her clean up after the broken window and wall damage from the brick event. He said he'd be there in a jiffy.

She took a minute to wander across the tidy lawn toward the lake, a line of boulders demarcating the difference between yard and shore. The grey, weathered remains of a dock moved rhythmically, mostly lost under the water, broken and slick with dying green and brown algae. She didn't get too close. The mist from the water was chilly on her cheeks and stung her lips, chapped because Frankie kept stealing her lip balms from her purse.

She allowed herself to think about Greg, and specifically about his ashes, cast from that boat cruise just as he'd wanted, and set adrift on the current that would no doubt take him here, to Higgins Point. She knew his remains had dissipated, that he wasn't actually here, but she felt him close, and she knew she'd done right in buying this place. It would be a lot of work, and the costs to modernize and restore would be huge, but in her belly, she felt close to Greg, even closer now than she felt in their bed at Red Maple Drive.

She was ready, at last, to say good-bye to the house in which she had been Mrs. Ellis, and make Mrs. Blymhill's place her permanent home.

Chapter Thirty-Three

Sunday, November 2. 4:30 P.M.

That afternoon, the first breath of winter dusted Derby Harbor with a light, slick layer of snow, filling the air outside the precinct windows with flurries. Dean Jagger had the best desk in the station, in his opinion, from which he could see Lake Ontario past the Queen Elizabeth Highway when he stood up to stretch or when he was returning, as he was now, from fetching coffee. He sat, leaning into his chair to give his back a stretch, then got back to his files, alternatively scanning the computer and the paperwork.

"Hey, Jag," a voice said behind him, and Dean didn't immediately look up, just nodded to acknowledge the speaker. Officer Thomas "Tombstone" Jones shuffled up to his shoulder, manila folder in hand. Despite his reputation as a loose cannon when he'd worked the beat – in addition to carrying a non-standard-issue hand cannon of his own, having gone meticulously through the paperwork to use his personal Ruger Super Redhawk revolver – Jones excelled when it came to spotting finicky details in writing that other people might miss. Tombstone's quirks hadn't endeared him with most of his colleagues, but Dean Jagger hadn't been one of those who shunned the man.

"Bobby McIntyre..." Tombstone said, and that got Dean's attention. His head came up. "Wasn't she one of the people you questioned in the Deacon case?"

Jagger made an affirmative noise and took the file Tombstone passed him. "When did this come in?"

"Thirty-first," Tombstone said. "Think there's anything to it?"

Jagger sat back in his chair to run it through his mind. *Poison*, he mused. *Antifreeze*. He drummed one thumb on his kneecap, deep in thought. *So how does it go? Bobby loves Frankie, Frankie gets engaged to Mike Deacon, therefore Bobby hates Deacon. Poisons Deacon to get Frankie for herself. But that isn't how it ended, because Frankie didn't turn to Bobby next, she went on to a different guy...* Dean shuffled through his papers to find the name of the man Frankie Farmer started dating three months after Mike Deacon's disappearance and couldn't immediately lay his hands on it.

"Dunno," Jagger admitted. "Who's looking into the allegation?"

"Uh, Broderick."

"Cheryl?" Jagger said, "Or that new guy?"

"Cheryl." Tombstone's tone spoke volumes; he approved.

Jagger nodded with equal approval. Cheryl Broderick had been on the job as long as Dean had; they'd been to school and the academy together. He couldn't think of a better person to work with, if their cases crossed paths.

He flipped through the paperwork and noted that Cheryl had taken a statement from Barb McIntyre, sister of Bobby McIntyre, from a hospital bed in St. Catharines, and that her blood work had come back with enough indication of antifreeze poisoning to put her on medication and treat her with hemodialysis.

Barb had given permission for police to search her home in Sugarloaf, where antifreeze had been found in various drinks in the tall fridge, and in a plastic bottle under the sink. Residue had been found on most of the dirty dishes around the sick room, where a very unwell Barb McIntyre had spent the last few months. Constable Broderick had ascertained that most of Barb's meals and beverages had been made by her younger sister, since Bobby moved into the residence.

Bobby McIntyre had not yet been located.

Dean Jagger slapped the file folder closed and picked up his phone.

Chapter Thirty-Four

Sunday, November 2. 5:10 P.M.

Gillian Hearth nodded at the news, though she knew Constable Jagger couldn't see her through the phone, and she said, "Thank you. I'll let you know if I see her. What a mess. Do you know if Barb is going to make a full recovery?"

She glanced behind her at Bruce, who checked the plywood on the shattered kitchen window before starting to pick large pieces of glass out of the sink and put them in a rubber bin so he could carry it to the construction dumpster outside the new place. Bruce was minding his own business, and she trusted he wouldn't listen-in on purpose, but even still, she left the kitchen and started to put space between them.

"I'm sorry," the cop told her. "I don't have any information on her condition at this time. There's a note in the file that the anonymous caller who alerted dispatch to the abuse indicated that Bobby McIntyre may be responsible for poisoning other people, including her mother Olivia. Do you know anything about that?"

"I wish I had information that could help you," Gillian said honestly, moving through the dark hallway, weaving through boxes. "If I think of anything, is it you I should call, or do you have a number for the officer in charge if the investigation?"

Dean rattled off a name and number; Gillian told him to hold on a second, and went into her bedroom to grab the closest piece of paper, a page out of the back of one of Greg's old Super Challenger crossword puzzle books, still resting on his night table as though he'd return to it any evening now. When she turned on the lamp to go into his night table drawer for a pen, she froze.

The drawer was open. Wide open. And it was completely empty.

"Hold on," she barely breathed into the phone. "Hold on... I just..." She stared at it, not surprised but feeling deeply violated. Her heart gave a funny palpitation and she remembered to breathe, sucking air deeply, feeling light-headed. In this drawer, she'd kept most her private things, including personal lubricant, sex toys she'd enjoyed, both with her husband and on her own, and in a plain brown envelope, a very old naked Polaroid photograph of her husband's nude body in a playful pose, and one of her that she'd taken at his request. Her mind began a deafening litany of *oh god, oh god, oh god, oh god* which drowned out any coherent thought or logic. Humiliation avalanched through her.

The constable was still talking in her ear, and now his inflection told her he'd asked a question that she hadn't heard. "I'm sorry, what?"

"Are you all right, Mrs. Ellis?"

Gillian didn't correct him to Hearth. "I, uh..." *You have to report this. He's going to keep getting away with this shit if you don't. He's got a green light to do anything if you don't show him you'll do something about it.* "I've had a break-in. Things are missing."

"Mrs. Ellis," he said, "this morning, your sister reported that a break-in occurred early Friday morning and a theft. Her diaries. Could this be related?"

"I think so," Gillian admitted. *Frankie reported the robbery? Paul must have given her a talking-to.* She felt out of the loop, like things were starting to unravel quickly. A woman who was used to being in control of her life, Gillian now felt as if she were drowning.

"Could it also be related to the possible poisoning of Barb McIntyre by her sister?" Dean asked her. "By that, I mean, do you believe that Bobby McIntyre could have stolen your things? Because Ms. Farmer believes Ms. McIntyre is harassing her."

"It's one possibility, yes," Gillian said, her cheeks flaming. *How are you going to report missing sex toys? They're going to want a description of the things. How are you going to look him in the eye and describe your dildos?* "Or, it may be the man who threw a brick through my window."

"Don't touch anything," the cop said. "I'm bringing someone from forensics."

Bruce shuffled in the threshold of the bedroom door and Gillian glanced at him, knowing her face was likely pale and horrified, but ready to give up hiding it. Her friend's face, already concerned about the brick through the window, went through a series of grimaces and twitches as he looked at hers. He didn't know what was wrong, but he could tell it was ugly.

Gillian answered the constable. "May I clean up the broken window?"

"How about you leave it until after we've taken another look?" Dean suggested. "We'll try to be there within the hour."

Gillian hung up, clutched her phone to her chest like a tiny shield, and stared at Bruce helplessly. "You're not going to believe this," she said. *If you can say it to Bruce, you can say it to cops. Better get used to talking about it.* "Someone stole my..." She choked on it, and tried again. "Private things."

Bruce's eyes cut left to her dresser against the far wall and he frowned. "Like what?"

Gillian turned to see a drawer open there, too, the top one where she kept her underwear and socks. She approached it with a dry mouth, suspecting what she would find but not wanting to confirm it. When she got close enough to see into the high drawer, her heart sank; there was a single pair of white socks left in the very middle of the drawer, unrolled from their tidy ball and placed in an X pattern. All of her other socks, and all of her bras and panties, were gone.

Gillian set her shoulders and exhaled angrily through her nostrils. "My underwear. My socks, almost all of them. My sex toys." Her voice vaulted up through the octaves and she yelled, *"My private things!"*

She felt Bruce's big hand on her shoulder, heavy but gentle. "Okay," he said soothingly, "it's going to be okay. We're going to sort this out. You're not alone, Gillian. You've got people who will stand behind you no matter what."

Gillian shook her head, clenching her fists. "He's going to use this shit to humiliate me."

"He can't," Bruce said. "Think about it. Are they engraved with your name? Who's to say they're even yours? He can show people anything he wants, but if you say they're not yours, then how can he prove they are? And who cares, anyway? I don't know a single woman in my life who doesn't have, you know, stuff." His big, round shoulders danced upward. "Seriously, you've got nothing to be embarrassed about."

"My lingerie…"

"So what? Gill, seriously, think about it. We all wear underwear. Wanna see mine?" He showed her a lopsided smile and put his hands on his belt. "It ain't pretty. Hell, it might not even be clean. But if it'll make you feel better."

Gillian squawked a half-sob-half-laugh and said, "Bruce!" to stay his hand.

He chuckled, and the sound of it reassured her. "Hey, look, you've got every right to be pissed off. It's a violation. No doubt. This is your bedroom, for fuck's sake. Your private things. No one has any right to do that. But don't let this pervert make you think that you have anything to be ashamed of."

The naked pictures, Gillian lamented. *My Greg. Oh, Jesus. I need that one back before it shows up on the goddamn internet.* She didn't even care about her own body being seen; she only cared about protecting the memory of her husband. "I'm not sure I can accept that right now."

"Okay," Bruce said easily. "Feel your feels, lady, totally. What can I do for you? What would help the most?"

Some of the tension drained from Gillian's tight shoulders and she gazed up at the big bear of a man, so grateful that she hadn't been alone when she discovered this. She had considered soldiering on alone this morning, calling a taxi instead of bothering a friend, cleaning up and lifting the garbage herself, relying on tenacity instead of logic. Thank goodness she'd swallowed her stubborn pride.

"Will you stay while the police are here?" she asked.

He nodded once, sharply. "Absolutely. What else?"

"Will you come with me to the new place afterward?"

"Of course," Bruce said. "I'll hang out as long as you need me to. What else?"

Gillian managed a weak smile. "Stay for dinner with me tonight so I can thank you properly with a good meal?"

He pretended to consider this seriously, studying the bedroom ceiling. "I dunno… are you home-cooking or ordering in?"

"I was planning a big pot of vegetarian chili for Frankie, but she's gone to stay with Henry," she said, waiting for him to crack some jokes, grateful for the distraction from his worries.

"Oh hey," he said, "chili sounds good. How about we stop by the grocery store and I'll buy salad fixings and some fresh bread to have with dinner?"

Gillian heard the front door and her phone vibrated in her hand simultaneously. It was too soon to be Constable Jagger, unless he'd been right around the corner, and she wasn't expecting anyone else. She felt a spike of fear which flipped immediately to anger. She marched to the kitchen, grabbed the boning shears from the knife block, and stormed to the door, ignoring Bruce's uncertain warnings behind her.

Not bothering to check who it was, she tore the front door open to a gust of snow flurries and a delivery man whose eyes cut down at the scissors in her fist. He said, "Uh, Mrs. Gillian Ellis?"

"What?" she clipped.

"Um, these are for you?" he said, wide eyes wary, not taking his eyes off her weapon. The long white box in his hand was offered cautiously.

"What is it?" she demanded, exhaling harshly from her nostrils like an agitated bull. "I'm not expecting anything."

"Flowers?" Again, it was said uncertainly; the drum-bellied blond man looked like he wanted to back away but was afraid to make any sudden moves.

Gillian felt her eyes narrow suspiciously. "From who?"

"I..." He shook his head rapidly. "I have no idea, I just bring them. There's probably a card?"

"Open it," she told him. "I'm not touching those until I know who they're from."

Bruce got closer behind her, literally backing her up. "How about I just take these?" he said, tapping the back of her hand and trying to peel the scissors from her fingers. "Thank you."

Gillian released them to him and took a deep calming breath. "I'm sorry," she told the delivery guy. "I've had a very bad week."

"Yeah, sure, you want I should open this, or...?"

"Please," she said. "Do that."

He raised a knee to balance the box and opened it and fished out the little envelope containing the card. Gillian got a glimpse of white and purple Freesia sprays and pink roses before he closed the box and held it under his arm. Opening the envelope with his thumbnail, he slid the card out, and his mouth did an unhappy twist.

"What. Does. It. Say?" Gillian said, her voice deadly low. Bruce's big hand landed on her left shoulder and he rubbed it soothingly.

The delivery guy swallowed hard and shook his head. "I don't get it." He turned the card to face her.

It said, *SOON*.

After a long silence, the delivery man cleared his throat. "Should I take them away?"

Gillian felt a cold smile settle on her lips. "No. They're mine. Thank you. I'll take the note, too, please. Have a lovely day."

The delivery guy shot Bruce a troubled look and nodded, backing away now with relief. "Have a better evening," he said, and hurried back to the white van.

Gillian shut the front door quietly. *SOON*, it said. She stared down at the little card, just a white piece of card stock with four little letters on it. *SOON*.

Her fear vanished under a riptide of fury. *Soon is right*, she thought. *Last straw, motherfucker. Soon is absolutely right.* "Bruce, there's a crystal vase in the bottom box in the stack near the kitchen door. Would you be a dear and dig it out for me? I don't think I could lift things…"

"Hey, are you okay?" Bruce asked. "Your face is the color of my Cream of Wheat."

"Oh?" She smiled tightly. "That's odd, because I *feel* wonderful. Look, someone sent me flowers. Aren't they pretty?"

"Uh huh." He wasn't buying it, but he didn't seem to know what else to say. "They're real nice."

"And I shouldn't let such beauty die."

"*Oooookay*. A vase, eh?" he said. "Yeah, I can find it."

He started in on the boxes and he'd just found it when there was another knock on the front door. Gillian wondered for a moment where Bruce had tucked her boning shears, put her flower box down, and answered the door with a murderous brand of calm that she hadn't felt in ages.

Chapter Thirty-Five

Sunday, November 2. 5:50 P.M.

Constable Jagger had brought a few people with him, which was fine by Gillian. She sat at the kitchen table staring at the pink roses and speckled Freesia, mesmerized by the howling maelstrom raging just beneath the skin of calm on the surface of her mind. *SOON*, the card in her pocket promised. The idea of that soothed her frayed nerves. *It's almost over.* A quiet, distant part of her warned, *We can stop this.* But the rage agreed. *Yes, we can and we will.*

Bruce had waited until forensics were done in and around the kitchen window; when he got the all-clear, he began piling long pieces of broken glass in the rubber bin, pulling demolished terra cotta flower pots and their resident herb plants from the sink, disposing of the dishes that had been in the sink, as well as the broken china cups on the floor and under the kitchen table.

Dean Jagger was scribbling in his note pad, taking down all her words, glancing curiously now and then at the cut glass vase of flowers in the center of the pine table.

"Those are pretty," he said.

Gillian felt a little smile twitch her lips. It felt smug. She heard herself say, "Funeral flowers so rarely include Freesia. It's a nice touch, don't you think?"

Bruce's shoulders went up, and he rolled his neck.

The policeman observed her for a long beat, his gaze calculating. She met his eyes with something approaching serenity, though she knew this was a trick her mind was playing on her. A dark shape had taken over, and she was happy to release responsibility to it; it would take care of things now. *SOON.* She sat ignoring her tea, daring the cop to read her mind if he could. There was nothing he could do to stop her. Not a damn thing. That smug twitch of a smile made an appearance again, and she reached her fingertips up to touch it, amazed at it.

Dean's pen moved across his notebook but his eyes didn't leave her face. "You said private things were missing?"

Gillian tapped a neatly trimmed fingernail on the saucer under her teacup. "All my underwear. I don't know how many pairs I had, to be honest. All my socks except for one pair. You'll see them in there, unrolled and crossed in an X shape in the drawer. From my husband's night table drawer, all my sex toys are missing; a black eight-inch dildo, a small pink vibrating egg, and a remote control butterfly-style clitoral stimulator that you wear inside your panties. He also stole a tube of regular lubricant and a strawberry flavored one. There was an envelope…" Here, her voice failed her, but she tried again. "Two nude Polaroid photos inside."

She watched as he noted this without any outward reaction on his face, like she was listing the groceries she needed. *Of course he's heard worse*, she told herself; still, she was glad he had chosen to look at his notes and not directly at her.

"No note left behind? Or any damage to the room?"

She took the note card from her pocket and flipped it across the table top at him. It slid and spun in circles on the high-polished pine, and he stopped it with a thick fingertip, spun it to read the single word on it.

"This came with the flowers?"

Gillian murmured and smiled coolly.

"You don't seem worried."

"I was," she admitted. "I'm not now."

Dean leaned back in his chair and sighed unhappily. "Mind if I ask why?"

"You know the answer to that," she said, motioning to the note. "He promised it would be over soon."

"Some women would be absolutely terrified by that implication."

"Do I look terrified, Constable Jagger?"

"No," he said, "and that's what worries me. Do you own a firearm, Mrs. Ellis?"

"I don't go by Mrs. Ellis anymore," Gillian told him. "Mrs. Ellis was the wife of a policeman. And a policeman's widow. I'm a Hearth girl. I'm my father's daughter."

He didn't seem to know how to take that. "The firearms?"

"No," she answered honestly. "I don't own a firearm and you will find no such weapon in this house or my other." *Because Colin hasn't brought it yet,* she thought.

"I would caution you not to deal with this person yourself," Dean told her.

Bruce coughed loudly, and Gillian knew it was a cheeky form of piping up in agreement.

"Of course you would caution that, officer," Gillian said.

"Who sent the flowers, Gillian?"

"Can you arrest a man for sending a lady flowers now?"

"If it was part of a pattern of harassment and he'd been warned to stop, and I could prove he sent them, yes, I could make him sorry. I could at least get you some protection."

"Like a restraining order?"

"Perhaps—"

"I might as well write 'fuck off' on the back of that card and mail it to him." She smirked. "It would do as much good, and you know it."

"As I'm sure Paul Langerbeins has advised you, if we build a solid series of reports against him and he continues to harass you, he *will* serve time."

And he would blab all my secrets to the world the minute he was in an interrogation room, Gillian knew. *If he isn't blabbing already.*

"And by 'serving time' you mean he'll stew in a jail cell and come out a few months later an angrier and more dangerous man," she said flatly. "Sounds great. Sign me the hell up, officer."

Dean tapped his pen on the table and scribbled something in his notes. "Why do you think this man is targeting you?"

"Because he's a fucking asshole?" Bruce ventured beneath his breath from the sink, tugging on his heavy leather work gloves so he could gather the smaller pieces of window glass there.

Gillian smiled sadly at the big grumbling bear and wondered if Bruce would be so quick to protect her if he knew all the things she'd done, all the ugly secrets she'd kept. She realized he probably would, no matter how ugly the secrets were. That made her even sadder, and her smile faded.

"What you're seeing here is the efforts of a small, empty man trying to feel big," she told the constable, reaching one pale hand out to tap the base of the crystal vase. "The only way to win is to ignore him. That, sir, puts him firmly back in his place."

"And where is his place, Gillian?"

That felt like a dangerous question but she couldn't resist. "Obscurity."

"So you're choosing to ignore him?"

Gillian gave what she hoped was a casual shrug. "He broke a window." *Fucked with my car at the grocery store. Left me threatening messages.* "He stole some socks and sent me flowers." *And sent a rape fantasist to my house late at night.* "The nude photos bother me, I won't lie about that. I was startled by the other things. I feel a bit violated, yes. But if I send cops to his place, he'll know he's winning, don't you see? He'll know he's scaring me, getting under my skin. And I cannot allow that. I won't."

"It's not about winning," Jagger told her quietly as the forensics team began to bring their equipment back out to the van in the driveway.

"That's where you're wrong, constable," she said, "and I always win."

***

With the police and forensics gone, and her bedroom tidied, Gillian collected her work clothes, some old jeans for doing outdoorsy work, and all her pairs of gardening gloves. She got some cleaning supplies from under the bathroom sink, and the bleach from the laundry room. Bruce carried the cartons of broken glass and swept-up garbage into the back of his truck for her, while Gillian collected her glasses, contact lens supplies, a roll of duct tape that hadn't been opened yet, and her medications. Bruce called her name and she shouted that she would only be a second and to go ahead and start the car.

She took the envelope from the flower note card that said *SOON* and used it to scribble her new address on and a quick note: *Colin, if you need me, I'm staying at my new place. Auntie Gillian.* She waited until Bruce was in the truck and putting on his seat belt, and, feeling like the spider expecting the fly, slipped it in her mailbox.

Then she loaded her overnight bag in the truck, went back for the flowers, locked up the Red Maple house, and joined Bruce in the truck's cab, where the heater was blasting and the seat warmer was cozy on her rump. She rested the cut glass vase between her thighs and ignored Bruce giving her serious side-eye about it.

Will I be seeing you tomorrow? Gillian texted to Nancy, the owner of Those Buns Dough.

Nancy texted back, *I can bring a dozen assorted loaves for around four? Rye, pumpernickel, white, twelve grain, etc?*

Gillian texted back, *Yes please, and a tub of the chocolate chunk cookie dough.*

"Can we drop by the department store real quick, first?" Gillian asked him, buckling up.

"Sure, what for?"

"Nancy from the bakery is bringing me samples, frozen dough that I can bake fresh in the mornings. Trouble is, Frankie got rid of her old chest freezer a few years back," she said, staring out the passenger side window, "and I haven't needed one at Red Maple, living on my own. But I'll need one now, won't I?"

"Better have that delivered," Bruce said. "There's no way you and I are carrying a big chest freezer down those stairs. That Paul fellow you hired can't help, what with his bad hip. You're *not* holding up half a freezer with that shoulder of yours, lady. Not happening."

"And I'm going to need the biggest one they have," she told him as the night rolled by outside the truck. *Man sized*. She'd get them to rush delivery. She wanted it tomorrow.

Bruce took the on-ramp to the Queen Elizabeth Highway heading for the city, and Gillian began to place furniture in her mind.

Chapter Thirty-Six

Sunday, November 2. 6:45 P.M.

Travis Freeman was at Red Maple Drive when he saw the most marvelous thing he could have ever hoped for. It was as if the universe was presenting him a gift on a silver fucking platter.

He'd driven past the whore's street twice, casting only a glance down the dead end road to check if the truck, car, and van full of people carrying cases were there. He figured they were law enforcement types, and that the whore's house was a temporary hot zone for him, but he couldn't resist a peek. He wasn't stupid enough to go down the firelane, though. He swung into the church parking lot two streets over and wandered the cemetery, pretending to pay his respects to a grave that had a perfect view of the street while keeping him relatively sheltered by the side of the church itself, at least from the direction of Red Maple. He'd been out in the cold, not feeling it in the least, for a good twenty minutes before the white van rolled to a stop at the intersection and sped away, followed by the black SUV. He returned to his car and waited for the blue truck he'd seen parked next to the whore's Jeep at Pleasant Pines Cemetery a few times. A coworker, a big one. Travis wasn't interested in him, either.

With one hand, he took the big, black dildo out of his backpack and whapped it on his knee rhythmically to the beat of the song on the radio. He lifted it to his nose, but it only smelled faintly of rubber and some sort of antiseptic, probably a sex toy cleaner. No matter. He'd smelled enough cunts to know the whore's fragrance.

When he saw the blue truck go by, and spotted Gillian Hearth in the passenger seat, staring out at the night, he felt a hot jolt of glorious hatred, and squeezed the spongy dildo hard enough to whiten his knuckles. Rolling his tight shoulders to loosen them up, he waited until the truck had turned and disappeared before turning on his car and driving quickly to Red Maple, where most of the trees had shed their red leaves. Their claw-like limbs seemed to grab a nearly full moon. Travis parked beneath one, two doors down from the whore's house. He was about to get out when a little crotch rocket style motorcycle zipped past him and pulled into the whore's driveway. The lean guy who rode the bike without a helmet engaged the kickstand and bounced off the Kawasaki, bounding up to the front door with the energy of youth, and knocked on the front door, glancing around at the lack of exterior or interior lights.

Travis waited. Watched. The biker opened the mailbox and fished around. *Would she be stupid enough to leave a house key?* Travis knew she wouldn't. Not after his break-in. Not after the humiliating slap he'd given her. *She'd be paranoid about security now.*

The twerp withdrew what looked like a little piece of paper. It was getting dark and harder to see. The biker must have thought so too, because he turned and tilted the paper under the moon glow to assist. Then he started back to the bike. Travis felt a momentary surge of anger; if he'd been a minute or two earlier, he'd know what that note was about. But then the universe's gift came, and it was better than he could have hoped.

A small shadow in a white t-shirt darted out from around the dark side of the house, a second young man, some blond twerp who looked all of twenty. *A couple of the whore's many suitors,* Travis was sure, but that thought had barely formed when the blond guy threw himself bodily on the biker, lunging and throwing fists.

Travis felt his mouth pop open and turn up into an amazed

smile. The biker dropped the note and swung back, but the blond guy's reactions were quick and merciless; Travis watched his elbow pump several times and then he stepped aside and the biker stumbled, clutching his midriff. Blood quickly seeped through his t-shirt, bright and stunning. The twerp held his knife down alongside his leg, carefully not dripping on his shoes or touching his jeans. Travis powered his window down a touch, but if any words had been exchanged, he'd missed them.

The biker on the ground spewed a jet of blood and shuddered. The blond twerp looked down the street both ways, but far too quickly to take in too many details, in Travis's opinion. Then the twerp delivered a finishing blow, sliding the knife into the biker's throat, a clean shot delivered with precision, like he knew his anatomy. Without withdrawing the knife, the guy leaned over and hooked the slightly larger man under the shoulders and began dragging him across the driveway and into the cover of the dark back yard.

Travis forgot he was holding a black dildo in his lap, forgot everything but what had just occurred in front of his eyes. He couldn't believe it. He just couldn't believe it. *A dead body in the whore's yard. A fresh dead body.* And only he and the twerp knew that she hadn't murdered this one.

Travis had yet to track Mike Deacon's remains. From what he'd read in Frankie's diaries, he knew that Frankie and Bobby McIntyre had put Deacon's body in Frankie's freezer until the EMS guys had taken Gillian away, and then left it there, not knowing what else to do, until Gillian was released from the hospital. After that, the details got fuzzy; Gillian Hearth was careful to keep her activities vague, so Frankie hadn't had much to report to the page. But there was no doubt that Gillian had taken control of things the minute she was physically able, despite the sudden loss of her husband and the funeral arrangements and the mourning. Gillian was a stone cold bitch; Travis Freeman knew one when he saw one.

And he knew something else, too. Felt it in his bones. Frankie had written in her diary that what Gillian did must have been self-defense. That Mike Deacon was dangerous, and that they'd struggled, and that he'd hurt Gillian a lot before she even hit the stairs or the cement floor.

But Travis Freeman had no doubt that Gillian Hearth was capable of excising anyone from her life if she felt they no longer served her purposes, and getting rid of her sister's men was not a problem for her. Not until now. Travis wasn't going to let her get away with it. He was sure that Gillian had shoved Mike Deacon down the stairs. Purposefully. One hard shove. Maybe she felt she had no choice, Travis allowed. But in that moment, faced with a chance to get rid of someone she wanted out of her life for good, Gillian had acted. She had stepped forward and made it happen.

If he could find Mike Deacon's body, police could probably link it to the Hearth sisters. He had failed so far. No matter. There was a dead body in her yard right now. All he had to do was call it in.

And yet, his hand stalled on his phone. Tapped the waterproof cover. Watched the twerp come back into the moonlight with a garden hose. It surprised him into a soft, incredulous laugh. *Kid, seriously? You're just going to wash the blood down and… what? Walk away?* Where was the body? Under a bush? Behind the garden shed?

It didn't occur to him until then to wonder just who these two young men were. The blond guy gave his boots and the bottom of his jeans a rinse, too. That water must have been damn cold, Travis figured, but he was trying. Stupid kid. He should have used his fists, not a damn knife. *Who are you, boy? Why are you so quick to strike like that?*

Having put the hose away, the twerp picked up the note, got on the biker's crotch rocket, double-checked what the note said, and took off. Travis was very tempted to go snooping around for the dead biker to see where he'd been dumped. It couldn't be far.

But that would be stupid. What if he got caught near it? What if he left evidence behind? No, that wouldn't do. He put Gillian's dildo away in his backpack, his plans having changed dramatically. He needed to be seen for a while in public, just in case.

He turned around with his lights off and drove out to the cross road, where he put on his lights and head for a pub called The

Nimble Fiddler in Sugarloaf, a ten minute drive from Higgins Point. There was no rush. The time had come to give the whore a late night visit. He knew exactly where the Hearth sisters lived now; he'd followed Gillian home from the hospital the other day.

He hadn't been the only one.

Chapter Thirty-Seven

Sunday, Nov 2. 7:05 P.M.

It was nearly a full hour that Paul Langerbeins had been sitting in the bakery across from the road from the Alibi Alley café in Derby Harbor. He should be in the café, but that wasn't safe. So he watched her through the plate glass window of Those Buns Dough, staring into the plate glass window of the other building as Bobby McIntyre sobbed into her coffee.

She'd pull herself together briefly, and then melt down again, using a napkin to cup under her leaky nose and hide her crumpling mouth. Earlier that day, he'd traced her using a partner (a guy called Beaner who did odd jobs) from Frankie's house to the new house at Higgins Point, and back to Frankie's. He wasn't entirely sure how she'd learned the Higgins Point address, though he suspected he hadn't been careful enough when bringing Gillian home from the hospital. No matter. It was almost over.

Bobby seemed frantic at the last visit to Frankie's, cupping her hands around her face to look in the windows, running the try the side door, then back to the front. Running, full speed, tripping over her feet in her frenzy. *She's lost her*, Paul thought, somewhat relieved. He put in a call to Constable Cheryl Broderick regarding Bobby's whereabouts, updating her when Bobby moved. He was waiting now to make sure she was picked up by cops.

Nancy, the owner of Those Buns Dough, offered him another free cookie; he declined, though it was the first time he'd ever turned down a cookie. He'd been smelling bakery scents for over fifty minutes, and that once-wonderful fragrance was starting to be too much for him. She smiled at him, and repeated her offers of goodies, whatever he wanted; when she'd found out he was there doing a little security job for Gillian of Hearth House, she'd been quick to offer any help he needed. Paul promised he'd take a loaf of bread home to his wife. Looking satisfied, she toddled off to count her till for the evening. It was almost closing time for her. He'd have to go back to his car soon.

He saw Bobby get up, take a pack of cigarettes out of her purse and go out to the empty patio, weaving among the wrought iron furniture until she got to a spot that pleased her before lighting up. Paul saw she'd left her purse on the table inside. Not many customers, but a strange thing to do. Her mind was elsewhere. He opened his phone, but paused, as she hadn't gone anywhere; he hoped Cheryl would come herself and not send a patrol car, or that Bobby would go back inside before the cops arrived.

It was not to be. A patrol car started up the street and Bobby dropped her cigarette and melted into the dark alley, abandoning her purse inside Alibi Alley. Paul dialed Cheryl to report her direction, at the same time launching out the front door as fast as he could on his bad hip, shouting to the cop and pointing.

He knew it wouldn't help. He texted Beaner, who was now sitting in his SUV in front of the big house at Higgins Point, standing guard. *Watch for BMc.* Beaner had photos taped to his dashboard: Bobby McIntyre, Travis Freeman, and, on a private recommendation from Bruce Wertheimer, Aaron Fletcher from the cemetery. Bruce had a gut feeling, and when he'd said that, the big, gruff lumberjack-type had looked a little spooked. Bruce had brought him a picture from the landscaping crew's personnel files; the blond kid didn't look scary. In fact, he looked fairly harmless. That dissonance between Big Bruce's fear and the actual look of this Aaron kid was enough to convince Paul to add him to the watch list.

The conversation had been brief, when Paul dropped by the cemetery looking for Gillian on Wednesday. She hadn't been there, and Bruce had taken him into the office to talk. He'd started by saying, "Look, this might just be a little crush or something, but…" Paul had listened, had absorbed all the information, and had come away with a bad feeling.

He added a simple text, *Lost her in Derby Harbor*, to Dean Jagger. Jagger had asked to be kept in the loop. All the loops.

After a moment, he added, *Going to the big house. Keep you posted.* He got no reply but hadn't really expected one.

He paid Nancy in the bakery for a loaf of caraway rye, Julia's favorite, knowing it would be treated with disdain, but trying anyway. He had no intention of giving up on mending his marriage; he'd been to therapy and marriage counseling — alone — every week for the last four months. The last time he'd asked Julia to come with him, she had paused before saying no. That was, in Paul's eyes, a baby step forward. Someday, she would agree to go. It would take a while, but he was willing to be patient.

He put the loaf in the passenger seat of his Audi and was surprised when his phone dinged twice with a single vibration, which indicated a text from Jagger. He checked it, and was surprised again. It wasn't usual for cops to info-share with private investigators, but it seemed Jagger was in a talkative mood tonight.

The flower shop has an online order listed for a bouquet of pink roses and purple and white Freesia, paid by MasterCard, by Aaron Fletcher on the first, the cop texted.

Paul replied, *Does GH know yet?*

Jagger answered, *I'll tell her.*

Paul didn't think that was good enough, but he texted, *Great.*

He called Gillian. When she didn't answer, he left a voice mail. "Hey, it's Paul. You received flowers from Aaron at the cemetery crew. Jagger traced it. On my way to your new place. I have a man there. Black SUV. Name's Beaner. No need to worry. If you need me at Red Maple instead, let me know." He hung up and started north to Higgins Point.

Chapter Thirty-Eight

Sunday, November 2. 7:10 P.M.

It wasn't until Gillian took out her credit card to pay for the freezer that her sanity finally flooded back in and she came to her senses. She would put bread in this freezer. Food. For her clients. Because she was going to have a wonderful, successful business like she'd always dreamed. Her and Frankie. She had to fight for that future. They'd figure out their problems and they'd decorate the bed and breakfast, go antique shopping to fill the bedrooms, paint the walls, plan menus, and enjoy their beautiful future.

But what about the diary? And Bobby's big mouth? What about Mike Deacon? There is no future for you. Not if the police find out what happened.

Bruce was browsing big screen TVs, pointing to several with a broad wink. "While you've got the plastic out, Sugar Mama," he said leadingly.

She managed a half-smile for him. "Yeah, yeah. You're not gettin' one."

"Party pooper," he accused. "We better get back to the car soon. Cold tonight. Your flowers are going to freeze out there."

She handed the salesman her credit card and asked him about rush delivery. The freezer she wanted was sitting in the back, and could be brought in the morning for an extra fee. Delighted, she paid for them to do so and gave them the address.

Just for food. No matter what comes next. She pushed away the dark thoughts, cleared her mind, and reminded herself that she was not that person. She just wasn't.

Her phone vibrated silently again in her back pocket. She checked the display. *Colin?* She was supposed to see him tonight; with everything that had happened, it slipped her mind. She planned to call him back when she got some privacy.

Another vibration alerted her to a message from Paul: the flowers had been sent by Aaron Fletcher. Gillian was hit by a one-two punch of relief and surprise. Aaron? She barely knew him. Bruce's gut feeling about the kid had been right. She'd have to speak to Aaron and let him know that his attentions weren't welcome. That was bound to be uncomfortable, but it was the least of her worries tonight. *But what did he mean by SOON?* Had it been just a clumsy romantic overture?

"Pssst," Bruce whispered.

When she turned around again, he was holding a bedside lamp up in front of his face, its filmy, crimson shade hung with dangling crystal ribbon, and he slowly lowered it until just his eyes were showing. He wiggled giant, bushy eyebrows suggestively.

Gillian let out an unintentional snort-laugh and motioned for him to bring it. She told the salesman, "Could you just add this on my bill?"

"You're gonna get this?" Bruce smiled bemusedly. "Not really your style, is it?"

"For my sister."

"Ah yes!" He raised two fingers beside his head and motioned clicking a light bulb on with an imaginary pull chain. "It all becomes clear now."

"You do know how to cheer me up, big guy," she admitted, shaking her head ruefully.

"And that's why you should marry me," he said wistfully, giving her a faux-sad shrug and sigh. "Then *alllll* this could be yours." He proceeded to rub his broad belly and chest with one giant hand. "Well, most of it. My heart belongs to poutine."

"That's going to lead to heartache," Gillian warned, signing the sales papers and taking her credit card back from the salesman. "Or at the very least clogged arteries."

"Worth it," Bruce said cheerfully. "Where to now?"

"I promised you dinner," she said, "though it's a bit late."

"Better late than never," he said, offering to take the lamp. She handed it over, pulling her purse strap up over her left shoulder and cupping her right arm. Her shoulder was still throbbing, but once they got to Mrs. Blymhill's house, she could take one of her pills, or maybe a cocktail of them with a coffee to make sure the pain didn't blossom into a migraine.

They struck out into a blustery winter night; the temperature was dropping fast, and the flags outside the store snapped loudly, casting shadows in a parking lot lit by street lamps. The asphalt was uneven, but Gillian watched her step carefully most of the way. When they hit the truck, though, a patch of ice lurking around the corner near the passenger side door caught her heel and her foot went out. She threw out her dominant right hand without thinking and grabbed the truck for support. The bad angle was too much for that shoulder and she went down with a high-pitched shriek. Pain tore through her arm, and tears instantly blurring her vision.

Bruce ditched the lamp in the truck bed and ran to her side, his boots loud on the asphalt. "Oh, God, Gills, what happened?" His big hands hovered, waiting to help her but wary to touch the wrong spot.

She couldn't speak. The pain was incredible. Her breath whistled in and out of lungs constricted by agony. She rolled onto her back and held her right arm tight across her torso, her left hand cupping her injured shoulder. The sky was velvet black nothingness pricked with broken glass, an endless hole filled with bitter shards above her. Pain swallowed her thoughts and then mercifully receded enough for her to form thoughts and words. She found her voice at the same time as her breath came easier.

"Slipped. Grabbed the truck with the wrong hand," she said, her voice husky through shock. She hated that she was so easily injured and reinjured over and over. Nothing to doctors had tried had helped; physiotherapy, cortisone shots, it had been useless. She tried to sit up and Bruce's hands again hovered close.

"What can I do?" he asked, close enough that when his breath fogged, it clouded her vision.

"Give me your arm," she said. When he held out one massive slab of muscle masquerading as an arm, she used her left arm to hook under and around, and pulled herself up as he rose smoothly from a crouch to standing, easing her up slowly with him. His strength was reassuring, his closeness a comfort. He reached past her to open the truck door and maneuvered his body so she could use him to get herself where she needed to go. He moved to reach for her seatbelt to help her when she looked up and noticed for the first time what a lovely shade of hazel his eyes were, and how kind and gentle, and before she knew what she was doing, she leaned forward and captured his mouth with hers.

Bruce made a surprised little noise into her mouth but did not pull away; he froze for the second that the kiss lasted, and when she broke contact, he did not attempt to reconnect. Instead, he blinked rapidly at her, and arched one eyebrow.

"So, that just happened," he whispered playfully. "Did you hit your head, too?"

Gillian's jaw dropped. "I'm so sorry. I didn't mean to do that."

He chuckled and buckled her seat belt for her, making sure the belt fell well clear of her injured shoulder. "Do you hear me complaining?"

He shut her door and crossed in front of the truck, giving his beard a scratch as he came to the driver's side and got in. As soon as he was settled, she said, "I mean it, Bruce. I shouldn't have done that. We're not... I mean, we don't..."

"It doesn't have to mean anything," he said. "It's only a little interesting thing that took place on a Sunday night for no reason whatsoever."

"Right," she said. Then she nodded and repeated, "Right."

He started the car, turned the heat up to maximum, and cast a huge smile at her. "I hope you don't mind if I wear this smug grin all the way home, though, because that's also a thing that's happening."

She groaned but couldn't help but laugh with embarrassment. "Bruce, don't tease me about this."

"Oh, I'm teasing you," he said. "For sure. A lot. Forever."

"Bruce!" If her arm didn't hurt so badly, she'd have slugged him.

"Severe pain makes Gillian kiss me," he noted aloud, and mimed drawing this on an imaginary chalk board in the air. "Documented for future reference."

"Bruce!" she scolded through a laugh.

"Does this mean I'm staying the night?" he asked, wiggling those massive eyebrows at her.

"No!" she insisted.

"Okay," he said with a bobbing nod. "I'll go home after the hubba-hubba sexytimes." He purred in her general direction like a big jungle cat and growled.

Gillian promptly dissolved into a giggle fit, which she knew damn well was his intention all along; the laughter erased her embarrassment and relieved a good deal of pain, and when she tried to rotate her shoulder experimentally, it wasn't as bad as she'd feared it would be.

"I feel I need to inform you that you're incorrigible," she said.

"You love it," he said.

She snuck a side-long glance at him, starting to wonder if maybe she did.

Chapter Thirty-Nine

Sunday, November 2. 7:25 P.M.

Bobby McIntyre stood at the curb on Red Maple Drive staring at Gillian Hearth's dark, quiet house; it was the one logical place she hadn't looked for Frankie, and it was clear that no one was here. It hadn't been safe to show up here, she knew that much. She also knew that she was dying, *dying* inside, and if she couldn't find Frankie, her whole life was meaningless. All her carefully laid plans, all her dreams of the future. A pit of churning acid gnawed in her belly. The pain was unbearable.

There must be a man.

Bobby's heart lurched sickly and a cold bolt of jealousy stole her breath. Of course that was it. *She's not home because she's with someone*. On a date. Out to dinner. Maybe drinking again. Maybe letting him touch her soft, pale skin, or reach under her clothes to stroke her. Bobby's fists tightened further and she took out her phone, knowing that was also not safe. She dialed Gillian's number. When she didn't pick up, she did it again, and again, and again. Finally, she let it go to voice mail.

"I *told* you that I always clean up everyone else's messes. And I would have cleaned this one up, too, if you'd given me more time. I *will* get rid of him. I *will* fuck him up. Just stop running me off like an ungrateful bitch. Everyone's always running me off. I'm just sick of it. After everything I've done for you two?" She paced at the curb, kicking through drifts of dried leaves, and ran a hand through her short red hair. "You don't even fucking know. *You don't know!*" She tried to keep from yelling, eyeballing the neighbor's houses. "I'm all-in when it comes to my loved ones." She started walking back around the rear of the yard where the cover of night was heavier, and lowered her voice. "There's time. There's still time. I can fix this. Whatever he's done, he'll pay for. I'll make him disappear. Just don't shut me out, Gillian. I—" Her anger turned to misery rapidly, and a sob escaped her. "I can't—" Her breath hitched and she dissolved into tears, unable to speak until she got a handle on them. "I can't believe you'd let her abandon me again. *Again.* Why do you make her do this to me? It's so mean, *you're so mean!* You and Barb, you just don't get it. Always treating me like shit, when I do everything for you. You owe me *everything.* You're not getting rid of me this time. I know your tricks. You throw a bunch of men at Frankie to make me feel like garbage, and she messes around in front of me, and then I leave. Well, I'm not leaving this time. You're *not* running me off. And after I fix this one, you're going to owe me again, and don't you fucking forget it." She hung up, exhausted, wiped the running snot from her upper lip on her sleeve. There was a funny smell out back near the shed, copper and shit and something worse. A dead raccoon in the bushes, maybe. Or down closer to the lake.

Bobby McIntyre wouldn't have been the least bit surprised if she'd taken four more steps and tripped over the rapidly cooling corpse of Colin Keller, but she did not take four more steps. She turned and picked her way in the dark down toward the lake, finding the easiest path down to the water's edge, where there was the tiniest strip of driftwood-dotted sand mixed with the shells of zebra mussels and water-softened chunks of glass. Careful not to turn an ankle, she let the moonlight guide her down the shoreline, crouching slightly when she got close to private properties, and headed west toward Higgins Point.

The walk would take her an hour.

She imagined there was blood on the wind, and she was not wrong.

**

Dean Jagger sat at his desk thinking about pizza and Mike Deacon and a French fry truck by the canal and missing dildos and a vase full of roses and Freesia ("funeral flowers," she'd said, the color in her cheeks vivid on her shock-paled face). He thought about Bobby McIntyre bringing Frankie Farmer carnations the morning that Mike Deacon disappeared. Gillian not seeing them in the kitchen that day. Gillian tripping down those long, hard basement stairs. The painkillers in her purse. The drug dealer who called her "Auntie." The statement of the nurses of Gillian's absolute silence after her injury. He thought about the gunshot wounds in Paul Langerbeins' hip and the way he didn't use a cane. He thought about Cheryl Broderick's call regarding Bobby McIntyre slipping away. He thought about the package he received that morning; a green leather diary with no name inside and some of the pages missing, torn out messily. The brick through the window, the slight man in the baseball hat. *Was it a man?* He looked at the picture of Bobby McIntyre. Same height, weight. Short hair. Boxy shoulders. *Could it have been her?* He thought about the gully at Pleasant Pines Cemetery where he'd dropped a receipt-wrapped stick to see where it would fall. He wanted to go back and see if anything else was being dumped there, garbage, whatever. If so, his stick may be disturbed. He'd need a team. Late now, though. Dark. And besides, he felt it wasn't a body hidden there. Something, but not a body.

That's too close. It's not there. But it would have to be close, he reasoned. How else would she move it? He couldn't, try as he might, picture Gillian Hearth slicing up a body into more manageable pieces. It was far too gruesome, and just didn't fit. But the ATV that the landscaping crew used, the one with the flatbed trailer on the back, he thought, made a lot of sense.

There must be a path elsewhere, a hole in the fence at the far end, perhaps, some place the ATV could get through.

For some reason, his brain showed him Gillian Hearth sitting in her kitchen, and his gut gave a telltale flutter of intuition; he listened to it, exploring the image, chewing the inside of his mouth absently. *Over her head.* The photographs. *What of them?* Roses.

So what? He figured there were a ton of roses in a cemetery. She'd likely planted some herself at the Red Maple house, and maybe she would at her new place at Higgins Point. *Why did they matter?*

They did, though. Because they weren't just in her kitchen. The pictures were on the living room wall, too. And hadn't there been one in her bedroom? The same rose, a single, open flower, the stem bristling with thorns.

He flipped through the green diary again, near the end, one of the more recent entries, dated October twenty-ninth. Light, looping script, very tidy. *New project, very happy. Gillian wants pink roses. Of course. Not even the pretty ones, but those plain single flat-looking flowers. She doesn't get it. I'm doing irises. It'll look perfect in that bedroom. Can't wait to get started!*

The back of Dean's chair tilted slightly on springs as he leaned back, bouncing a little, extending his muscles to stretch again. Flipped pages. *Aubergine and vanilla cream for the second bathroom upstairs, fern accents. Should look perfect with the fixtures that are already there. Must find a better mirror. Big. Walnut, maybe.* Two pages later. *I can't wait to open this place. I should have everything settled by May, June.*

I should, he thought. *Not we should.* Dean lowered the diary and stared into the distance in thought. *Does that mean anything?*

He got a text from Cheryl Broderick; they'd found Bobby McIntyre's car, a red Fiat with tinted windows that matched the car that Frankie Farmer drove, parked in Derby Harbor near the service road at the Gas N' Goods. That was a five minute walk from the main strip where Alibi Alley was. No sign yet of Bobby. Barb McIntyre had contacted police about an hour ago; her kidney tests came back positive for oxalate crystals, confirming ethylene glycol ingestion. *Antifreeze poisoning.* Barb was adamant that she had not consumed antifreeze in a suicide attempt, but was hesitant to blame her sister outright, hopeful some other explanation could be found. *Denial*, Dean thought.

He began to go over the day that Mike Deacon disappeared one more time in his mind. But his belly gave a sick twist. He stared out the plate glass as the last of daylight disappeared into a thin, crystalline night, black as sin and twice as shady. *What are the chances that Bobby McIntyre is still in town?* The answer hit him like a punch. *She isn't leaving town until she gets what she wants.* Which begat the question: what did she want?

She wants her sister dead. Why? Money? Vengeance? If she wanted her sister dead, the doctor had told him that it would have only taken a single large dose. Why had Bobby not done that? *She wants Barb sick but not dead.* Why? *She wants to be needed.*

By everyone? He scratched that into his notepad, his pen digging into the paper more forcefully than usual, trying not to let his personal disgust cloud his perceptions. He was still missing something important, some link. He wrote his missing person's name in the middle of a fresh page, then jotted down names around him: Frankie Farmer, the fiancée, Gillian Hearth, the sister, and Bobby McIntyre, the unstable friend. His eyes kept straying back to McIntyre; this was the one who'd proven herself to be harmful, and she had been at the Farmer house the day Mike Deacon went missing.

Before Mike Deacon's visit. *During?* he wondered. What had Gillian said when he asked her about that? He referred back to his notes. *I don't know when Mike Deacon arrived at my sister's house, but I know I wasn't there when he came or left*, were her exact words. That didn't mean she wasn't there at the same time as Mike, Dean thought.

His phone dinged, and the ringtone was the theme from Bonanza. He smirked; he'd changed it when Tombstone Jones started wearing cowboy hats to the shooting range. When he answered, Jones wasted no time with small talk.

"Broderick let me know that Bobby McIntyre has been using Barb's ID to work out at a gym called Wilcox Wellness in Derby

Harbor. Gave them a shout, and lo and behold, the Wilcox twins are a *very* cooperative pair. Yoga Boy has a record and he's not too eager to run afoul of the law again."

Sensing Tombstone's gloating tone was the beginning of a rant, Dean prompted, "What'd you manage to dig up, Tommy?"

"They sent over a list of their other patrons," Tombstone said, "and guess who else pinged on the client list?"

When Tombstone told him the name, Dean bolted out of his chair, grabbed his jacket, and hustled to his car.

Chapter Forty

Sunday, November 2. 7:55 P.M.

When Bruce pulled into the driveway at Hearth House, Gillian saw the big house with fresh eyes; its towering roof, its good bones, its long, floor-to-ceiling windows on the main level, its little round windows in the attic. Hers. Her and Frankie. Moneywise, technically hers. Frankie didn't have much money of her own, and certainly what little alimony and child support she got from Henry went to supporting the kids. It was no matter. Gillian was comfortable with Frankie owing her a bit of money now and then. Greg had left her a fairly large chunk in life insurance, and spending it to make the Hearth sisters' dreams come true was worth it.

Bruce pointed out the black SUV near the road and Gillian said, "Paul said he had a man watching the house. Someone named Beaner."

"Then where is he?" Bruce asked. "Nobody in that car."

"Maybe he's doing a walk-around? Checking the yard?" Gillian carefully undid her belt and slid out into the night. "He'd better be careful. There are still three old bear traps in the herb garden. If he steps on those, he'll snap his leg."

She closed the passenger side door and came around to get her lamp from the back. The box was dusted with snow. Bruce popped out and came around the back of the truck. "I didn't know you had a dog."

Gillian spun around and blinked with disbelief; Doogie, Frankie's mostly deaf yellow lab, was wandering down the front yard toward the shoreline, wagging his tail. She called his name and whistled, though she knew he wouldn't hear her.

"How'd he get out?" Bruce wanted to know.

Gillian dug out her house keys, watching the house uneasily. "I don't know. Maybe I forgot to lock up?" *Not even possible, being as paranoid as I have been lately.* "Maybe Frankie came home and left the door open and he slipped out? We're the only ones with keys."

Bruce sighed unhappily. "Maybe someone didn't use a key, Gillian. Want me to grab the dog?"

"He won't come without his leash, I'll grab it."

"Well, I'm coming in with you. There's no way you're going in there by yourself," he said. "Better yet, give me your keys. Let me go in first."

Gillian gazed up at him and opened her mouth to retort when he lowered his brow at her and said, "Seriously? You're going to argue with me about this? Lady, you have a death wish. If something bad happens, let me take the brunt of it. I'm a big dude."

She dropped her key ring into Bruce's huge mitt and she followed him up. The porch lights were on a motion sensor, and she expected them to blink on when they approached. Still, when they did, she gave a nervous start. The wind blew the hanging lamp-style lights to and fro, casting shifting shadows around the wicker chairs and tables on the covered porch. The wood planks creaked underneath. Gillian remember how she'd been charmed the first time she'd heard that noise, but now it ratcheted up her nerves.

Bruce glanced back at her, and motioned for her to stand directly behind him like he was a massive human shield. They approached the front door cautiously; it was closed and locked. As the key turned, Gillian set the lamp box down beside the door, wanting her one good arm free in case she needed to defend herself. She was tempted to pick up the metal shovel beside the door, but she knew with her right shoulder in so much pain, she'd never be able to swing it.

Bruce stood listening to the interior of the house before crossing the threshold. He slipped her house key back to her hands, fiddling with it until she was holding the key between her knuckles. She nodded at him.

Bruce whispered, "What did you say the name of Paul's watch guard dude is?"

"Beaner."

He nodded and cleared his throat to call, "Beaner? You in here?"

Silence answered them, a dead calm. Gillian whispered, "I left the light on over the sink in the kitchen. We should be able to see that from here. And there's a night light in the bathroom. If the door was open like I left it, we'd see that, too."

In the hallway, pure darkness, the kind you only find far from town where there are no streetlights to break the night's cover. Bruce nodded grimly, and said, "Might be time for a police sweep, lady. I don't like this."

"Me either," she agreed, and reached for her purse. It was not over her left shoulder. She'd left it in Bruce's truck. "Need your phone."

"In the truck," he said with a soft curse. "Time to get the fuck out?"

Nodding, Gillian spun around to retreat.

And slammed face first into Travis Freeman.

Chapter Forty-One

Sunday, November 2. 8:05 P.M.

Craning up at Travis in horror, tongue glued to the roof of her mouth, Gillian could only shake her head. A little whimper escaped from deep in her throat.

Travis' mouth slid into a knowing smirk. "Hey, Featherweight."

Bruce reacted quickly, stepping forward with both fists raised in front of his face, but Travis held up a rusty orange diary flagged with colored tabs and rocked back on his heels.

"Whoa, whoa, whoa." He wagged the diary meaningfully at them. "Settle down, there, Wide Load. I'm only here to talk."

Gillian recovered enough to look him up and down. "Talk about what?" she demanded. "How I'm a whore? How I'm a nut?"

"Actually, no," Travis said, his eyebrows rocketing upward. "May I come in? It's cold as balls out here."

Gillian, confused and uncertain, glanced up at Bruce. Bruce did not look impressed, and said, "If I can pat you down for weapons, and the lady says it's okay."

"Lady," Travis repeated. "That's rich. But whatever. Pat away." He dropped an open backpack off his shoulder and spread his arms wide, tolerating Bruce's big hands searching his body from bottom to top. Gillian watched this carefully. Travis snort-laughed. "You want to cop a feel too, honey? Be my guest."

"I'd really rather not," she said tightly.

Bruce found a pocket knife on Travis and put it in his own pocket. "Gills?"

The cold air blasting through the open door made her eyes water. Shaking from the shock of actually speaking to this man after the hell he'd put her through, speaking semi-civilly at that, she demanded, "Did you let the dog out?"

Travis frowned and glanced over his shoulder. "Who, dumb-dumb-Doogie? No." He whistled sharply; the dog's head came up and he loped over, his tail wagging his whole body, his hang lolling out. He cozied up to Travis' leg for a stroke and a head scratch before running into the house, yapping.

"It's nice to know I was missed," Travis said, smiling again.

Gillian didn't take that bait, and backed up a few feet so Travis could come in. When he did, Bruce shut the door behind him and stood there, flanking the newcomer. Travis shot a look over his shoulder and said to her, "This one's a lot bigger than the last man you fucked. And I don't mean your husband."

Gillian fumed but did her best to keep it off her face, asking coolly, "What does that mean?"

Travis slapped the diary open to a little blue sticky note and read aloud, "May third. Dear diary. My sister, that slut!" He said the word with delight, drawing it out. *Sluuuuuuut!* "I can't believe she fucked her husband's partner. She said it was 'an accident.' Did Ken's dick just fall into her? So disappointed but not at all surprised. She's always doing shit like this."

Bruce made an unhappy noise but Gillian held up a hand. She didn't believe for a second that Frankie had actually written those words. The diary looked like Frankie's, but those words... no, those were not Frankie's words. Gillian had never touched Ken. There *was* no affair. Why would Frankie make that up in a diary that only she would ever read? Why would she write lies to herself?

"Is that what you came here for after all this time?" she asked coolly. "To talk about my sex life?"

"I came to return some things I borrowed," he said, pointing at the backpack.

She felt her eyes narrow at him, crouched to peek inside, saw her sex toys and her underwear, and left them in the bag. "Keep them. I'll buy something else."

"I didn't do anything to them," Travis promised, wearing a lewd grin. "Promise."

Gillian just glared at him. "And my pictures?"

"They're in there. Nice tits, by the way." Travis side-eyed Bruce, and then insisted, "No, I mean it. They're cute."

"That's enough," Bruce said.

"Where are the other diaries?" Gillian asked. "You had more than one."

"Oh, the green one? Yeah, that had some interesting stuff. Oddly, it overlapped with this one. I sent the cops the other. Sorry 'bout that. I was in a bad mood," Travis said. "The orange diary was the most interesting by far, though."

"Oh?" Gillian said tightly, but was now too afraid by the thought of policemen reading the green diary and whatever Frankie might have written in it to form any intelligent inquiry.

"Did you fuck around? It's no big deal," Travis said, "but I've been calling you a whore, and if it isn't true, I'd like to apologize."

Bruce moved fast, grabbing Travis by the shirt front and heaving him backward and around, his feet coming clear of the floor. The front door shuddered loudly with the impact. Travis laughed, spreading his arms in a gesture of surrender, holding the diary high. Bruce pulled him off the door once to give him another solid, punishing slam.

"Well, *somebody* doesn't think so," Travis noted. "Wanna call off your pet bear, here, Featherweight?"

"Stop calling me that," Gillian insisted. Then, softer, "Bruce."

Bruce stepped back but not very far, using the size of his body to intimidate.

Travis rolled his eyes. "So that's a 'no?' Look, there's a lot of other bullshit in here about you. I'm trying to pick out the facts."

"No," she said, voice thick with emotion, "not that it's any of your business. I never slept with anyone but my husband during my marriage."

"Not even the big guy, here?" Travis jerked a thumb at Bruce.

Bruce growled, "You want another fucking thump, asshole?"

"I loved Greg and was never disloyal," Gillian said. "But I don't need your apology. Your opinion means nothing to me."

"Now, now. Listen. I was sitting in the pub just now, reading the last bit of this diary, and I started thinking, what is the likelihood that *all* of this is true?" Travis shook his head, turning to another page. "Which made me wonder, of course, if *any* of it was true. Did you tell Frankie to ditch me?"

"She asked me what I would do in her position," Gillian said. "She was unhappy. I told her to make herself happy. That is all I said about you. Make of that what you will."

Travis nodded, deep in thought, and then read aloud, "September second. Dear diary. Bobby is the only one who understands what it's like to live with that psycho-bitch. Bobby and I should run away together, but I'm afraid of what Gillian would do to us, especially after what she did to Mike."

Gillian glared. "You're full of shit. It does not say that."

Travis showed her the page. She stared in shock, reading each word one at a time, over and over, feeling it sink in. "She had a bad night, I guess. Wrote something in anger. Half of what's in a diary is nonsensical ranting and garbage."

Travis read, "October seventeenth. Gillian told me if I don't break up with Trav, she'll make sure he ends up chopped up and buried under rose bushes just like Mike Deacon. I wonder where she put the skull? She never would tell us."

Silence fell in the room and Gillian felt Bruce's eyes cut her way. She shook her head mutely. Mike Deacon *was* buried under roses, but neither Frankie nor Bobby knew where. She had kept complete control of that little detail. There was no way she could risk anyone else knowing.

She watched Travis' finger slide down the page and he continued, "Gillian shot him. I don't know where she got the gun. Maybe it was Greg's." Finger slide. "When I got downstairs, it was too late. He was already dead. She put the body in the freezer, warned me not to tell. I was afraid if I told anyone, she'd kill me next."

"What? How? I... That's completely false," Gillian barely breathed, head swimming. She saw little stars. "That's not how it was. I don't understand."

"Gills?" Bruce said. "You need to sit."

"I need a drink," she said, swallowing hard.

"Frankie's chair is in here, right?" Bruce said. "Come into the dining room and sit, and I'll get you a drink."

Travis followed them down the hall, boots clumping. Gillian had almost made it to Frankie's Papasan chair when she noticed the dog wasn't in his favorite place by the hearth. She wondered where the hell he was now.

"Bruce, can you make sure the back door is closed and locked?" she asked.

He nodded, casting one last suspicious look at Travis before leaving for the kitchen down the dark hallway.

Travis handed her the diary. "So, I ordered another beer, and I really thought about it. She wrote that you fought with Mike Deacon at the top of the stairs and you both fell."

She nodded and heard Bruce thumping around in the kitchen, slamming the fridge door and the cabinets. Two thumps that sounded like he removed his boots and dropped them. Then silence. She listened, worried. Another thump that sounded like the back door.

"The fall is true," she admitted, feeling the urge to fetch her purse and phone, though it no longer felt like an emergency. "Bruce?"

"Then, according to Frankie's muddled diaries," Travis continued, "which were thoughtfully dropped in my mailbox, by the way, you shot this guy and hauled him up into the old chest freezer and threatened her if she told. Which would have to mean you carried a gun. But your husband was a cop. He wouldn't have let you traipse around with a gun, not in Canada. Lots of stuff that doesn't make sense, here."

Dropped in his mailbox. "You didn't break in and steal the diaries?"

He shook his head. "I did deliver one to the police, that was on me. But I received two as a gift. Say, how did you lift Mike Deacon's dead body if you were so badly injured that you needed an ambulance?" Travis grimaced doubtfully. "And why wasn't there blood all over from the gunshot? Gunshot residue? Some evidence of a crime when the EMS guys got there to take you to the hospital for your fall? If you shot him…"

"I didn't," she insisted hoarsely, looking at the pages, page after page of ugly lies about her mixed with just enough truth to be believable on first read. "It was a fall. I didn't put him in the freezer. I didn't even know." She realized she was confessing, but looked up at this man who knew her secrets. "Someone else did that while I was unconscious, to protect me. I didn't know he was even dead until I got out of the hospital. I was scared stiff to say anything until I knew for sure what had happened. And by then, it looked way too suspicious to tell anyone about. I was going to jail. There was no way out of it."

"But then, I noticed this. You've got to see this," Travis said, and leaned over to take a small section of the last diary pages and fold them over.

The lovely, loopy script handwriting in the early pages of the diary was wildly different from the pages of accusations; the writing was sharp, all-caps, riotously slanted in the later pages. He opened the front of the diary to show her Frankie's worried words about her increasingly abusive relationship with Mike Deacon and her fears about leaving him, and then pulled back the pages to reveal the nasty things that were scrawled about Gillian in the end of the book, and she knew those were not Frankie's words.

Gillian heard a small, rapid series of floor squeaks and had a mere half-second to wonder why Bruce was running into the room at them when Travis grunted and fell at her hard, throwing the chair backwards and both of them to the floor. The cushion flew sideways as Gillian hit the floor on the back of her head, and Travis' weight slammed her in the chest, knocking out her breath.

The baseball bat swung high again. Bobby's eyes were wide and empty of emotion. This time, the bat whipped straight down at the pile of them. She whacked Travis in the back of the skull hard enough to drive the front of his head into Gillian's ribcage. Gillian's breath whooshed out. She tried to cry out for Bobby to stop but it came out a croak. Trying to buck Travis' heavy, unconscious weight off of her, she wriggled, using both arms for leverage. Her right shoulder screamed, freshly aching, but she ignored it, desperately scrambling backward. Bobby raised the bat again. It came down with a sickening crack on Travis' skull. Gillian screamed Bruce's name. Slipping free of the bulk of Travis' weight, she flipped to hands and knees and crawled a foot until she could launch to her feet. Gill bolted past the fireplace and ducked down the back hall toward the rear stairs. She didn't make it that far.

Bobby leaped over the body, right on her heels, closing in fast, ordering her to stop. Gillian took a chance and dropped into a crouch. Bobby slammed into her bent back at knee height and went flying. The impact screamed through Gillian's bad shoulder. Sailing over Gillian, Bobby sprawled, losing her grip on the blood-splattered baseball bat; it spun out of her hand, clattered and rolled, coming to a stop against the wall.

Gillian sprang up; she doubled back down the hall, and slipped into one of the empty rooms, shedding her noisy shoes and sidling into one dark corner behind the slightly open door to plan her next move. Cupping her bad arm, she pinched her lips inward and refused to cry, refused to think of the bashed-in skull in her dining room or the blood on her shirt, anything but the crazy bitch in her hall. *She's lost her mind. Bobby's finally lost it.* She knew she had to get out of the house. She couldn't hide in these empty rooms.

She had to check on Bruce; he must be down, otherwise he'd have come running at the commotion. What had Bobby done to him? Did she only have the baseball bat? She worked to quiet her panting, breathe slowly, and listen hard for sounds in the hall.

A shuffle. Heavy breathing. Gillian's eyes darted to the crack in the door. A shadow slid across the wall.

"Am I going to have a problem with you, Gillian?" Bobby called out warningly. "You sent her away from me. You tried to break me.

You tried to break me but I'm still here. I'm stronger than you. Smarter. I can do the things you can't do, won't do." Her breath was ragged. "Poor guilt-ridden Gillian. You actually think you killed Mike Deacon? Fuckin' joke. *A joke.* Bobby cleans up the messes. Bobby does, not you!"

What the fuck does that mean? Gillian bit her tongue and sidled in her sock feet to the far side of the room where the shared bathroom led into the front living room. From there, if she was quick and stealthy enough, she could reach the kitchen and the back door. Where the hell was the damn dog? And where was Paul's guard, Beaner? Was Travis dead? Had she hit him that hard?

Bobby's voice floated through the room, closer now. "No more games. You need to know the truth. Frankie doesn't tell you shit. I cleaned up the last one. Surprise-surprise, tough girl, you didn't fix anything. You didn't save Frankie. *I* did. *I* finished him off."

Gillian forced herself to inhale slowly, quietly, though her lungs were constricting and her heart thundering hard.

Bobby's footstep was soft. "Pillow case and a hammer," she said, as if to herself, "like a fucking rat. Twitched a bit and then pop, one more. Sank his battleship, you betcha."

The door swung further open on noisy hinges just as Gillian was slipping into the en suite bathroom, and she paused and strained to hear the direction of Bobby's footsteps; was she coming into the room, or passing it by to go to the kitchen? Gillian, with no weapon and no phone, couldn't afford to be wrong. She heard nothing. No breathing, no movement. Was Bobby standing still, also listening? Gill's eyes darted around the dark room, adjusting quickly, looking for anything. A toilet brush. Some tissue. Her toothbrush and a plastic cup for rinsing. She hadn't moved anything useful in yet.

"You need to tell me where the body went, Gillian," Bobby called out. "It's mine. *I* need it."

What the hell for? That thought was followed quickly by, *If you tell her where it is, she'll have no reason to keep you alive. It might be your bargaining chip.*

Bobby's voice wavered on the edge of brittle. "Nobody said you could steal it away. It was supposed to stay in the freezer where I put it. It wasn't yours to move. Now… if you tell me where you buried him, and tell me where you put Frankie, I'll let you live."

Gillian knew better than to fall for that and held her tongue.

"How's that for a deal?" Bobby called, shuffling closer. "Best deal you're gonna get tonight, I promise you that, bitch. *Only fucking deal you're gonna get.*"

Gillian heard a creak in the hall, another soft footfall, and knew Bobby was passing the room to go directly into the kitchen. Seeing stars, Gillian paused for a second to take a few slow, steadying breaths, and then came back out into the dark room, revising her kitchen exit plan. She'd have to run in behind Bobby and catch her unawares, hoping she didn't have to stop and spend precious seconds unlocking the back door. She was maybe twenty running strides from freedom, tops. She could do this.

Pressing into that dark corner behind the door, she listened with her heart hammering in her chest as Bobby's steps, quiet but audible, left the hardwood of the hall and hit the tile in the kitchen. *Let her get a bit further. Wait. Hold on. Out the door, around the side yard to Bruce's truck. Get the phone. Call for help.*

Gillian pumped herself up for her sprint, willing her body not to fail her, demanding high performance. No slips, no falls, no pain; she wouldn't allow it. Hands clammy and trembling, mouth dry, she counted down from five, listening to the warning sirens screaming in her head.

It was then that she heard the groan. *Bruce!* It was coming from the kitchen. Rustling. Shuffling, a slap, like a palm hitting tile.

She slipped quietly out to see him lying passed out on the kitchen floor next to the breakfast bar. Wary of Bobby's passage, she crouched near him. She didn't know if he could hear her or not, but she leaned over and whispered, "I'm going to get help, hold on." She took his key ring off his belt loop and crept to the back door. It was already unlocked. She fought the urge to rip it open, but as soon as the cold air hit her face and freedom was at hand, she couldn't hold back anymore and bolted.

Her foot hit something soft but unmoving and she tripped over it, flying forward down the porch steps. She instinctively threw both hands out in front of her face, and the jolt hit her bad arm. An unwanted yelp of pain shot from her mouth. Scrambling up, she craned back at the porch to see what was lying there.

A strange man. Blood. No time to think.

Bobby's hate-filled roar rushed toward the back door. Gillian launched into flight, pelting into the dark garden, heading desperately for the closest solar light, a barely-lit beacon in the night. At the last minute, she jumped, her heart in her throat, leaping the bear trap buried in the overgrown mint. Bobby ploughed right through it.

Gillian heard the wet snap of bone. Bobby's shriek was high and airy, full of a primal agony. Gillian landed and sprawled again, this time knee-deep in a wiry old thyme bush. She rolled onto her back panting, holding her aching shoulder, all the pain flooding back through a haze of adrenaline. She wept up at the black sky. *Is Travis dead? Will Bruce be okay? Is that Paul's man Beaner on the back porch? Is it over?*

She got her answer soon enough, but it wasn't what she expected.

Chapter Forty-Two

Sunday, November 2. 8:35 P.M.

Bobby panted and hissed, seemingly unable to scream for her pain. She snarled through her agony and threw her baseball bat in a final effort to punish Gillian, but Gillian was beyond that. She could see a figure moving through the shadowy back garden, and at first, it made no sense. She could hear the tinkle of crystals and the jingle of her favorite dangling earrings, the metal clink of bronze and copper bangles on her slim wrists. The breeze blew Frankie's blonde curls over one shoulder.

For a second, Gillian nearly wilted with relief at the sight of her sister, but then she saw Henry behind her; the gun in his hand didn't immediately register as a threat until he pointed it at Gillian's head.

"Well, that was messy," Henry said with disappointment. "This is what you call taking care of things? Stupid crazy bitch."

Gillian floundered until she realized that Henry wasn't talking to her.

Bobby sobbed. "It hurts, it hurts! Get it offffff. It hurts *ithurtsithurts.*"

Frankie's expression crumbled when Gillian gaped up at her. She half-sobbed, "He's got the boys, Gills. I don't know where they are."

"You were supposed to deal with this," Henry snapped at Bobby, ignoring the sisters. "And now you're going to fucking whine to me? You ran into a bear trap, moron. Of course it fucking hurts."

"Frankie—" was all Gillian could manage.

There was another shadow in the dark yard, moving just behind Henry and Frankie, but Gillian couldn't bear to tear her eyes off her baby sister, standing there frozen and terrified. Gillian swallowed and heard a dry click in her throat.

"Bobby killed Mike Deacon," Gillian said finally. "Frankie, you told me I did it. The fall. You told me you put him in the freezer to protect me."

"And you bought it," Henry said, rolling his eyes. "Get over it already. *Gawd*, you're such a fucking whiner. You've always been such a fucking whiner, Gillian."

"Let Frankie go to the boys. Let them go," she begged.

"I'm going to have to go with *no*," Henry said, and then barked a short, ugly laugh. "That's not part of the plan, darlin'."

Gillian swallowed her horror to ask, "Why are you doing this?"

Henry ignored that and asked Bobby, "Okay, where are we going to put her? We have to hurry before Travis shows up. This isn't going to work if he—"

"Travis is dead," Gillian interrupted. "Bobby killed him. Inside. In the dining room. With a baseball bat."

Henry's lips thinned and his dark eyes narrowed to slits. "She what?"

"Was that not the plan?" Gillian asked, dreading the answer, trying to figure out what Henry could possibly be up to. *Of course.* Bobby and Henry were going to kill her and frame Travis. The police would buy it; Travis had been legitimately stalking her. *Or had he?* How much of it had been Bobby setting things up? *Did* she *leave me notes?* She had access to Frankie's house, as did Henry. Did Bobby write the end of the orange diary? Did Henry?

Bobby moaned and let out a throaty gurgle. Henry looked down at her with disgust, aimed, and fired once. Chunks of what had been Bobby's head hit the mint an instant before the rest of her did. Gillian let out a breathy squeak and crammed her eyes shut, waiting for the next bullet to tear through her. When it didn't, she peeked up to see Frankie vomiting in the basil, bent over with the force of it.

"You're a goddamn sociopath, Henry Farmer," Gillian said. "What do you want?"

"You say sociopath like it's a bad thing," he drawled, his wrist flopping the gun from side to side like a wagging finger. "You know what's funny? You actually believe I give a shit what you think. Now, it would help enormously if I had that body, please."

"I don't know where Bobby put it," Gillian lied.

"I'd rather have that body floating around linking my dearest ex-wife to a murder, lady," Henry said. "I need Frankie. I don't need you."

Gillian moved her hand slowly behind her in the dark, scraping her fingertips into the cold, hard dirt; November had begun to stiffen the ground, and the soil beneath the crispy, frost-damaged herbs was gritty. She watched her ex-brother-in-law roll his eyes up at the night sky and sigh as though heavily burdened; the wind shifted, and Gillian caught a sharp hint of blood and something worse from Bobby's direction, but she tried desperately not to think about what that might be. Dark memories of moving Mike Deacon's frozen torso from the back of her Jeep to the ATV at Pleasant Pines assaulted her. *That was not my doing. I did not kill that man.* Her guilt was stubborn, though, and it insisted, *you tried. You intended to. You wanted him gone. You pushed him. You did the wrong thing more than once. His death is on you.*

She vowed she would call Constable Jagger and confess her crimes if she got out of this alive; even though that did not seem likely. Henry began muttering under his breath as Frankie's sobbing returned; he snarled something about incompetence and mental fragility, and brought his attention back to Gillian. He clucked his tongue as though considering his next move. Gillian folded the hard, cold dirt in her left hand; she only needed a few seconds.

Gillian shot her gaze quickly past Frankie's left side with a faked expression of relief. Henry bought it, glancing there angrily. Gillian used her good arm to fling the dirt just as Henry looked back. Some of the dirt caught Frankie but most of it pelted Henry in the face. Gillian launched up, panic making her reckless. She lunged at Frankie and threw her to the ground, then rounded to bat with both hands at Henry's gun. Frankie's cry of surprise did nothing to help. Gillian barreled into Henry full speed. He squinted, shaking his head to clear the dirt, but there was enough in his eyes to confuse his sight. The gun swung wildly. Gillian used her good hand to chop at Henry's wrist. He brought the gun up to pistol whip the side of her skull.

Gillian swooned, seeing stars, but managed to keep her feet. She brought her knee up for a groin shot. He blocked her with his thigh. Frankie flew up from the ground, baring her fingernails like claws, slashing at Henry's face. Gillian bared her teeth and locked onto Henry's wrist, bearing down hard. He shouted sharply and tried to shake her off, using his free hand to punch out half-blindly at both sisters. There were lights, headlights, someone pulling in. Gravel crunching. Doors slamming. Frankie clawed and kicked and the gun went off, deafening next to Gillian's head. The kick made her jaws release and she fell back. A strange male voice shouted in the distance. Frankie moved in on her ex-husband in a flurry of chiffon and feathered hair and flying hands. The gun went off again, two sharp reports in the night.

Frankie fell back, her face falling, her mouth a silent, perfect O. A horrifying scarlet spot bloomed and spread across her abdomen through the diaphanous fabric.

Gillian snapped, felt the gut-deep tug of retribution and murderous temper and gave herself over to it. She snatched the solar light from the cold ground. Heard that male voice shouting something over and over, repeating whatever command it was. Knew it was a cop. Ignored it. Clutching the solar light, sharp end out, she darted forward at Henry. The cop bellowed. Repeated. Henry dropped the gun, raised both hands. A flashlight beam swung back and forth behind him, turning his lean body into a dark target. She felt the rage swell and the power behind it felt glorious. She thrust the sharp rod forward but at the last minute aimed lower, driving it through denim and into Henry's meaty thigh.

Henry howled and dropped, flesh sliding off the metal rod with a sucking sound as he fell. Gillian folded her hand around it and raised it above her head for a finishing blow. Locked in on the back of Henry's neck. Aimed for raised vertebrae and the soft tissue between. Heard Dean Jagger call her name. The rustle of a gun leaving a holster.

But it was Bruce's shout, "Gillian Hearth, drop it!" that stalled her, made her blink with surprise.

She'd never heard him raise his voice. She cut her eyes at the back porch, where Bruce leaned unsteadily against the railing. Gillian vaguely registered the quick movement of Dean Jagger in her peripheral vision, felt a rough hand on hers, tugging gently at the solar light.

"Let's have that," Dean Jagger said softly next to her ear. "C'mon, it's all over now. Let me take care of it."

Gillian felt a shudder go through her and her core went cold as ice. She released her grip on the light and Dean whisked it away before bending to snap cuffs on Henry Farmer and call for an ambulance. When he started reading off Frankie's injury, Gillian's shock began to fade enough for her to feel fear.

She whipped around and hurried to her knees beside her sister's fallen form.

A moment later, Gillian's agonized shriek lanced through the night.

Chapter Forty-Three

Wednesday, November 5. 10:10 A.M.

The snow was gritty, flying directly into their faces as they strode through the frozen weeds and across hard, uneven ground. Her work boots scuffed a layer of hoarfrost off the soil in a pair of parallel tracks. She had always made an effort to hide her passage, had never dreamed of having company on the grim walk.

When they hit the tree line, Gillian took the lead, covering the last few hundred feet by memory, spotting the rose bush under the trees. Stripped of leaves by the cold wind, sprawling out in the shade, laden with rosehips, the rose protected her secret well. Tangled in its roots would be a ribcage, a length of spine, collarbones. Gillian had skeletons in her closet, but she'd placed them here to rest, wallowing in her guilt and shame, trying for years to justify it to herself.

She turned to say something to the silent cop behind her and found him watching her with quiet calculation; the look on his face — a combination of disappointment, resolve, and frustration — took any attempts to launch some sort of defense right out of her mouth. There was no excusing this and she wouldn't try.

Instead, she said, "It was about the insurance money, wasn't it?"

The stolid cop didn't answer her; it was far too soon to know, and she was the last person on Earth he'd be confiding in. At least, not before her trial.

"Yeah," she said, answering the unspoken agreement she imagined, nodding to herself. "Henry always was horrible with his own money. I bet he owed a bookie some heavy cash. My sister had nothing, but if I was dead, she'd inherit everything I owned. The new house, the money I'd collected from Greg's death. I don't know how he figured he'd get Fr—" Her voice broke and she couldn't say Frankie's name. Tried again. "My sister to give him anything. Maybe he thought they'd get back together if he sweet talked her. Used the boys as leverage. And how he got Bobby to help him, I'll never know. Especially not now that she can't tell…"

Dean let her talk, tucking his hands in his pockets to keep warm and keeping his face blank.

"I shouldn't be talking about any of this without my lawyer present, should I?" she said, not sounding especially concerned.

Dean's lips turned up in a sad half-smile that was barely more than a brief shrug. "I can't advise you on that, Mrs. Ellis. Hearth. Ms. Hearth."

Behind Dean Jagger, near a gully at the north end of Pleasant Pines cemetery, a crew worked with police to lower forensics into the space safely to retrieve the skull and the chainsaw that Gillian had used to dismember Mike Deacon's frozen body in her sister's basement.

"I heard from Bruce. He's doing better," she offered. "Says he's got too hard a head to incur any lasting damage." She gave a soft, defeated laugh. "What about Paul's fellow, Beaner?"

"He's pulling through. Just a knock on the head and injured pride."

"Pride? Whatever for?" Gillian said.

"He was there to protect you," Dean said. "He got clocked from behind from one of the people he was meant to look out for."

Gillian sighed. "Is Travis Freeman going to pull through? Paul Langerbeins told me that he might?"

Dean's shoulders fell but he remained silent on that score, too.

Gillian read his body language. "Well, shit. Colin. Bobby. Travis.

My Fran… Frankie." She got the name out this time, but not without her breath hitching. Her eyes filled with the hot sting of tears but she bit down fiercely on her bottom lip and refused to let them spill. "I still have no idea why Colin was dead in my yard. That makes no sense at all."

"We'll figure it out," Dean said confidently, giving no indication if he believed her confusion or not.

She took a deep, shaky breath and let it out harshly. "He's under the rose. Mike Deacon, I mean."

"Thank you for telling me," Dean said.

"I should have told you sooner," she said. "I should have told someone right away."

He didn't argue that. "How'd you keep the animals from digging him up?"

"Rat poison upon burial," she said quietly. "And I laid branches of the common buckthorn tree above the mulch around the rose. In time, the rose's own thorns made a good deterrent. This species is bristling with them."

"Where are the buckthorn branches now?"

I moved them so I could see a bone that had been heaved up by the freezing ground, she thought but carefully did not say. *I wanted to see it. I needed to see it.* "My sister's diaries are full of misinformation," she told him. "But I suppose you already have an analyst looking at the handwriting inconsistencies. Bobby stole them. Wrote lies in them. Delivered a couple to Travis to bait him into a confrontation and to use as evidence of trouble between us. There were more than two stolen. She must have kept a couple of them."

Dean's mouth did that lip shrug again.

"I didn't bury Mike Deacon because I was covering Bobby's crime," Gillian said. "I didn't know she killed him. I thought I had. I buried him to protect myself."

"I believe you," he said, and glanced over his shoulder as voices approached over the squawk of police radios. A line of evidence technicians were approaching with a trio of cops from the homicide division, their breaths fogging in the November air. "Anything else you'd like to tell me before we hand the scene over?"

"Henry must have promised Bobby that she could remain in their lives, in Frankie's life, but only if she helped him," Gillian said, reluctant to call an end to this. She'd be seeing her lawyer next, a man who reminded her of a hound dog with his long, dour face and did nothing to reassure her that her punishment would be light. She was preparing for the worst.

"You used the ATV?" Dean supposed. "To move the body?"

"To the back fence. From there, I took it on foot. On my back. A duffel bag. It was only a torso," she said, grimacing when it came out of her mouth so nonchalantly. "I'm sorry. That was..." She drifted off helplessly, shaking her head.

"Did your husband know?" Dean asked, his voice carefully low.

Gillian's jaw dropped and then snapped shut. "God, no." She struggled with her words for a moment, and then said, "The body was in the freezer while I was in the hospital from the fall. Frankie didn't tell me it was there right away. I was dealing with my injuries. And then Greg died, and I found out about the freezer, and..." She shook her head hard. "I was picking out a casket and flowers and I couldn't deal."

"Until you could."

"One day," she agreed. "Yes. One day, I decided I could. I had to. It couldn't stay in Frankie's basement forever. What if the boys stumbled across it?"

The team was upon them then, and Dean stepped aside to speak quietly to the homicide detectives. Gillian let her gaze creep back to the rose, her rose, where her bones lay hidden. She picked out the tiny yellowed bone showing through the dried leaves and icy earth. It would be the last time she saw Mike Deacon's remains until the trial.

Dean Jagger escorted her back from the woods, through Pleasant Pines cemetery, past the retrieval crew at the cliff. Their vehicles had chewed up the lawn, and for some bizarre reason, that troubled Gillian more than the prospect that she'd be serving time in prison. When they ducked the yellow police tape and got to Jagger's vehicle, he clicked the key fob and opened the door for her. She hesitated.

"He said he'd stick by me," she told him. "Bruce, I mean. I told him what I'm telling you. He said he'd be here with me, regardless." She searched Jagger's face for condemnation but found none. "He probably shouldn't."

"We don't decide who we fall in love with," Dean said. "We only decide what to do about it when it happens. Sounds like he's decided."

"I've no right to be starting a relationship with anyone," she said.

The constable didn't argue for or against that.

"I'm a mess," she continued. "My whole life is in ruins. I've demonstrated I can't be trusted. What is he *thinking?*"

That made Dean smirk, and he offered, "Some guys like to sleep with one eye open."

"You're a very good listener, officer," she told him, smiling reluctantly. "If I had confided in you sooner, maybe I could have…"

"No sense in doing that," Dean said, and nodded for her to get in the car.

"You're right," she said, taking one last look at Pleasant Pines. "It's all over now."

***

Gillian ducked into the car and Constable Jagger shut the door behind her. He circled the car, glancing once more at the team working at the cliff behind the bench. Someone had backed their van into the fountain, and someone else from the Medical Examiner's office was yelling at the driver. So far, no media. That would change when word hit the street. A sleepy little town like Derby Harbor wasn't home to murder every day, and certainly not a veritable slaughter like this one. As if summoned by his thoughts, a van sporting the local TV station logo started down the cemetery road, prompting Dean to hurry into the car and leave the bones behind.

***

Aaron Fletcher was eventually arrested and charged with the murder of Colin Keller; he served three years of a life sentence before he died of a brain aneurysm in prison.

Barb McIntyre recovered from antifreeze poisoning. She refused to attend her sister's funeral and maintains contact with Gillian Hearth by mail.

Bruce Wertheimer quit his landscaping job and went to work for Paul Langerbeins doing legwork, something they both make grim jokes about.

Paul Langerbeins and his wife, Julia, are seeing a marriage councilor to work past their grief regarding the loss of their son, Simon; Paul bought his first cane, though he often forgets to use it.

Henry Farmer was killed before he made it to trial; speculations about horse racing debts and a bookie are unsubstantiated at this time.

Frankie Farmer's sons, Matthew and Kirk, and her dog, Doogie, all went to live with Henry's parents in Quebec. Word has it they are doing very well, though the boys miss their mother every day.

Gillian Hearth is currently serving time for obstruction of justice and committing indignities to a dead body.

Many Derby Harbor residents who heard the stories regarding Mrs. Blymhill's eccentricities claim the old house at Higgins Point is cursed.

Hearth House would lie empty for the next five years.

About the Author

A.J. Aalto is the author of Closet Full Of Bones and the paranormal comedy series, the Marnie Baranuik Files. When not writing, she can be found singing old Monty Python songs in the shower, eavesdropping on perfect strangers, stalking her eye doctor, or failing at one of her many fruitless hobbies. A.J. cannot say no to a Snickers bar, and has been known to swallow her gum.

www.ingramcontent.com/pod-product-compliance
Lightning Source LLC
Chambersburg PA
CBHW030355020726

47493CB00003B/826